MISSING

INTREPID WOMEN
BOOK 8

A MEYERS SECURITY STORY

KATHRYN JANE

Missing
By: Kathryn Jane
Cover by The Killion Group
ISBN: 978-1-988790-09-1

kathrynjane (dot) com

To the Blain family.
You are a testament to extraordinary heritage and parenting.
I am honored to know you.

1

Well, fuck.

Dying wasn't on today's agenda. But with a six-hundred-pound bear in front of him and a four-hundred-foot drop behind him, things weren't looking good.

While he perched there on the rock wall—not daring to climb over the ledge and onto the plateau—Mamma grizzly grunted at her cubs and sniffed the air. Looked right at him.

Broughton eased his left foot from a thin gap in the rock, lowering and searching for a toehold he'd used moments earlier.

If the grizzly charged now, he'd be in a pickle.

Positive thoughts. Couldn't afford anything else. She wouldn't come over the side, so any move she made would be intimidation tactics. No need to even flinch. Hah, like try and turn off that reflex.

He was a warrior, a survivor, the higher the odds, the better, and today's odds were right up there.

He found purchase with the sole of his boot. Ran his fingertips across the rock, and down until he found the tiny crevice.

Sixteen.

This was one of those times when his bizarre counting habit was going to come in handy. The climb up this section had taken sixteen moves. That made it fifteen more to get both feet on solid ground

Broughton?

Crap. This wasn't exactly a good time for a telepathic conversation. *Hey, James, what's happening?*

Fifteen.

Thought I picked up an SOS from you a minute ago. You okay?

Fourteen.

Yep. All good here…if you didn't count his right foot being suspended in midair, searching for a landing. Got it.

Thirteen.

Lying bastard. What's going on?

They definitely knew each other too well.

Found myself in a tight spot, but I'm good now. Just trying to decide my next move. Literally. Right hand.

Twelve.

What put me on your radar? He hadn't heard from James in over six months, which was totally normal, because although they could communicate telepathically, they rarely opened the psychic channel unless they were on a mission together.

New op. Putting a team together and your

name came up.

Yes! *About time. I'm heartily sick of being on the bench.*

Down. Over.

Eleven.

I hear ya.

A bit of gravel trickled across his knuckles and he glanced up. She wasn't visible, but had to be near the rim. Good thing the top of his head was finally beyond her reach.

Team meeting at HQ at nineteen hundred if you want in.

A year ago, his quads would have been burning and pain blasting through his knee like gunshots, but today, thanks to modern technology and a physical therapist with zero sense of humor, he was steady.

Ten.

Timing's going to be tight.

Where are you?

On the side of a mountain, north of the forty-ninth. An hour out of Revelstoke. And an hour from his rented SUV.

Nine.

He should kiss his PT's feet for every time she made him go up that wall, and then back down. A thought crossed his mind. Had she known? She *did* work for ETCETERA, and precognition was a fairly normal gift in that place.

How's it holding up?

James would understand Broughton's need to test drive the knee.

Feel like I'm a kid again.

James laughed. *Good luck with that. Angie's on her way to do a drop-off only an hour or so away and will have to refuel the Steed for the return. Might as well pick you up at the same time. Revelstoke airport in three?*

Barring complications. Mamma grizzly should only be concerned about protecting her cubs. No way she would circle down and get below him…he hoped.

I'll be there.

Six? He'd lost count.

#

Parked near the flight service station, Broughton watched for the fancy helicopter. The Steed was a modern marvel both invisible to the naked eye, and capable of silent flight. Engine and rotor noise was absorbed and contained within the craft itself, which meant passengers and crew had to wear superior ear protection. A mild nuisance, but no big deal.

The illusion of invisibility was created by a special skin which acted like a screen, showing what was on the other side of the bird, or acting as a reflector.

Today, however, the pilot brought it in noisy, and visible, and once it was shut down, Angie hopped out looking like a boy in her black flight suit.

Before getting busy with the refueling process, she tipped her chin toward Broughton and tapped the side of her shiny black helmet—a subtle reminder.

He opened the passenger door and grabbed the

helmet hooked to the inside handle. Slid it over his head, and her voice came through the built-in speaker. "No dogs?"

"They're with a friend."

"We could be tied up for a few weeks. Do we need to pick them up?" Along with six seats in the back, the helicopter had a special place set up for dogs so their ears would be protected.

"My PT has them, and I wasn't due back for a couple of weeks, so we're good." Where else? With what other outfit was there concern for the four-legged? Broughton's weren't service dogs like James's Swagger, but still, they were afforded the same respect and care, and that went a long way.

Angie climbed in beside Broughton as soon as the tanks were filled, and he watched, marveling at the gazillion things she did to get them off the ground, and he stayed silent because Angie had strict rules about chatter during takeoff and landing.

Once at cruising altitude, she said, "Welcome aboard."

"Thanks for the last-minute ride."

"Good timing," she said. "You up here climbing?"

"Yep. Testing the new knee."

"How'd it go?"

"Great until I ran into a mamma grizzly and two cubs this morning."

"Ran into?"

"I was coming up over the edge of a plateau and there she was, looking at me like I'd just committed the sin of all sins."

"Bet ya had to change your shorts."

"Ha-ha, close. But the knee? Not even a twinge, and backing down the face of a cliff was one hell of a test run for it."

Angie laughed. "So, how is Alexandra?"

He should have known she would pull no punches. "I don't know. We kept in touch for a while after she went home, but then with my surgery, and communication through ETC being shut down, we lost touch." What a cop-out.

"Looks like I'm going to win a bet," said Angie. "But I'm pissed. I didn't *think* you'd let yourself get into a relationship, but I was hoping you wouldn't be able to resist her charms. Her being related to Mom's side of the family and all."

"Timing was wrong. She had a lot of shit to get over...past...whatever. The Minnows really screwed with her head, and she needed space to get it sorted out. Didn't want to be leaning on anyone."

"You're telling me she was the one who put a halt to that off-the-charts chemistry?"

He sighed. "Not exactly." He pushed her away the first time, turned down her invitation to come in after they had dinner at a restaurant close to her place. She knew the owners and introduced him as a friend of her cousins, which had then required explanation of finding family she hadn't known about.

The couple immediately sat down at the table with them. Asked for details, and Alex supplied them. Broughton was surprised by their genuine concern, by how easily Alex leaned into their emotional support while blatantly leaving out important details of the past few weeks—like being kidnapped and paralyzed by some freaking rare poison.

That's when reality kicked in, and Broughton saw her for the first time as a real person, not just an interesting shell of a woman lying in a hospital bed, hooked up to monitors. She had friends, and people who treated her like family, long before she discovered she was related to the Meyers.

The chemistry and connection between him and Alex was tied up in what they'd gone through, but had nothing to do with reality.

When they got back to her place and she invited him in, he shut her out. Lied to her. Said his flight was leaving in an hour.

After a few days, when regret set in and he called her, she was too busy to talk.

Broughton thought it was for the best. Their connection developed while in the middle of a situation where she was completely vulnerable, and he was her rescuer. As a professional, it was his duty to keep his distance from her.

When they landed on the helipad beside Angie's house, they were met by her husband, Matthias, and their son, Dhillon—one of the smartest, wisest, and funniest kids Broughton had ever met. Considering his parents, it shouldn't be a surprise.

"Yo, Broughton, you bring your dogs?" asked Dhillon. "I can look after them if you get deployed—right, Mom?"

"Sorry, kiddo, they're with the warden at ETC."

"Warden?"

"My physical therapist. She's okay when she's not torturing a guy in the gym, and the mutts like her. Where's Chance?" It was unusual to see the teen without his dog.

"Inside on kitten duty. Eve brought three strays home, and Chance adopted them, so we brought them over here from the big house. I have to force him to go outside to pee."

Angie laughed. "He's like a mother hen. Looks ridiculous too, stretches out on his bed with those little balls of fluff tucked in between his front legs, and when they wake up hungry, he whines and whines until we get their bottles ready."

"No wonder he was a failure at the racetrack. He never got the sighthound gene," said Broughton. Chance, a tall, leggy greyhound, had been rescued from racing after failing miserably at the game he'd been bred for.

"Yep, Dad says he's a lover, not a killer."

"Speaking of," said Matt. "How's Alex?"

"Good, far as I know. I never had a chance to stretch after I came down the mountain, so I'm going to head for the big house now and get an hour in the gym before the meet."

Evasive tactics, but absolute truth. Which was good, because once in Meyers territory, you wanted to be very careful when dishing out bullshit. There was too freaking much psychic power floating around this place.

Which reminded him, he needed to strengthen his mind blocks, and now would be a perfect time to get it done. Make sure no one would be privy to his every thought, although with their built-in bullshit detectors, there would still be no lying. But that was okay.

Aside from his feelings for Alex, he had nothing to lie about.

Well, almost nothing.

2

Once they were all gathered in the Meyers boardroom, James dove right into the meat of the problem.

"Millions of people were displaced by Hurricanes Harvey and Irma."

Not like that's news, thought Broughton, and James pinned him with a stern look.

Well, fuck. Guess the block I created is somewhat substandard. James's eyebrow went up, and Broughton's mouth twitched while he fought a grin. It was good to be back.

"None of this is news," said James, with a half-smile for Broughton before his glance moved to the others at the massive table. "But what several of you don't know is, prior to the Texas event, Meyers was hired by the Federal Emergency Management Agency because we have technology designed to withstand just about anything the universe sends our way, *and*, while we were close to the locations most likely to be affected, we were not in Harvey's predicted path." He brought up a map of the US on the big screen at the far end of the room.

"When the hurricane hit far harder than expected, we stepped up our game, and while I was working intel and logistics, Julia put together a team." James passed his wife the laser pointer.

"We were not only boots on the ground, but among the first in," said Julia. "We rescued people from the floodwaters in these three areas." The red dot swirled around county names.

"Most were dropped off at the closest rescue centers. Some we put right in the care of site coordinators. Many of those we transported had pets with them, and when the evac centers balked at more animals, we set up a relay system to bring them here. More specifically, next door to Haven, where they would be cared for until evacuees were safely home and able to look after them. Rachel's territory."

She nodded toward Quinn's wife, who took over the narrative.

"We kept meticulous records in the beginning, but with floodwaters rising, time was of the essence, and filling out paperwork was wasting that precious commodity."

Julia slid the keyboard toward her. "Plan B," said Rachel. "We used our phones and did this."

A video came up on the screen. It was an old man, with sun-weathered skin, tufts of white hair on his head, and stubble on his chin. Hugged tight to his chest was a brown and white dog, some kind of hound cross.

“What is your name?” Broughton recognized Quinn’s voice asking the question.

“Jackson Ford.”

“Tell us your address and phone number, Jackson.”

The man’s voice was shaky, and he stumbled over the phone number, muttering about never calling himself.

“Next of kin?”

“My brother’s boy, I guess. Never saw him after he went to college. There’s a girl too, don’t know where she lives.”

“Tell us about your dog, his name, and what he likes and doesn’t like, so we can look after him for you.”

“He’s my life.” A tear tracked down the old man’s cheek.

“We’re going to take good care of him. You can’t get dog food here in the shelter, and others might not be kind to him here. We’ll make sure he’s safe and happy, and bring him back to you.”

“He’s Digger. He’s seven, and he likes everybody. Even cats.”

“What kind of food does he like?”

“It’s a big blue bag, with red letters and the picture of a police dog on the front. I get it at the grocery down the street.”

The video ended.

“Before we were done, there were three hundred and twenty-seven of these clips. Haven took in four hundred and twenty-two dogs, a hundred and sixty-five cats, and nearly a hundred other critters from the scaled to the feathered.”

Broughton and Rachel were near-phobic about legless creatures. "How'd you handle the, uh, unmentionables?" There was a family pact to not use the s word unless a life was at stake. And lives… Well, hell, they were in Texas, so there was always that to consider.

"A reptile rescue group stepped up, thank the heavens above us."

"Perfect."

"Anyway, when the dust settled, or more specifically when the flood waters receded, we were able to return the bulk of the pets to their owners, and there was much rejoicing... For the most part."

"We reached out to everyone who didn't contact us," said James. "Touched base with dozens who were looking for somewhere else to go because they had lost their homes. Let them know we would keep the animals for them indefinitely."

Rachel smiled. "At Haven, we believe in the power of souls connecting with souls, and knowing their pets would be okay was something people could hang on to while they struggled to find housing and get their lives back to some kind of normalcy. There were those who seemed helpless. Loss of home and livelihood took a toll on relationships, and it was freaking hard on the heart some days, but we made a difference."

Quinn touched the back of her hand. "We really did."

"Stepping off my soapbox and going on," she said. "In the midst of the 'recovery and return' process, we were not surprised to discover that some people seemed to have vanished completely.

There were those who were taken in by kin or friends, or perhaps even traveled to other states." She shrugged.

"Then the spidey senses kicked in, and we did some investigating. Accessed evac center registrations. Turns out we have vids of twenty people we dropped off at rescue centers, I mean right at the doors, but they never registered, and there's no record of them at any other shelter either."

"Maybe they got picked up and moved elsewhere because a shelter was too full to take them," said Broughton, more or less thinking out loud. "And, of course, you've pulled that thread already. And twenty is a tidy number. Could be a busload."

Human traffickers often preyed on victims of natural disasters. Exactly why this big team was about to mobilize.

Broughton scanned the faces of the assembled. James at the head of the table with his wife to his left. What a pair. Born leaders, stubborn, talented, fit, and vibrant. Grandparents several times over, but who would know by looking at them?

James had been through hell and back while conquering PTSD, and Julia stayed at his side up until he disappeared a few years back. Then she took up the reins of the family business and led Meyers Security with an iron will until her husband returned. Now they shared leadership.

Quinn, their son the psychologist, didn't often participate in ops, but he was apparently in on this one along with his wife, who had given birth to twins only months earlier. In addition to that monumental task, she was the energy behind Haven—a property bordering the Meyers ranch—where they rehabbed people and animals recovering from physical and emotional trauma.

Angie, Matthias, and Dhillon sat across the table. She was a pilot, he a research scientist, and their son was...not your average teenager. With a mind like a computer and a memory that let go of nothing, he loved being on the team almost as much as he adored his dog, horses, rescuing kittens, and farting.

The kid's talents were epic. Weird to see him without his sidekick, though. Chance was usually glued to the boy's side.

Rather like the service dog lying quietly at James's feet. Swagger had dragged his master back from the edge of a PTSD implosion numerous times, but it was good to see the dog relaxing today.

"If you're assessing the team," said Dhillon, who was also a master at observation, "Merlin's on this one too."

"Merlin?"

"The white cat some people think can talk, or at least communicate his thoughts to select humans. Not that he's ever said squat to me. I think he talked to Alex when you were here before. You know, when she couldn't move or speak."

Alex. Not bad. He hadn't thought about her in at least an hour. "I remember her saying something about Merlin having a sarcastic streak."

"Whether or not the cat is involved," said James, "we did some investigating, one thing led to another, and Rachel learned of similar situations in Florida, after their hurricane."

"Except they didn't have the video records we did," added Rachel. "So they didn't have much to go on."

Broughton's curiosity was well stirred now. "What or who do you suspect?"

"I thi—"

"Dhillon." Angie's voice was quiet, yet commanding. The boy buttoned his lip and appeared to reconsider an eye roll halfway through. Which made his expression darned comedic, but didn't take away from the seriousness of the situation.

Broughton didn't like the sound of things so far. Innocent people being scooped up during a frightening time? Was it a sophisticated operation? Or a random crime of opportunity?

"None of the Texas evacuees appeared to have much in the way of family," said James.

"On their own except for a pet?" asked Broughton.

"Twenty men, who are connected to seventeen dogs and six cats we have in care," said Rachel.

Broughton didn't like how easy it sounded. "Adult males with no one to report them missing. A perfect setup for organs or slave labor." Thank God there were no children involved. Less than a year ago he intercepted a shipment of kids plucked off the streets of various Third World cities and smuggled into the States. Before that, he'd scooped four boys and three girls from a semi on its way out of New York. He'd be happy to never work another case with a kid factor.

"Every federal agency you can think of jumped on board." James stroked his dog's long ears. "Started butting heads and getting nowhere until they agreed to let us do the legwork and provide them with solid leads."

"What's the plan?" Broughton didn't like the odds. There had been hundreds, if not thousands of strangers in and around the flood zones for weeks. Everything from the national guard to an amazing flotilla of rescuers from Louisiana.

"We have hundreds of hours of video from news sources, from security cameras, and from social media. Everyone in this room, and a few of those working remotely, will put in a full day tomorrow reviewing footage." James tapped the keyboard in front of him and images filled the wall screen. "These are the people we're looking for."

Broughton sucked in a breath.

"Yes," said James. "It's not hard to see the common thread."

All men of color. "Targeted."

"Sure looks that way."

"Have you found any data on them besides what you gathered when you took the pets?"

"We've created full profiles from canvassing neighbors, finding employers, the usual." Rachel smiled. "Got quite a bit from their pets, too."

Okay, that was just too far out there. "I hope you're not sharing that with the government agencies."

"No," said Julia, giving nothing away with her expression. "Nor have we shared that you're on the roster because of your psychic abilities."

Ouch. "A palpable hit," he said, trying not to smile. Everyone in the room had skills other than those listed on the average job application. Mind reading, truth detection, and telepathy only scratched the surface, and nicely complemented special ops skills like Broughton's fluency in four languages, and his ability to pick off a target at a half mile.

"Grace," Julia continued, "will be joining us as soon as Logan returns from his current mission. For now, she's one of the remote researchers."

Grace was Julia's niece and had mad psychic skills. "I guess she's already tried communicating with the victims?"

"Yes, and no luck. She can't just tap into a mind. It has to be open and seeking connection, which is why most of her success is with children. Also," she hesitated the slightest of beats. "Alex has completed her training and will be arriving with Grace and Logan."

As a veterinarian, he imagined Alex often did training updates for new procedures and things. It would be interesting to have her here, to find out if there were still sparks between them. Her strength of character impressed him and her family tree was packed with powerful women. Grace was her cousin, and Julia their aunt…all because of one man who traveled the world as a polo star and left a scattering of pregnant young women in his wake. He'd been a player, and a cad, and had bedded the rich and famous as well as those working for them. He loved women, and they loved him back...for as long as he stayed in their city.

Broughton shoved thoughts of being under the same roof as Alex into a remote corner of his mind. "What about data on those missing after the Florida hurricane?"

James clicked his keyboard again, and a screenshot of sixteen men appeared—all young, able-bodied, and not white. "This is what we have so far. The twins are there, digging for more."

Broughton liked the twins, possibly the youngest of the Meyers children—there were so darn many, Broughton lost track. Nathan and Tyler were mid-twenties, and full of life. People were drawn to their light-heartedness, and to the tall, curly-coated black dogs constantly at their sides.

"They took Puck and Stick with them," said Dhillon, and Broughton was reminded that the kid was very intuitive. Always seemed to know the direction his thoughts had gone.

"Seems funny for this room to not be filled with mutts."

"If you need a fix," said Rachel, "I left two of my charges in the kitchen with Consuelo. They're well-adjusted, but still missing their own people."

"I'll visit with them after." Broughton was used to being without his dogs for long stretches, but it was always good to connect with a canine. Grounded him somehow, and would help him deal with the prospect of Alex.

3

Alexandra Davidson stared across the room at Grace. "Say what?"

"The team we're about to join includes Caleb Broughton." Grace waited a beat. "If you think you'll have a problem working with him, you'd better get over it. By this time tomorrow we'll be in Texas."

"What if I don't want to see him? And I can't believe I haven't even known his first name till now. Caleb?"

"It means a dog, in Hebrew, which is fitting, don't you think?"

Before Alex could respond, Grace continued, "As for you not wanting to see him? You'll go anyway, because that's who you are. You signed on to help find the missing. You're invested. And you're not a quitter."

Alex couldn't stop the smile. "Dammit, you really are good."

"The best." Grace grinned when Alex threw herself onto the couch. "Come on, you know you're dying to see him."

"I wish I could say that wasn't true, especially considering the son of a bitch brushed me off the last time I saw him—*after* I pretty much invited him to my bed. Yet here I am with my knickers all in a twist at the thought of seeing him again. What am I, twelve?"

"What you are, is in love with a difficult man. The kind who will love you and respect your brains and brawn, yet still try to make decisions on your behalf."

"Sounds like a great catch." She didn't roll her eyes, but…

"I figure you'll have him beaten into submission within a year."

"If only."

"Look, from what I've seen and heard, he's a good man, and has the utmost respect for women, whether they're authority figures like Julia or domestic workers like Consuelo. Well...Consuelo really doesn't count, because she's more family than anything else. But still, he treats everyone well, and dogs love him."

"Even Merlin had a soft spot for him."

Grace's gaze narrowed. "I'd forgotten you connected with the cat."

"He's a funny dude."

"So's Broughton occasionally. But for the most part he has major issues—all the good ones do—and getting him past them will be work, but you're just the woman for the job."

"As long as I have you to coach me."

"Unh, uh. Nope." Grace shook her head. "Once we land at the ranch, you're on your own. Not," she held up a hand. "Not that Julia and I won't be there for you if you need us, but you and your man need to work out the wrinkles on your own." She raked her fingers through hair, as thick and curly as Alex's.

"Julia and I will, of course, be available to mop tears if necessary, but you need to know it's not our forte."

Alex would have laughed if her throat hadn't closed upon hearing a sentiment incredibly close to what her mother would have said.

In spite of never meeting, or for that matter even knowing each other existed, Julia, Grace, and her mom were strikingly similar in their strength, stubbornness, and inability to deal with people and emotions. Could handle the toughest of situations, stand up to the bad guys, soothe frightened animals, or tackle a wall of granite standing between them and where they needed to be. But if a human needed comforting? All three—make that four, because Alex had the same affliction—would run for the nearest exit.

Such a shame Mary never had a chance to meet the others. In her work as a veterinarian, Alex often marveled at how nature stamped siblings with similar personalities. But nurture also had a role, and it played out with these women as well. They'd all grown up isolated. Mary in a home run by nuns, Grace dragged around the world by a woman who was a performer first and a mother second. Or third.

Even Julia had grown up differently than most kids. Her single mom had fought to keep her, and they moved from town to town, dodging the authorities trying to track them down. Julia had grown up quickly while her mother worked two and three jobs to support them.

How Alex wished Grace and Julia could have been at her mother's side to help her battle for her life, and give her the comfort of knowing Alex wouldn't be alone after.

Giving her head a shake to dislodge her morbid thoughts, Alex changed the direction of her thinking.

"What time are we leaving?"

"Angie will be here at seven."

"That gives me a day to get used to the idea.

"A.M.," Grace said, straight-faced.

"That's less than twelve hours from now."

"Time to suck it up, buttercup."

"Good thing I was taught to respect my elders, or I'd say something about your cruel streak."

Grace blinked. "Elder? Seriously? I don't even have ten years on you."

It was Alex's turn to grin. "But every one counts. Hah, you'll be a senior long before me, too." Grace's comical expression had Alex laughing so hard she was wiping tears away when Grace's husband joined them in the solarium.

"What's so funny?" asked Logan.

"She was being cheeky. Called us old."

"Did she, now? There shall be punishment for such behavior." He tapped his chin as though thinking. "Perhaps I should sing?"

"Oh, please no," said Grace, covering her ears and closing her eyes.

Logan took advantage by slipping his hand around the back of her neck and pulling her to him. Planted a noisy kiss on her lips.

Cute. They were cute together. And hot. Alex could nearly hear the air sizzling between them. They were the epitome of a power couple. Strong, sexy, capable, and madly in love.

Could she have something like that with Broughton?

Broughton. Until today she hadn't even known his first name. Would she ever be able to think of him as Caleb?

She'd never forget his soft breath on her cheek and his whisper in her ear when they met. "I'm Broughton, and I'm going to keep you safe…" And she had immediately trusted him, in spite of the precarious situation. In the days that followed, while she lay helpless, paralyzed by a drug no one could identify, he became her constant companion, helping move her, keeping her company, and entertaining her through the long hours of immobility and uncertainty.

They'd even once communicated telepathically, just as Grace and Logan were probably doing right now. Hell, for all she knew, the pair of them could be tapping into her thoughts.

Going back to the Meyers ranch would mean being surrounded by people able to slip into her mind, which meant she'd best work on the blocking techniques Grace taught her.

Time to shore up the internal entryway, make

sure the illusion of firmly locked doors was what an intruder would encounter upon attempting to access her thoughts. Communicating telepathically while her mind was configured with the secure entryway was a hard-won skill, but she'd had little else to do while the paralytic was in her system, and she'd become quite adept. But now, nine and a half months later, she was rusty.

Good. Practicing the process would give her something to do tonight, because sleep wasn't likely to be her friend. Not with the prospect of seeing Broughton, of hearing the voice that helped her hang on to her sanity. And then there was his scent, clean and masculine. She would wake up and know he was in the room even before she opened her eyes.

When she wasn't sleeping, he hung out, asking if she preferred silence or talk, and she was able to respond to his questions with eye blinks for yes or no.

When she wanted the comfort of his voice, he talked to her about everything from training his dogs to the paintings he did while in hiding on a reservation in New Mexico. He spent several years there, with only his three Belgian Malinois for company. He understood the complexities of solitude.

Some nights he told her stories of special ops missions he participated in, and each time he prefaced by saying he was changing some of the details. She liked that he remained loyal and true to his pledges, even when the incidents had happened many years earlier.

One night he laughingly asked her a number of questions, and, using her yes/no eyeblink answers, created a profile he then illustrated with a few pen strokes on the back of an index card he stole from Eve's desk. He was talented. The caricature was simple. It was all about her froth of curly hair, her eyes wide open, and her mouth ticked up on one side—a habit she'd had since she was a kid.

But the fun part was the rest of the little things. He'd put her on a mule, with a cat under one arm, a dog under the other, and her legs folded up, jockey style.

She planned to keep the drawing, but couldn't find it when she returned the day after she regained mobility. But things were wild then, with another abduction, lives threatened, and thank God an eventual happy ending.

That's when Broughton kissed her, and she told him he could do better. And he did. It was like Fourth of July fireworks, and she thought he felt it too. He followed her home to Kentucky because he said he wanted to see more of her. She took him to her favorite place for dinner, and when they came back to her place, he left her at the door. A chaste kiss, and—poof—gone.

"Dark thoughts," said Logan, making her look up sharply.

She imagined the sound of a slamming door, and he didn't flinch. "Not nice to trespass."

"No need. Your face was giving you away, although I'm not sure whether it was anger or sadness winning the battle."

Alex sighed, and Grace said, "Anger and

determination will win. It's in her DNA."

"Of course it is." And Logan would know. He was married to a woman who looked like Alex's older sister, and they had a lot more than looks in common. "Until I met Julia, I thought James was the reason they had such strong, pigheaded, brilliant children. Now I know they had no choice, because they got it from both sides."

"Are you suggesting Julia, Grace, and I are also pigheaded?"

Logan grinned. "If you're half as stubborn as they are, absolutely."

Alex thought about that, and the upcoming meeting. Yes, she was absolutely stubborn enough to deal with the man who kept her awake at night. A smile lit her from the inside, and she nearly laughed with the joy of it. Broughton had no idea what was about to hit him.

4

Up and working before first light, Broughton was taking a break from the computer screen, and was in the kitchen helping Consuelo put together the lunch tray when a new swirl of energy and hum of voices joined those already inside the sprawling building.

He recognized the colors of Logan, Grace, and Alexandra, and all three were locked down like pros.

"Hard on the food that way, young man."

He dropped the crumpled slice of bread. Felt like an idiot. "I—"

She held up a hand. "You spent a great deal of time with her last year, and barely got to hear her voice, but you know it. And know it well, because you heard her telepathically from the moment you met her."

No one had known. Even Alexandra. He opened his mouth to deny. Closed it again. Shook his head. "Is there anything going on in this house you don't know about?"

"As a matter of fact, yes. What's none of my business is none of my business, but that young woman was in a very bad position, and I feared for what could be going on in her mind, so I kept tabs." She sliced another sandwich and added it to the pile already on the cart.

"Wheel this thing to the boardroom for me, would you? Everyone's going to be feeling awkward, and food will help."

He leaned down to kiss the top of her head. "You're an amazing woman, Consuelo."

"I know." She flapped her hands at him. "Now get."

The newcomers were still standing when he pushed into the room.

Well, hell. That thud he heard just might have been his heart landing at his feet when he set eyes on Alexandra. Did she have any idea how powerful that smile was?

"Hey." More a sound than a word.

He cleared his throat. "Hey back. Nice to see you upright. I brought lunch." That was the best he could do? "Consuelo said it was time for the team to take a break."

"I agree," said James. "Then we'll get everyone caught up."

Grace helped him transfer the plates of sandwiches, bowls of salad, and trays of desserts to the wide counter at the back of the room while James and Julia pulled dishes and utensils from the cupboards, and cold drinks from the fridge.

The business of getting food seemed to keep everyone occupied for a short time. Long enough for Broughton to study Alex surreptitiously, at least. She looked good. Healthy and well, unlike when he'd seen her last.

She'd only been back on her feet for a few days at that point, and was still pale, and had a breakable quality about her. Today, she was as fragile-looking as an athlete at the peak of her career, and he wondered what it was that gave her such a fitness edge.

In spite of spending nearly twenty-four seven with her for ten days at the end of last year, he knew freaking few details about her life.

She wasn't able to talk then. Swallowing and blinking her eyes were the grand total of her physical abilities.

"You gonna eat that?" Dhillon was pointing at the slice of chocolate cake on Broughton's plate.

He eyed the boy. "You didn't get any?"

"Sure. But it was looking like you didn't want the rest of yours, so I figured I could take care of it for you."

Broughton had forced down a sandwich, but the rich cake was beyond him. "Bet your mom said you could only have one slice."

"Chocolate is bad for the dogs, which means it will be headed for the trash, and we hate wastefulness around here."

"You'll owe me."

"Only if Mom doesn't catch me eating it."

"Deal," he said, and had to stifle a laugh when the kid shoved half of it into his mouth. He was at that gangly stage Broughton remembered well. Always hungry, and tripping over his feet while suddenly towering over the other kids at school.

Along with the memories came the darkness of going from being a normal teenager to a traumatized youth on the run.

"Mmmm." Dhillon had inhaled the rest of the cake and was licking his fingers when his mother stopped beside his chair and eyed the bowl at his elbow.

"Seconds of salad, I see. Nice try. I'm not fooled, but you're getting a pass this time because there's important business at hand. Doesn't mean I won't revisit this later, though, so consider yourself warned." She knocked his forehead with a gentle knuckle and moved on to help her father fill the trolley with the dirty dishes and leftovers.

When James returned from the kitchen, everyone found a seat, and silence descended.

"We've turned up three of the missing, alive and well. Rachel and Quinn will be making contact with them to follow up about their pets later."

"So we're down to seventeen," said Dhillon.

"Dhil—" Angie's admonishment was cut short by her father.

"Young man. In these briefings, no one besides the person leading the meeting speaks unless spoken to. You see the notepads in front of each person? That's where your questions go. That way they will be handy when it's time to ask them later." He glanced around the table.

"For those of you just arriving, this is Dhillon's first time as an official team member. He campaigned hard and was granted apprentice status. He was also apprised of the rules, which means if he breaks one a second time, we'll remove one of his thumbs."

Broughton could almost feel the contained snickers, but not a sound came from anyone.

"Now, to continue," said James. "While our original numbers did come down to seventeen, during the process we identified five more people who were headed for evacuation centers but never registered anywhere. The total is now twenty-two."

He put a photo on the screen at the end of the room. It was a huge warehouse with a big "evac" banner draped near the front door. "This is the location where all the missing were dropped off. The entire building is monitored by security cameras. However, the ones at the back of the building were miraculously out of commission."

Having narrowed the possibilities to a single building was huge. Gave them something concrete to work with.

"We need to canvas for video footage. Best case we'll get a view of the rear doors. Besides that, we're looking for vehicles going in and out of the area during the hours after we dropped off those who are missing. Of note, the five new victims were left by friends during the same hours we were doing evac."

Julia reached to use the keyboard in front of James. "Meanwhile in Florida, using a new software they developed, Tyler and Nathan have ID'd three panel vans leaving evac centers with more weight in them than when they arrived. Not conclusive evidence by any means, but if we get some vehicle footage from the Texas evac, the software might come in handy." The image she posted was side-by-sides of a white panel van. Numbers below them suggested a difference of six to seven hundred pounds.

"The tags on the vans were stolen, so nothing to go on there," said James. "I want two pairs working the Texas zone today. You'll have about four hours of daylight to ferret out cameras and witnesses, get us some video footage. Grace and Logan will be one pair."

His gaze settled on Alex. "You are new to the team, so you may choose to pair up with Broughton or stay here and review video."

"I need field work." She flicked Broughton a look he thought might be a challenge, but when she didn't follow it up with words, he had no idea what was going on in her head. Apparently she had mastered blocking access to her thoughts.

And James calling her a member of the team wasn't sitting well. She was a veterinarian, not a security agent. What the hell were they thinking?

"Angie will drop you off and return for pickup when you're ready for her, and you'll send what you can via your communications units, enabling us to review footage while you're still in the field. These people have been missing for too damn long."

"Getting some bad vibes the past few days and not liking it at all," said Rachel, who had a weird yet interesting relationship with the dead, a kind soul sometimes used as a conduit for connection with this side.

"Quinn and I will be mostly at Haven because of the number of evacuees still with us, but we're available to zip over here if needed," she added.

"Matthias and Dhillon, you're on research," said James. "And now is the time for questions, Dhillon. "You have anything?"

"Alex is getting field experience on her first op. Maybe I should too."

Nicely said, and without whining, thought Broughton. Smart.

"They'll all be armed, and you're not legal to pack in the city. Anything else?"

"No, sir." Nice touch.

James stood. "Safety first." And that was the signal to disband.

"Landing strip in twenty," Angie said.

"Not taking the Steed?" Dhillon asked.

"Smarter to take a jet when time is critical." She grinned at her son. "I'll be back almost before I leave."

"Ha-ha, only if you take up teleporting."

With this family, Broughton didn't doubt that's exactly how they'd travel one day. In the meantime, he needed to grab a few things from his room before they took off.

He headed out. Stopped, and with barely a glance over his shoulder, said, "I'll meet you back here in five, or at the strip in fifteen." And beat a retreat.

In his room, he took a deep breath and let it out slowly. As much as he'd love spending the next few hours in her company, he wasn't happy about James allowing Alex to step outside the compound. She was green as grass, and she'd be packing. Was she proficient? Could she defend herself if someone didn't like them poking around? Could she possibly have his back if he got in trouble?

Not that Matthias would have been a better choice. He was a doctor. Research scientist. Not exactly a think-fast-on-your-feet kind of guy.

Broughton wanted to ask James to rethink the assignment, but nothing short of a gun to his head would get him to do that.

Chain of command.

And Broughton had trusted James with his life more times than he could count.

5

Alex had to squelch a nervous laugh when Broughton spotted her in the boardroom. He clearly hadn't expected her to wait for him, silly man.

"You're surprised," she said.

"Yeah."

"That's it?"

He pinned her with a searching look. "Helluva move, ditching vet medicine for a job in security."

Talk about cutting to the chase.

"Seemed like a good idea at the time. And speaking of which." She tapped her watch. "When we have some, I might explain my decision, but for now we need to get a move on." Not a chance in hell she was going to be late for her first assignment.

She left him standing there flat-footed, but he was quick to catch up and fall into step beside her while she strode down the long hallway.

The security offices were located in one of the

spoke-like wings of the ranch's main house, and there were always vehicles parked at the far end, at the ready.

She pushed the door open and eyed the selection. Perfect. She was barely able to keep a straight face while passing by two golf carts and an SUV.

"Hop on," she said, and slid her leg over a camo-panted four-wheeler.

He was quick to settle in behind her, and when his arms came around her middle she said, "Not so fast," and passed him a helmet she unclipped from the handlebars.

It would only be a five-minute ride, or less, but accidents… She'd lived through paralysis less than a year ago, and a head injury wasn't something she wanted to add to her list of accomplishments.

When his hands once again gripped her middle, she eased the machine onto the road instead of the dirt path—no point getting coated in dust—and picked up the pace steadily until hot air was buffeting them. Not as good as galloping on horseback, but not completely unlike it either, and during her training with Grace, Alex had come to love blasting around the back roads of Paradise.

The place was such an amazing facility, like this ranch in some ways, but also very different. Hundreds of acres of wilderness and pastures and small homes, fancy barns, and a country inn complete with tennis courts, formal gardens, and an indoor pool. A person could become spoiled by the lifestyle of the rich and famous while staying there, but Alex's days had been filled with long hours of work and study.

Odd, or so she'd thought at the time, was how comfortable she was while learning to ride a four-wheeler over uncertain terrain, and commanding the vehicle instead of simply riding it. She'd learned offensive and defensive moves she'd hopefully never need. But now she was able to command virtually any land vehicle from an eighteen-wheeler on down.

She'd worked her ass off, and damned well deserved to be going into the field today, even if Broughton didn't think she was capable. She considered making a fancy move now, but it would be irresponsible with him on the back and unprepared.

Instead, she slowed appropriately when making the turn for the airstrip, then blasted the straightway just a bit because it felt so damned good.

His arms tightened, and she poured more gas, enjoying the sensation of *him* hanging onto *her*. Depending on her this time. If their helmets had been miked she could have said, "I'm Alexandra, and I'm going to keep you safe."

If the others hadn't been climbing aboard the pretty jet when they came into sight, she'd have driven past, then circled back, just to keep Broughton hanging on to her. But instead, she eased to a stop beside the hangar where the other vehicles were parked.

Broughton climbed off right away, passed her the helmet, and she hung both just as she'd found them. Stared at Broughton's back while following him to the plane. Was he annoyed? Who could tell from here? She started to hustle to catch up, but how undignified. She slowed instead. Waited until he was aboard before climbing the stairs.

Angie came in behind her and closed the door, latched it, then joined Trent in the front while Alex took the only empty seat in the passenger area. Beside Broughton.

What a riot to be wishing for the closeness of economy class on a commercial flight when instead the upholstery was buttery soft leather and the seats were not only huge, but had a narrow aisle between them. There would be no being forced to touch your seatmate on this ride.

Probably just as well, because distractions were never a good thing, and today she was determined to shine. To hold her head high and make Grace proud.

"You will," said Grace from the seat behind Broughton.

Alex frowned. Her mind block must have slipped, and that was unacceptable. Grace was chuckling.

"What's so funny?"

"You looked so annoyed."

"You shouldn't have been able to read my thoughts."

"I was guessing, which wasn't hard, considering. You had that stubborn, I'm going to slay this set to your shoulders."

"That's just mean, making me think…" No, Grace was, as always, trying to teach her something. Perhaps a need to pay more attention to her body language. Keep her thoughts and emotions to herself so no one could play her. "Got it, thanks."

#

Broughton stepped onto the tarmac first and scanned the area while the others deplaned.

Quiet. But not eerie quiet. More the kind that came from a place mostly inhabited on weekends by hobby flyers. On weekdays only the retired hung around, polishing their planes, swapping stories with their comrades.

Landing at small airports with something as fancy as the jet usually caused a stir, but Meyers had a hangar here, so the locals were used to their comings and goings.

"Hey, Angie," said an old guy wandering their way.

"Hey, Del. How's it goin'?"

"Oh, 'bout the same as always. You?"

"Good air, smooth trip. You been up?"

"Not yet. Kid coming later needs some night hours for his commercial. If your bird's still here, he'll want to see inside."

"I'm just dropping off, but I'll be back to pick up later. If he's here, bring him over."

"Will do." He touched his forehead in mock salute, then ambled away.

"Okay, troops, I'll be back in three hours," said Angie. "Need me before that, just shout."

"Where you headed?" asked Broughton.

"Here and there. A few things to pick up, but I'll never be more than thirty minutes away if you need me."

Which meant she was likely on her way to the nearby military airport. Good. That tied up the last loose thread. He liked knowing where the whole team was.

Solid with the plans they made during the flight, Broughton headed for a car parked beside the small Meyers hangar. He slid into the driver's seat, with Alex beside him and the others in the back.

Stopping at the security panel inside the gate, Broughton got out to enter the code and slide his hand into the palm reader. When the gate rolled open, he drove them through and waited for it to close before leaving.

Less than twenty minutes later he parked behind the warehouse used as a receiving center for hurricane evacuees. It wasn't much more than a stopgap, but enabled those with boats to easily go back and forth, getting people out of flooded homes and to a safer location. They were then transported to one of the large centers.

During the storm, the only viable route away from the building was to the north, so Grace and Logan would go northeast while Broughton and Alex went northwest. On foot.

The task was to find security cameras which could have captured an image of a person or vehicle, and secure copies of any pertinent footage. Seemed like a simple enough assignment, but that made it the kind most likely to go off the rails. Add in a greenhorn partner, and the odds were definitely against them.

He couldn't depend on a greenhorn to have his back, especially one with not even the tiniest bit of relevant background. What the hell could a veterinarian bring to a project like this?

"Will you be acknowledging my presence any time soon? Perhaps even speak to me?" asked Alex as soon as the others were out of sight. When he didn't turn around right away, she grabbed his arm, but he continued to scan the area, as he had since they arrived. There were so many nooks and crannies for an enemy to hide.

"It's a job, Alex. We need to be vigilant, and, as decided earlier, we'll walk the routes a vehicle would travel until we get to the end of our assigned zone. Then we'll work our way back and check out any possible pathways not accessible by a car or truck."

"There's no need to repeat what I already know. I simply wanted to remind you we're a team."

He stopped to study her expressionless face, and was reminded of Grace when she was in work mode and locked down. Professional, and just a bit scary. Didn't help that Alex could pass for Grace's sister.

"You are a very inexperienced member of this team."

"I'm well trained."

She'd never survive boot camp. "Training is good. But experience is better." A thousand times better. Until you've looked an enemy in the eye…

"I don't expect you to talk, or point anything out to me, but I do expect you to at least acknowledge me."

He heaved a sigh. "I see you and hear you. I'm aware of your presence even when I can't do either of the above. That's all I can offer." He bit his tongue before he said he didn't do "chat," because that would be waving a red cape, and he'd deserve getting slapped down for it.

Sucked that he even had the thought, dammit. Meant there was something wrong with him. Sexist? No, he'd have said the same to Dhillon, or any other agent wanting him to converse.

Working alone was his preference, always had been. Could sit in a tree for hours at a time, waiting for as long as it took to pick off a target.

He'd even been called the Silent CO on a long mission in Columbia. Perhaps the animal reference would make more sense to Alex.

"My call name was Dobie, because Dobermans are notorious for their silence." And then he wanted to kick himself, because the last thing he wanted to do was start a conversation.

"Well, that certainly fits."

He waited, but she said nothing more. Good. She was a quick study. But hadn't he learned that months ago while he sat those long hours with her? Because he had tapped into her thoughts from the get-go—a necessity to keep her safe—he was fully aware of how her mind worked constantly, even when her body was frozen in place.

Staying connected wasn't exactly necessary in the following weeks, and he should have let her know he could hear her thoughts. But he didn't then, and now, when he could have used the insight, she was apparently adept at keeping others out of her mind.

6

Alex resisted the urge to smack the man upside the head. And Dobie...seriously? Her specialty might be horses, but she worked her way through school as an assistant at a small animal clinic. Not a dog she couldn't handle. She stifled a smile. This poker face thing was making her teeth ache.

Meanwhile, she used her observational skills to pick out three cameras mounted on buildings they approached. Had Broughton seen them first and waited for her to notice them? Perhaps. Did speculating make any difference? Yes. It distracted her from her job, so she shoved it away.

"There," she said, keeping her voice low. "Top edge at ten o'clock."

"Got it."

"Pointed at the parking lot makes it more promising than the last ones." Cameras trained on a building egress didn't give much for peripheral views.

"Yep."

They went inside.

"Hello?" The woman's eyebrows disappeared under her bangs.

They approached the wide wooden desk in what looked like a reception area, but clearly the woman sitting behind it wasn't used to people just wandering in off the street.

"Hi, we're hoping you can help us."

"If you're looking for the furniture warehouse, hang a left out the door, and it's two blocks down."

Alex wanted to engage, but stayed in line, waited for Broughton to speak.

Unhurried, he flipped open a leather case to display his identification, which happened to have FBI in bold letters at the top.

The woman did a quick scan, stared down at his boots, then her gaze tracked upward, taking in his cargos and T-shirt. "They wear suits on television."

He flashed a killer smile. "Those guys have plush offices, too. I missed out on both. I'm hoping you can help us out."

He started with "I" and finished with "us," so she supposed that was him trying. Maybe he'd remember "we" next time.

Broughton explained that they were looking for people displaced by the storm and matching them with their missing pets. Close enough to the truth for it to have a solid ring, and after short introductions, Margaret was very accommodating.

Twenty minutes later, they said goodbye to their new friend and left with a memory stick that just might be worth its weight in gold. Margaret wasn't the least bit tech savvy, which meant having a file sent to them for forwarding to Meyers wasn't going to happen, but she was happy to give them a backup USB stick of what was downloaded for insurance purposes before the cameras were reset a week or so after the hurricane.

"Interesting how quickly she bought your phony ID," said Alex.

He quirked an eyebrow. "You got that good a look at it? I must be slipping."

"Grace is a thorough trainer. There," she said, pointing at the camera perched high on a corner of the next building. They went inside, came out twenty minutes later with more potential evidence to be sorted through at HQ.

Alex could have danced with excitement by the time the foursome met for the ride back to the airport. But she maintained her poker face.

"Anything?" she asked Grace.

"About a dozen files, but only the last two look promising. Sent them to HQ about twenty minutes ago. How about you?"

Alex waited for Broughton to speak, but when he stayed quiet, she filled Grace and Logan in on what they had come up with.

"Gut feelings?" Grace asked.

"The best footage is on the USB stick."

"From the sound of the location, my money is with yours," said Logan, and Alex mentally rubbed her hands together with glee. *She* was going to be instrumental in bringing this case to a successful conclusion. And that was huge.

Funny, though, she hadn't expected parallels with her work in the horse racing industry. Today's success rated right up there with one of her patients recovering well.

And if it turned out to be "too late" for those who were taken there, she'd face it like other losses she'd experienced.

Her life had always been about doing what needed to be done and accepting what was beyond her control. Even when her mom was diagnosed with stage four breast cancer. There was nothing Alex could do to change the prognosis, but she could change how those few months together played out.

That was the first time she stepped away from vet medicine.

She and her mom had gone to the Derby, and to Breeders' Cup. And although Mary had worked at a first-class breeding farm from the time she was sixteen, and worked with some very good horses, Alex thought she should meet some of the all-time greats.

They visited a farm famous for fields and barns filled with retired champions, and her mom got to feed carrots and peppermints to winners of every leg of the Triple Crown.

They sat front row at a Keenland Sale. And visited the Kentucky Horse Park. Mary bought photos that day, and other mementoes, as though she believed she would be around to enjoy them. Two years later, there was still a hole in Alex's heart.

She glanced over her shoulder at her cousin

Grace, who appeared to be having a telepathic conversation with her husband. The average person would never guess, but there was a softening of expression that gave them away to Alex.

When she once asked Grace what it was like to always be privy to her husband's thoughts, she laughed, and said, "Staying connected all the time would likely be enough to ruin any marriage. We keep our thoughts to ourselves, and only share words, just like any conversation."

"So he never knows what you're thinking?"

Grace hesitated. "Our telepathic skills are different from our other gifts. We are capable of thought-sharing, but don't use it on a regular basis since it can feel intrusive."

That made sense to Alex, because she wouldn't want someone in her head any more than she would want to know Broughton's every thought.

Yikes, had she just thought of him as husband material? Not a good idea. He was obviously difficult, although not at all in the way of the controlling, manipulative, mentally abusive man in Alex's past. Hah. More of a dark knight, riding in to rescue the princess, then slipping away, into the shadows.

Good luck with that. Alex was one damsel who could take care of herself. And then some.

The jet was parked in front of the hangar when they arrived back at the airstrip, and Angie was shaking the hand of a tall, skinny kid.

"I've never seen anything like it," the kid was saying while his gaze remained glued to the aircraft.

Angie smiled. "When I was working my way to

commercial, I spent hours online looking at planes and dreaming of the ones I might fly one day."

He stuffed his hands in his pockets. "I'm trying to get my college degree in half the time, so I don't mess around online much."

"Impressive. What kind of degree?"

"Aeronautics, with a minor in security." The kid hadn't stopped staring at the jet. "One day I'll fly one like it."

Angie handed him a card. "Give us a call when you're ready. Who knows? We might need a new pilot by then."

"I'm enlisting as soon as I graduate. Air Force, so I won't be looking for a job for a while."

"You'll be an even better fit for us after that, because most of our people have military backgrounds."

Except me, thought Alex. But dammit, she brought a different kind of life experience with her, and that counted too. Of course, not everyone thought so. She glanced at Broughton and found him watching her.

She tipped her chin up a notch, and to her surprise, he smiled. Her heart skipped a beat, and she was barely able to squelch a responding grin. Instead, she turned away. Boarded the plane without a backward glance. She was not going to be a pushover. One smile didn't make up for his attitude.

#

Approaching the aircraft, Grace caught the brief exchange of looks between Alex and Broughton, and she sighed. Such a rocky road ahead, when all either of them wanted was a safe place to call home. Total loners, both of them, and that, too, she understood. Just like she knew how hard it was to give up the self-protective shields they wore.

She shouldn't worry about them, because after all, if she and Logan could overcome the odds and end up together, anyone could. Not a day went by that she didn't thank the powers above for his dogged determination to be in her life.

He'd heard her voice in his head just that one time, and somehow knew they belonged together—but oh, what a journey. She hadn't gone willingly. Not by any stretch of the imagination.

Alex and Broughton's dynamics were totally different, though, because both of them were pigheaded. But then again, Alex was a lot like Logan, and she would eventually decide Broughton was the man for her. Then she'd have her work cut out for her.

You're looking very serious, my love.

She met Logan's intense gaze. *Watching these two makes me think of the days before I decided that even though I didn't need you, I definitely wanted my life to be intertwined with yours.*

He winked. *They certainly do send off sparks.*

And they're just getting started. We'll all need heat shields before they're done.

Broughton's a tough nut. I hope she's got a big hammer.

She strikes me as being just as stubborn as you were, in which case it will work.

Speaking of work, you think she's going to stick with this gig? Leave the animal thing?

I suspect she's going to do exactly what's right for her.

He touched her cheek. Y*es, she has the same tenacity as you and Julia.*

Tenacity is such a pretty word compared to stubbornness.

"Call me a sweet-talker," he said, and lightly brushed his lips across hers.

She tugged on the front of his shirt. "I'll see you that and raise you one." She kissed him, aiming for cheeky and just a bit hot, but he slid a hand into her hair, held her there for more.

"When you two are ready, we can blow this pop stand," said Angie, bringing the kiss to an end.

"Well, that oughta hold me," said Logan.

Grace laughed. "You sure? We'll be stuck in this tin can for two and a half hours."

"Control is my middle name."

"You and my husband," said Angie. "A pair of smart-asses."

"Amen," said Grace. "It's the Y chromosome."

#

Once they were airborne, Grace pulled out her laptop, and Broughton passed her the USB stick to download. The file was way too big to be sending via satellite, so they reviewed it during the flight instead, each doing ten minutes before passing it on to the next person, and after lots of fast-forwarding, Alex was the first to spot a vehicle leaving the area, but it was a small car, not big enough to transport more than a couple of people.

However, the same small car made over a dozen trips.

Grace connected with Julia. *Looks like we have a hit. Gray compact, two door, no plates.*

Can you see the people inside?

Only to be certain there was at least one passenger each trip.

More like an opportunity seized than a planned event.

Grace agreed, but something was niggling at her, and she had no clue at the moment what it was. *Another thought. Those on the planning level recognized the possibilities and used local recruits to move people for them.*

If that's the case, the driver would be in danger once the job was done.

Absolutely. Whatever was trying to get through to Grace needed room. *See you when we get back.*

Everything okay?

Something's off. I should have a handle on whatever it is by the time we land.

See you then. Grace knew Julia would also be opening up some of her extra senses.

Grace closed her eyes. *Hmmm.*

Logan's response was instant. *What is it?*

Not sure. And she hated being unsure about anything.

Give me one word.

Darkness.

Ditto. He unclipped his seatbelt and in three strides was leaning over, talking to Angie and Trent.

Broughton's back went straight, and his gaze locked on the three of them. He had a gift for long-distance vision, but was his hearing also enhanced? Could he hear them in spite of the engine noise?

And what about his other senses? Had he also picked up on what she had?

Grace was directly behind Alex, so couldn't see much but the death grip their newest agent had on the arm of her seat.

This was real, and she needed to deal with it. An agent with Meyers never knew what might happen, minute to minute.

Tension swirled throughout the small craft.

Logan came back to his seat. "Angie's got it too," he said.

"Got what exactly?" asked Broughton.

Grace shook her head. "First, are you getting any odd feelings?"

"Darkness. With pinpoints of light."

Grace nodded. "How about you, Alex? Anything?"

"I'm not seeing darkness, but feeling it."

"That's everyone but Trent," said Logan. "He's not usually sensitive, but it seems odd to me that he's getting nothing."

"He never got off the plane. Never set foot in Houston," said Alex. "Perhaps what we're feeling is a manifestation of the sadness left over from the hurricane. People still suffering from the loss of their homes, their livelihoods." She shrugged. "I put what I was feeling down to the overwhelming emotional fallout from the emergency situation. I'm an empath with animals, so I'm used to being exposed."

Exactly the reason Grace had her empathic abilities well shielded. She hadn't wanted to bear the brunt, although, being particularly sensitive to children, she hadn't expected to run into much trouble while searching in an area filled with warehouses, which was why she hadn't reinforced her barriers when they arrived.

"What else did Angie say?"

"She's contacting HQ to make sure all's well there, but she's not entertaining any thoughts of turning back to Houston, because that will leave HQ without a helo pilot."

"I did wonder about protocol when Angie and Trent came on this run together." They were the only two who were certified to fly the Steed, so the rule was one would always be available wherever the helo was.

"What's the plan?" asked Grace.

"We deliver the USB stick to James in the war room and have thirty minutes to grab a meal in the kitchen while he reviews the footage, then we reconvene for a debrief. After that, this other unknown issue will be on the table."

Grace nodded. "In other words, we'd better get some rest now, because this is going to be a long night."

7

“Sit.” Consuelo pointed at Broughton. “I’m serving, and you will eat what I put in front of you.”

“I only offered to help.”

“And I thank you for the offer, but I can’t stand having so many full-sized bodies in my way, so sit.”

He did as he was told, and Logan patted his arm. “Good move, pal. She can take you down without breaking sweat.”

“Smart mouth,” said the woman wielding a soup ladle. “You get extra veggies.”

Alex and Grace both choked back laughter, which seemed to upset the two big dogs on the bed in the corner. They whined, and wagged just the tips of their tails, and Alex slipped out of her chair to go to them. Broughton liked how natural she was with animals, responding to their needs quickly, and apparently instinctively.

“It’s okay, we were just laughing,” she said, giving the pair a hug. The black one looked like a lab mix, the other maybe a German shepherd cross. "Are they from the floods, Consuelo?"

"Yes, poor guys. They've been waiting a long time for their people to come for them."

"Hopefully we made headway on finding some of them today."

Consuelo set steaming bowls of chicken stew on the table, and a big basket of fresh buns. "There's more in the oven if you want it." She untied her bright orange, yellow, and blue apron, slipped it over her head and hung it in the pantry.

"I'm taking these boys for a bit of a ramble." At the snap of her fingers, the two were instantly at her side, waiting for her to open the door. She grabbed a shawl from one of the hooks by the door and slipped out into the night.

"She's incredible," said Broughton. "And a bit scary."

"I bet she could have taken you down," added Logan. "I'm always amazed by how she handles the kids and dogs."

"Like a pied piper," said Grace. "Freaks me out when I come in here and she's surrounded by kids, dogs, and even a litter of kittens, plus a goat scrambling around in here once, and she looks totally happy in the chaos. Hell, I'm good with the four-legged creatures, but I'd be tying the rest to their chairs." Her shudder was so heartfelt it was funny.

Logan laughed. "You'd be happier in a room full of hungry tigers."

"Absolutely. I know and understand what they want. Kids? Weird, foreign beings who make no sense, but look at you like you're supposed to understand their garbled language. Even when they can speak in real sentences, they have a look that says they are superior beings. I have no idea what to say to them."

"This from a woman who telepathically connects with children in trouble all around the world," Broughton said. "*And* ensures their rescue."

"You see, that's different. I can connect when I know they need me to help them. But random kids? Just shoot me." She buttered a bun and passed it to Logan before buttering one for herself. And wasn't that interesting?

"I'm the same, except with teenagers," said Alex. "Those I can talk to like adults. I had a few clients with teen girls working in their barns. Dedicated, hard-working dervishes, looking to soak up information like they were writing an encyclopedia. Wanted to know every detail about whatever treatment I was there for." She smiled. "I really liked a couple of them."

"Kind of like that kid with Angie today," said Broughton. "Hanging on her every word, because she's a pilot and he's super interested in flying."

Alex nodded, and everyone was quiet for a few minutes while they ate, but Broughton could almost hear the wheels turning, and finally asked, "Was that where the darkness started?"

"He was leaving before we reached the plane," said Grace. "All I got was an impression. Tall, skinny, good posture, and his clothes were too big for him. He needed a haircut, and guessing from the big hands and feet, he's got a growth spurt coming on. Not the least bit athletic, but he's strong."

Alex was staring at her. "But you only got an impression."

Logan chuckled. "Trained observer. Anyone else?"

Alex nodded. "I got conflicting emotions. Sad but hopeful, and eager yet resigned."

"Broughton?"

"Being treated respectfully, with the shaking hands and being talked to like an equal, wasn't new to him, yet he was very grateful for the attention. Like a kid who grew up solid, and then something changed." Broughton knew what that was like because he'd lived it. But this kid didn't have the anger factor.

Broughton rinsed the dishes, and Logan put them in the dishwasher, while Grace wiped the table and Alex looked lost with no job left for her. From what he understood of her past, she'd been raised by a single mom. A hardworking woman who would have expected her daughter to help out with all household chores. Not really so different, he supposed. He, too, had learned to carry his own weight, help out in any way he could, and respect those providing for him. And grew up in a traditional two-parent home. At least until he was fifteen.

Logan turned on the dishwasher. "That's a wrap."

When the four of them filed into the boardroom, they found it in full "war room" mode. Lights dimmed, the center of the massive table raised to create a workstation at each seat, complete with computer monitor, keyboard, and phone. Giant wall screens displayed interactive maps, and codes.

James and Julia were hard at work, but James glanced at the bank of clocks on the wall. "Ten minutes."

Because it looked like this would be a long night, Broughton headed for his room at the far end of another long hallway, while dragging off the T-shirt he'd been wearing since four in the morning and unsnapping his jeans. Once inside he was naked in seconds. Turned on the shower, full cold, grabbing toothbrush and paste and stepping into the frigid spray. Not exactly icy, because...well, Texas...but it did the job.

Arriving back in the war room with only seconds to spare, he was surprised when Alex came in behind him. She too was wearing fresh clothes and, dammit, looked wet. He shut down his imagination. Could *not* go there.

#

Alex looked away from Broughton's damp hair and the dark spots where drips had landed on his T-shirt. She needed to ignore how sexy he was and concentrate on the meeting, because judging by the tension crackling in the room, something was seriously wrong. Even Angie's easy smile had been replaced by a somber expression.

"A quick debrief so we can move on to something else," said James. "We've tracked the vehicle you spotted doing transport from the rescue center. Houston PD confirmed it was abandoned in a washed-out area—along with many others. The owner is Thomas Park, and his address is currently uninhabitable. He did not register with any evacuation centers, and no one has reported him missing."

Alex wondered how many people were still unaccounted for, people with no family to report them missing, and the homeless. How many were gone without a trace?

"He's now added to our list," said Julia.

"Each of Park's return trips took approximately twenty-two minutes. The plan had been to send you back out to search for more footage in the areas five to fifteen minutes farther out, but we're putting that on hold to be revisited at the end of this meeting." James rubbed his hand over his face in a rare sign of emotion.

"New business. A flight plan was filed today for an aircraft leaving thirty minutes after yours departed."

Alex's stomach plummeted. The boy.

"The flight did not return as scheduled, and a search is underway. The plane is one of ours."

Had this been a group of average people, there would have been a collective gasp. But training prevailed, and instead every spine straightened. No one blinked.

"Del Andrews is a mechanic at that strip, retired Air Force instructor, and he's under contract to us. Sees to our hangar and anything we need when we're there. Part of his wage is free use of a Cessna trainer, and he often mentors a kid or two." James glanced at Julia, and she nodded.

"Meyers is also connected to the student he had with him," she said. "Ryder is part of one of our foster grad mentoring projects. For those of you not aware, we have a foundation which takes on foster kids about to age out of support, and we help them transition into careers that would otherwise not be available to them."

"Ryder is a very special kid," added James. "Sent to us by a friend in Canada. His parents were killed in a plane crash some years ago, and he was about to run out of time in foster care. My friend was impressed by the kid's smarts and his passion for flying and mechanics, and wanted to send him to aviation school, but didn't want him left alone in Houston. He contacted me, and we set it up with Del as his guardian. Now they're both missing."

Angie was suddenly on her feet. "I should have turned back. We all knew something was off, and I should have turned back, dammit."

"Wrong. You should have stuck to protocol, and you did."

Father and daughter stared each other down, and for the first time Alex saw the similarities. James might be a foot or more taller, his hair black but for the gray, and eyes blue, but his petite red-headed, green-eyed daughter had the same set to her jaw, tilt to her head, and grim look on her face.

Julia leaned back in her seat and appeared relaxed, but Alex suspected she was like one of those sweet thoroughbred fillies who could cow-kick you without flicking an ear or even looking your way. Yes, Julia would be able to hit hard and fast without the recipient even knowing she'd moved.

"You're both ignoring the facts," she said.

"They would have been in the air before you got there. Beyond your reach."

"The point," said James, "is that you stuck to protocol, which was correct. Whether or not it would have made a difference is irrelevant."

"But it makes me feel marginally better," said Angie. "Thanks, Mom." She sat back down, but James still looked ready for an argument.

He glanced around the table, and Alex steeled herself to not flinch under the laser-like intensity of those eyes. "Local authorities have a full-scale search underway. I have a call in to the commander, and will have a plan in place for when he calls back. Since both Angie and Trent were on today's flight, we are limited in hours available. That—" His jaw tightened. "That was a tactical error on my part, and highlights why adhering to protocol is critically important unless there is a damn good reason to deviate."

Was that the root of the thick knot of tension? Did he believe he was, or should be, above making mistakes? According to company protocol, two lead pilots never did the same hours, which meant there was always one available for emergencies, and able to log more flight time without fatigue being an issue. James had made an exception today, and one had to wonder why.

For Alex, this was a brilliant illustration about the importance of sticking to the rules, and one she was never likely to forget.

Nor would she forget what it was like to be a team member. She'd never been a part of anything like it. All these people had each other's back. Solid in support of each other and their diversity.

Julia and James were amazing to watch, and even when they disagreed, they seemed to be two halves of one whole, as though nothing could come between them, and yet...

The last time Alex was here, when she was lying paralyzed in the medical rooms in another wing, she remembered the stress, the pressure Julia was under while trying to relinquish control of the security team to her husband—who had only recently returned to the fold.

It was hard to believe that less than five years ago James was not only addicted to drugs, but was on the streets of Seattle. Just one of many vets—homeless, helpless, and living with the horrors of their past day in and day out, thanks to Post Traumatic Stress Disorder.

Even if she had seen a photo from those days, Alex doubted she'd be able to reconcile him being the same man standing here, commanding the room. The only tell was the service dog leaning hard against his legs. Alex felt for the dog, soaking in all that tension, but knew he was given plenty of down time when James was in their newly built home up on the hill.

Apparently the design and security features negated much of what created stress for James, giving him extraordinary relief just by walking in the door.

#

Grace couldn't take the pressure in her head any longer.

She held up a hand. Got slowly to her feet.

Headed for the exit on legs almost unsteady. "I'm going to step outside this tension for a while. I'll be in the quiet room, trying to connect with the kid. It's a long shot, but worth a try."

Without waiting for comments, she slipped out and across the hall to where walls draped in special textured fabric absorbed sound, and deep armchairs covered with soft blankets contributed to a feeling of peace.

She tried to draw a deep breath, but couldn't. Not yet.

Sometimes, the intensity of a group of Meyers was too much for her, in spite of all the blocks she had available to protect her mind.

Seemed ludicrous, considering she'd been learning since birth how to protect herself. In the beginning, her reactions to being bombarded by the emotions and thoughts of everyone around her created a problem for her caregivers, who used drugs to control her outbursts.

When she was just a toddler, and on set with her famous mother, the nannies slipped meds into her drinks, or they gave her cookies laced with whatever was handy.

But although their solutions quieted her, and made her less difficult to deal with, they did not dull the voices and pressure in her head.

That relief began by humming—internally, because she wasn't allowed to make any sound for fear it would be picked up by the mics. And somehow she began weaving the thread of that internal music to create a wall of sorts, which dulled the impact of what her brain was constantly being bombarded with.

With each passing day of her young life she gained more control, and eventually, as a young woman, was able to enjoy a reasonably normal life...until her father was murdered just a few years ago. That's when she shut down completely for a while, and was suffering for it until Logan barged his way into her psyche. Oh, what a ride that had been! One she'd wanted to escape as much as she wanted to enjoy, and in the end she gained more than she had ever dreamed possible.

Including an aunt and a career of sorts. One that was sometimes just a bit too much for her, but she knew how to deal with excess energy. How to defuse it or weave a new filter.

Today, however, she suspected she was only overwhelmed because there was someone trying to connect. Someone in trouble, as the children she often rescued were. It was her forte. She had a pathway which was often discovered by innocents who were desperately in need.

Grace settled into an oversized sofa-type chair and laid her head back, closed her eyes, and climbed inside her own mind. Strode with purpose along meandering corridors, pausing to open arched windows and allow the soft breeze to flutter through delicate fabric hanging from thin rods.

There were no doors, but the walls were lined with dozens and dozens of windows, and outside each one the scenery was slightly different. She whispered the boy's name at every opening, welcoming, promising she could help.

Yes, there was a chance the plane had crashed,

and he was beyond hearing her, but it wasn't what her heart was saying. She had barely seen the kid, almost taken no notice of him, but now she felt a preternatural connection.

With every passing minute since she left the cacophony of emotions in the war room, she felt closer to Ryder.

She brought his image to the front of her mind, but it was vague. Needed detail. She concentrated, starting at the top and working down, just like doing a police description.

White male. Wait. Was he tanned, or did he have a naturally golden skin color? Food for thought. She still had the gist for her image.

Red ball cap with scraggly black hair hanging almost to his shoulders. His whole face was in shadow, but she had an impression of dark eyes and a wide mouth. Nose could have been hooked, or not.

Shoulders weren't wide, but not narrow either, under a bright white T-shirt.

Jeans were black instead of blue, and belted. Crisp, as though new, and from under them black aviator boots were planted firmly on the tarmac.

Ryder had a quiet strength about him she hadn't noticed before now, but she was certain it was his, and not something she was creating for him.

"Where are you, Ryder? You're strong, and you're with a good man. Let me in, and I can help you. Take me to where you are."

She stirred the wind in her mind, making the curtains on the arched windows dance in welcome.

8

When James split the team, it was a good thing Broughton was with the group investigating the missing plane, or he'd have balked. But James would never have left him working a lukewarm case when there was a hot one on the table. And a missing plane—a missing *Meyers* plane, with two people on board—was smoking hot, even without whatever it was James wasn't telling them that had him hitting the top of the tension scale.

The more didn't matter. Because if it did, as a down and dirty, balls-to-the-wall leader, James would have told them. Nope, whatever he was keeping to himself wasn't relevant to finding the plane and its occupants.

Julia took over the evac center case with the twins—who were still in Florida—and Quinn and Rachel would join them remotely from Haven.

That group was now dismissed. Off the clock until oh six hundred. James, Angie, Logan, and

Alex remained seated. Grace, Matthias, and Dhillon were also part of the team, but not currently in the room.

The door had barely clicked shut when James posted a photo of Ryder on the wall screen and said, "We're bringing this kid back alive if it's the last fucking thing I ever do." James was as pumped as Broughton had ever seen him. "He's got no one."

James shot a glance at Broughton, and their eyes locked for a nanosecond. But whatever the message was, Broughton missed it.

"He's ours now, and we won't stop until we bring him home."

Broughton concentrated on the photo while listening to James recap what information they'd received from the authorities.

Was there some kind of connection he'd missed? Ryder looked to be of Native American heritage, but his build was similar to the men of the Meyers family. James had said his parents were dead. Were they his biological parents? Was the kid adopted? Perhaps a secret son of a Meyers man? James, or one of his brothers?

James was the kind who would never hide a mistake. His or anyone else's. If there was Meyers DNA, Ryder would be part of the family by now.

Tall, lanky, golden skin. It all fit with Grace, Julia, and Alex, who were the result of an Argentinian Polo superstar spreading his seed far and wide while he toured the world over thirty years ago. Could this kid be another of Francesco's grandchildren?

"Open for input," said James. "Logan?"

"Grace is working on connecting with Ryder as we speak, and if she has no luck, we still have Liz to fall back on. She's located kids worldwide using her empathic pathways. Bringing her and her husband on board also gives us another pilot certified on the Steed." Logan was licensed for fixed-wing only.

"So noted. Angie?"

"Matthias suggested contacting ETC, because their search department—the one Liz used to work for—remains fully functional in spite of the chaos."

Angie's husband worked at ETCETERA right up until last December, when all hell broke loose, and the fallout had been ugly.

"Broughton," said James.

"Suggest boots on the ground where the plane took off from. Gather the details the authorities don't even know are important. Video footage will be invaluable. Could show us exactly who is involved."

James nodded. "Alex?"

"May I ask a question?"

"Go," said James.

She swallowed hard, as though for courage, and Broughton fought a ridiculous urge to touch her. Reassure her.

"There's an aircraft missing, but you're acting like the young man, Ryder, has been kidnapped. What did I miss?"

"The darkness," said Angie.

Broughton nodded. "What we felt coming from the tarmac, and Ryder's presence prior to takeoff this afternoon, was darkness—which we have subconsciously identified as malice. Correct?"

"Exactly." Angie held out her hands, palm up. "Precognition of an event such as a plane crash comes in visual flashes some liken to slide shows. But what we were feeling was the presence of evil, or at least evil intent, because evil itself is a subject we don't need to visit right now. If ever." She shuddered before continuing.

"The feeling we were picking up was from a human source. And I would guess the person or persons it was coming from were only arriving as we were lifting off, which is why we didn't feel it while on the ground."

Alex nodded.

"Unless we learn otherwise, we work from the premise that he was taken," said James.

Angie clicked keys, and the suggestions each had expressed appeared on one screen and the abduction checklist on another.

"Motivation," said James. "Wrong place, wrong time, isn't ringing any bells, but there's nothing obvious. Matthias and Dhillon will dig, because there has to be a reason, and likely more than one."

Age-old theory. Every event was a product of more than one thing going right, or wrong.

And good thinking to put a teenager on searching the background of another teen. He would see things from a different perspective.

"Evidence." James glanced at Broughton. "I want you at the strip. Find the vehicle the perp arrived in, or footage of a drop-off. He/she could have come in by air."

Broughton was eager to sink his teeth into the assignment.

"While he's doing that, Alex will access Del's office and connect us remotely with his computer and any other devices she finds. If the authorities are not in the way, everything comes back here."

Good, a safe job for her to do while I'm outside.

"Logan and Grace will go with you, because I'm counting on them to pick up a psychic thread, something we can tug on. Follow."

James turned to Angie.

"Use the Steed. It will slow your arrival by twenty minutes, but leaves you able to move from there in any direction, and put down where necessary. Keep the craft visible and noisy. No point giving up an advantage we might need later." He hesitated, glanced from face to face.

"You are officially off the case of those missing from the hurricane, but keep it in mind, because missing is missing, and we don't believe in coincidence. Right?"

Everyone nodded.

"Vital information on Ryder's background," said James. "The people behind him are an outfit called Sunrise Ranch, and we need to make sure they're protected. Their mission is to make life easier for foster kids, and to help them explore their Native heritage and cultures. When Ryder was there for a summer camp and his obsession with planes was noted, they contacted Meyers about sponsorship. We got him into a good school, and Del signed on to be his mentor."

He hesitated, tapping a finger on the table as he always did when carefully weighing what he was about to say.

"Ryder's connection to us, and more importantly to Sunrise Ranch, is strictly confidential. Many of the Sunrise kids have been to hell and back. Have lost parents in one way or another, been subjected to stereotyping, bullying, and prejudice. The people who run the ranch help them deal, excel, and decide for themselves what their futures are going to look like." He touched the dog at his side. "PTSD is only one of the major issues they deal with."

And there was the reason James was emotionally involved. As a survivor, he spent a great deal of time helping others beat the symptoms and win their lives back.

"Sunrise is all about leaving the past behind and embracing the future. They believe it, and they live it."

James sent Broughton a look he wasn't able to interpret, but a tingle ran up his spine.

#

Alex was fascinated. Could have sat there all night watching the subtle interplay among the people in the room. Apparently James wasn't usually this jacked up when heading a mission, or that was at least how she interpreted the covert study Broughton was making of him. And there were a few looks from James to Broughton that were filled with mysterious undertones.

Judging from her expression, Angie had seen them too, and was also intrigued.

“If there’s nothing else,” said Broughton, “We should get a move on.”

James nodded. “Consuelo has supplies ready for you.” He glanced at Broughton, and Alex got the impression James had something more to say to her partner.

“I’ll grab my jacket and swing through the kitchen. Meet you at the door.”

She jogged the two hallways to get to her room. Needed the exercise, and extra oxygen pumping through the body was never a bad idea. If she’d let him get the food, she could have run to Angie’s place, but then she’d be sweaty, and who knew how long until she’d get another shower?

She slipped into her shoulder harness, checked her weapon, and grabbed the lightest of the three jackets waiting for her when she arrived. All were black, with a Meyers emblem, the same as the T-shirt she wore. She put on fresh boots. One of the survival tricks she’d learned while working split shifts as a track vet a few years earlier was never wear the same pair of boots for more than eight hours in a day.

Consuelo was waiting for her in the kitchen with two insulated containers. “Packaged meals in each, with lots of water and some caffeine as well. White plastic container has the snack food. Mind those meals get eaten, too. Nobody can work endless hours on cookies and chocolate bars.”

Oh, yes, they could. She’d done it for years. Was it healthy? Nope. But until her run-in with the Minnows, she hadn’t paid much attention to her own health. Now? Now it mattered.

"Thanks, Consuelo." She hugged the woman who had sat with her during the endless hours when she could do nothing but stare at what was directly in front of her, and listen. During those long days and nights, when Broughton wasn't at her bedside, Consuelo was, and Alex would never forget how she'd clung to that lilting voice and her matter-of-fact attitude.

"It's going to get messy," she said. "But you'll bring him home in the end."

Alex's gaze narrowed. "What do you know?"

"Just that you and the rest of the team are in for a wild ride. Now get going. That impatient man is beginning to pace." She held open the swinging door for Alex, and there was nothing she could do but go, even though she wanted to ask Consuelo for details. Details she was obviously unwilling to share.

A wild ride? She'd endured a few, and knew the best way to survive them was to get tied on, take a deep seat, and keep her face out of the way.

Broughton was indeed pacing when she got to the door, but, credit to him, he hadn't come in to hurry her up.

"Consuelo knows something."

"She always does," he said, taking the containers and placing them in the back of a golf cart.

"What does that mean?" Alex watched him from the passenger seat.

Broughton climbed in and started the engine, got them on their way. "She's a precog. Sees things."

"Then why wouldn't she share what she knows?"

"It has to play out. We can't change events, or how time passes, because everything is interconnected, which means other things would have to change. Consuelo shared once a long time ago and it went badly. Now she never shares more than whether it will be a hard case or an easy one."

"She said this would be messy, but we'd bring him home in the end."

"Hmm. Could mean alive, or dead. And how far away will 'in the end' be?"

Alex didn't like this much at all. "Why would she bother to say anything if it's so vague and open to interpretation?"

"Best guess? It's your first op and she didn't want you overwhelmed or confused or something when things didn't go as planned?"

"Makes sense." Alex sighed, and let it go. "She also said we couldn't live on cookies and chocolate. We were to eat the meals."

"I bet she packed peanut butter chocolate chip cookies. I'm breaking into those things before they go on board. A good sugar hit to get us rolling."

"When I was here before, I could always smell cookies baking, and I could almost taste them when Consuelo would come to sit with me and the scent followed her into the room."

She glanced over at him. "You, on the other hand, smelled like shampoo, or witch hazel."

"You recognized the witch hazel?" There was an odd tone in his voice.

"What's wrong with that?"

"Nothing except it's touted as having no lingering scent."

"Unless you work with racehorses and use it constantly as a base for liniment and leg brace. It was comforting." Her stomach tightened. "Like the way you talked me down from more than one panic attack. I was a hot mess."

"You were terrified, and with good reason. Hell, I was afraid for you. Felt helpless—which sits poorly—but there was nothing I could do to change what you were going through." She stared through the darkness at his tanned hands, barely able to see them on the tiny steering wheel, guiding the cart through the winding path. Thought about his gentle touch.

"But you did do something. And you made a difference. Every time you…" Touched me. "Every time you walked into the room, you made a difference."

They rounded the last bend, and there was Angie, with the Steed already uncovered, and doing a walk-around.

Before the cart came to a full stop, Broughton, with a light grip on Alex's chin, brushed his mouth across hers, then set the brake and climbed out, calling to Angie, "Got food to stow when you're ready." Then he began rifling through one of the containers.

Alex could have told him where to find the cookies, but her voice seemed to be stuck in her throat. The kiss had been gentle, and heartfelt, and…and nothing. She had a job to do. She headed for the Steed without looking back at him.

9

Thoroughly pissed at himself, Broughton watched her march away. They were on an op. Working. And kissing her was so far out of line he needed his ass kicked. Did he dare apologize? Would that be making too much of a minor brushing of lips? He was a professional. He was technically her superior. Had no choice.

"Alex."

She waited for him to catch up, and he was careful not to touch her. Not to put a hand on her shoulder and turn her to face him.

"I was out of line. Please accept my apology."

She turned then. Stared at him like he was some kind of foreign blip on her radar screen. "Seriously?"

"I had no right to touch you. Especially on the job."

"Broughton. *Caleb*. Let me spell this out and make it very clear. I'm interested in having a relationship with you. Little flyby kisses and the odd touch will not upset me, but they will lead me to believe you are also interested in a relationship. If that's not the case? Yeah, keep your mouth and hands to yourself. Meanwhile, you should probably finish digging for snacks and get the rest to the Steed."

She left him standing there with his insides at war. Caught between grinning like an idiot—because, gawd, he loved her attitude—or scrambling to shake loose from the hold she already had on his heart.

He could use a beer.

But a cookie would have to suffice. He dug one out and shoved the whole thing in his mouth, stuck the carton under his arm, and lugged the rest to the Steed.

"Whatcha got?" asked Dhillon, who was hovering close by.

"Consuelo cookies."

"Figured. She always uses that same thing to put 'em in. Gonna be tough to eat with your helmet on. Might as well leave them here."

"Funny guy," said Broughton. "But I'll share. Want one?"

"One? Sure, if that's all you're giving away." He rooted around in the container. "Gotta be the kind with walnuts in here. Consuelo hides something healthy in everything, and the walnut ones are to die for." He laughed. "She even packed you some bombs."

"Bombs?"

What Dhillon held up was as round as a golf

ball, about half the size, and a mottled brownish color.

"These suckers are like dynamite. Ri-*diculously* good, and hard to eat just one. When I was just a kid, I snuck a handful...well, maybe a few more than that...from the jar. Ate them all." He made an exaggerated full body shudder that looked more like a seizure, then glanced over to where Angie was in conversation with Alex. Dropped his voice to a whisper.

"Fucking things exploded inside me." He shuddered again.

Broughton couldn't resist asking, "What happened?"

"Gave me the runs big time. I was scared to fart for a week."

Broughton laughed while Dhillon took a wistful sniff.

"They even smell as good as they look, and they're made with dates and oats and honey and sunflower seeds and nuts. One is supposed to give you a big energy jolt, but nobody can eat just one." He dropped it back in and chose a cookie instead.

"Thanks for the heads-up. I'll stick with the peanut butter chocolate chip. A perfect protein and carb blast." He glanced around. "No sign of Grace and Logan yet?"

"They're inside talking to my dad."

"We're ready to go as soon as they come out," said Angie. "Decide who's riding shotgun, and get strapped in." She headed for the house.

Broughton needed to see where he was going, hated sitting in the back. "I prefer a seat with a view if you don't mind?" he told Alex.

"Sure, I'm good."

He snagged another cookie, then set the container on the floor by the back seats. "Go easy on the golf ball ones. Apparently they pack a punch."

Alex lifted her eyebrows.

"Roughage," said Broughton, with a smile. "A good combo with some of those prepack cheeses."

Alex's mouth twisted in a half smile. "So noted."

That, thought Broughton, put them safely back on the kind of solid ground a couple of agents needed to be on.

The flight was uneventful, with no conversation through their helmet audio until Angie announced they were ten minutes from their destination. The trip in the helo took much longer than in the jet.

"Comments, anyone? Ideas, thoughts?" prompted Broughton.

"Comment," said Grace. "Be wary of hitting the tarmac with all your senses at full throttle. Better to let them open one at a time."

Broughton didn't take offense at the warning, because he was sure Grace was offering it for Alex, and he was good with participating in training. "We need to protect ourselves from all the ramped-up adrenaline of search crews and the like, plus it's possible the darkness we experienced before could still be lingering. We should proceed directly to the hangar, work outward from there."

"I have the air," said Angie, meaning they needed to be quiet while she got clearance and instructions from the control tower.

Being a helo, they were not pointed at the well-lit landing strip where their downwash could create havoc for planes but sent way off to one side, where the designated landing zone was a glowing circle of light with an H inside it. Within seconds they had touched down about a hundred feet from the Meyers hangar.

"Ninety minutes to pickup at twenty-three thirty," said Angie, and the foursome stripped off their helmets, left them hooked to the seatbelts, and marched toward the building while the Steed went airborne.

Security lights blinked on, illuminating their path to the side door, where the SUV was still parked. Broughton opened the door to confirm the keys were still under the floor mat, then continued inside and directly to the office with the others.

But someone was already there. The man looked up from where he'd been studying the computer screen. "Hello?"

"Hey," said Logan. "Care to tell us what you're doing?"

"Looking for maintenance records on the missing plane."

"You won't find them there," said Broughton. "Got some ID?"

"Course." The guy fished a wallet from his back pocket. Flopped it open and pulled out a card. "Special investigator for the FAA."

"They don't hire outsiders."

"They don't advertise the fact, but I'm one of hundreds. Saves them a bundle in wages, benefits, and retirement packages."

Scab labor? Almost. Or an interesting cover story. Broughton glanced at Grace, and she winked back. Good. She was feeding information to Julia, telepathically. They'd know soon enough if this guy was legit.

Grace then did the expected. In her most compelling tone, the one designed to slip under a man's skin and make him do exactly as asked, she said, "Good thing you're finished here. Now you can leave and be out of our way. We have work to do, and you're done for the day.

She was good. Beyond good, and, Broughton suddenly realized, Alex could have inherited similar talents. He would need to be wary.

#

Grace studied the man gathering up his briefcase and jacket.

The ID is fake. Logan's voice slipped in.

I agree. Shall we detain him?

I don't think he's connected with whoever took Ryder and Del.

So we know for certain Del and the boy were aboard the aircraft? Grace had missed the briefing at HQ.

Yes. Both voices are on the recording from the tower. And checked against Meyers voiceprint files.

As soon as the man walked out of the glass-walled office, Logan flipped a switch that locked all the outside doors and said, "His ID is bogus. We can hold him or not. Opinions?"

"I'm not picking up anything from him," said Broughton.

"Nor am I," said Alex. "Could he be adept at blocking?"

"Darkness can never be completely hidden," Broughton told her.

"Do we let him leave?" asked Logan.

"Yeah, but Alex and I will go now too," said Broughton. "We'll open the door and keep an eye on him. Plus you have the security monitors." He pointed at the screens mounted along the top of the wall.

Grace watched the screens while Logan used an electronic wand to lift a set of fingerprints from the keyboard.

"He went straight to the command center," she said. The FAA was set up in the small coffee shop not far from the tower. Their mobile units were parked all around it, along with an array of law enforcement vehicles.

"All done," said Logan. "Your turn."

With his hand on her shoulder, connecting them physically, she shut everything out of her mind, including him. Waited for the lightness of psychic energy to spread through her, then set her fingertips on the keyboard where the stranger had been.

When no blast of dark or evil shot through her, she lowered onto the chair he'd used. A faint ripple like electricity danced up her spine, but nothing she couldn't handle.

She set to work. Allowed her instincts to lead her through the places the stranger had been. She opened files, folders, clicked on emails and other messages.

“Nothing much on him,” she said. Time to go deeper. Get the browser history so they could figure out Del and Ryder’s last moves before they took off.

She clicked keys, copied links and then hit on the dark energy hanging like mist on a sunny morning—not threatening, but not letting the sun touch the ground either.

She linked fingers with Logan. “Going under.”

“I’ve got you.”

She closed her eyes, waited. There had to be more. Something. A direction or a source. She slowed her heart rate, slipped into that place between. Between where she was and where there was nothing. Air passed through her nostrils, into her lungs, out again. Slower. She waited between breaths, made each last longer.

When the sparkle appeared behind her eyelids, she was deep enough to let go. Follow the darkness through the corridors of her own mind and out to where it wafted around the plane Del and Ryder were climbing into.

The boy stopped, and his posture was that of a wild animal sensing a predator. Muscles ready to spring, nose in the air, searching for scent. He glanced across the runway, then behind the plane. Over his shoulder. And in the way of one too young to know better, he climbed into the aircraft and closed the door, locking himself and his mentor inside with someone they weren’t aware of.

Ryder’s voice was clear when he requested permission for takeoff, and the tower responded, directing them to turn right at a specific altitude.

When the plane was a bit sluggish on liftoff, Del tipped his head to concentrate on the sound of the engine and Ryder compensated by lowering the nose. Reducing the angle of climb.

Del addressed the tower, requesting a left turn for a circuit. He wanted to land and check the engine instead of following the planned flight.

Tower cleared them into the pattern requested.

"Make the right turn, and know I have a gun pointed at the back of the kid's head." The voice was male, and darkness floated on the sound.

He climbed over the seats. "Not much you can do about me now, old man, so just turn back around and watch where we're going. And kid, stick to the flight plan you filed."

The ATC in the tower wasn't pleased when they deviated course. "Cessna 184, Charlie Victor Bravo One Seven Seven."

"What do you want me to tell them?" Del asked.

"Sorry, sticking to original flight plan."

Del repeated the words over the radio.

"Now turn it off."

"Not safe in this airspace."

"Bullshit. The right turn takes us away from trouble. Out to practice grounds. Shut it off."

Del flicked the switch and the radio went silent.

"What do you want from us?" asked Del.

"A friend of mine wants to have a chat with the kid. Seems they have a mutual acquaintance. One my friend hasn't seen in a very long time."

"Who?" asked Ryder.

"Couldn't say. I'm just the messenger."

All was quiet for a while, until Ryder said, "This is the practice area."

"Get this thing down to two hundred feet and head due north."

As they got closer to the ground, Grace's contact diminished and was finally gone. She waited and waited. Tried for a connection with Ryder, then Del, but nothing worked.

"Grace."

She opened her eyes. Blinked a couple of times and drew in a huge breath. Let it out slowly.

Logan passed her his water bottle, and after she drank, handed her a cookie from the container now sitting on the desk. Straight sugar from her emergency pack would have been better, but the cookie was delightful, and she worked on normalizing her heart rate while she devoured it.

When Logan offered her another she took it and asked, "How long?"

"Twenty-three minutes."

"It passed in real-time then. I rode along with them until they got under five hundred feet, then they lost me."

"What do we have?"

"Abduction of Ryder for info on someone he knows. Del is collateral."

"Meyers connection?"

"Didn't feel like it. Especially as the interest was only in the boy. Sounded like someone he knew before he came here."

Because her power was depleted, and she was unable to connect telepathically with Julia, Logan used the secure line, went through some coding, and eventually connected with HQ. Let them know what Grace had found out.

#

Once they cleared the security gates, Alex said, "I didn't get any of the dark feelings tonight, but there's a certain uneasiness in the air. Do you feel it, or is it just me?"

"Could be the accumulation of excitement and tension coming from the command center."

"No, that was a wave I recognized. This is something different. It had an insidious quality about it."

First Broughton used an electronic device to harvest data from the security cameras with a view of the road into the airport—possible only because Meyers had the codes to the system.

Then they drove the route they'd walked the day before, and she had to rearrange her focus from the missing aircraft to the people missing from the Hurricane rescue centers.

The buildings were all dark now, closed for the night. "Even if we find cameras, I don't like our chances of being able to access video when everything is shut down."

"Lots of trucking companies in this area, and they'll have twenty-four seven desks. As for the others? I have my ways."

Would he hack into systems, or go for straight B & E? Somehow she could see him doing either. He slowed when they got to the farthest edge of where they searched before. Now they were looking for where the gray car stopped and let out each passenger.

She kept her attention on the likely places for cameras and managed to pick out a couple in spite of the dark. "There." She pointed.

"This place is shut right down. We'll come back after."

By the time they reached the highway some miles away, they'd spotted a dozen cameras on closed buildings, and four others they were able to access. The four should give them enough coverage that they wouldn't need the others, but Alex wrote down addresses and business names for follow-up, slightly disappointed they hadn't needed to do anything more interesting, like burglary or hacking.

When they arrived back at the hangar, Logan and Grace were still working inside, and Broughton and Alex waited in the car for their all-clear.

Just when she noticed how alone they were in a small, dark space. Broughton asked, "Are you getting any feelings here?" and she nearly laughed out loud. Sure, she knew he was asking about the case, but that's not where her head had been.

She cleared her throat. "Ah, no. Maybe if I walked around outside."

"Good idea. But we'd best keep conversation to a minimum. You never know who could be listening from where." He sounded relieved, and that annoyed her.

"Is there a reason why we don't use silent communication?"

"I don't like having channels open. Makes me vulnerable to others with greater power than mine."

Are there really enough like that to worry about? He showed no sign of hearing her, which wasn't surprising. Even if he could hear, there wasn't much chance she would ever know.

While the security lights lit their way, his face remained in shadow thanks to the bill of his cap, and Alex found herself wishing she had the same kind of cover to hide behind.

You can hear me, of that I'm quite certain. Just like I think you could hear my thoughts and words while I was laid up all those months ago. You just maintained your distance by not letting on. And cheated me out of another, more intimate connection that would have made such a difference while I was feeling incredibly helpless.

Dammit. What was she thinking spilling her guts like this?

Perhaps the ground could open up, and she could just disappear now. She stopped.

No! She owned who she was and how she felt, and if it was too much for a big, brave guy like Broughton to handle, well then, he wasn't the man for her anyway.

Broughton?

She stopped at a dark spot between lights, and he stopped as well. They squared off and stared into each other's eyes. No way was she going to blink first.

Is this a standoff?

No. This is me trying to figure out what to do about you. His voice sliding into her mind, was everything she could have wished for. Low and sexy, with something both scary and gentle about it.

Why do you have to do anything?

Because you're trouble. You upset my balance.

Don't fit in any of the slots I have in my head.

Instead of finding a compartment to stuff me in, maybe you should just let things work out naturally.

The breeze across the tarmac sent a strand of hair across her face, and before she could shove it back, he tucked it behind her ear, and his hand stayed there against the side of her neck, fingers tickling the sensitive skin.

I live in a very simple, organized world, and you're messing it up.

You've kind of screwed with mine too.

What you said earlier about a relationship? That's a problem. I don't do relationships. I don't sleep with women who want more than sex, and I never deviate from that rule.

That's too bad, Broughton, because we'd be good together. Damn good.

A flicker of sadness tried to settle somewhere close to her heart, but a spark of something else pushed to the surface.

She could simply turn her head to kiss, taste the inside of his arm. But wanting more, she raised up on her toes and whispered, "Just so you know what you're missing." And she kissed him. Not hard and hot, but soft, teasing, and provocative.

When he came along for the ride, she let the kiss deepen while they both explored, and her heart pounded in her ears. She wanted him in more ways than one, but she pushed away. Stepped back.

The next move's yours, cowboy.

10

His move? Hell. Half of him wanted her naked and under him, now. Right now. Or up against the damn wall.

The other half was already three zip codes away, running like hell.

He jerked the lapels of her jacket together. Started to reel her in. And stopped. Let her go. *Can't go there, Alex.* Backed up a step. *For the record, I want you bad right now. But not on your terms.*

With grim determination to get control back, he opened the portal to Logan. *How's it going?*

We're done, come on in.

"They're ready for us," Broughton told Alex. "Let's get back to work."

She shook her head but said nothing. Seemed to shrug off the personal. Glanced at her watch. *We have forty minutes until Angie's back. Is there a plan?*

We'll wait and see what the others have come up with and work from there.

When they got back to the hangar, the others were in the lounge area.

"Sorry I had to start without you," Grace said taking the last bite of what looked like a sandwich. She was ghostly pale.

"What happened?" Broughton asked.

Grace glanced at her husband. "You tell it." She put two wraps and a handful of cookies on her plate, confirming Broughton's suspicions. Psychic events sucked the energy from a person, and food was desperately needed for a quick recovery.

"Grace tapped into the incident. Saw an unidentified subject hiding onboard the plane, and shortly after takeoff he threatened Ryder and Del with a gun, had them stick to their flight plan up until they arrived at a practice area. Then they dropped below five hundred feet and vanished."

"A sudden descent in that area would be normal, and then they could stay under the radar," said Broughton. "Could have gone any direction."

"HQ is searching satellite history."

"I find it surprising that a Meyers aircraft isn't equipped with a GPS locator," said Alex.

Logan pointed across the open space to a workbench spanning an entire wall. "According to the maintenance records, Del found a problem with it. Had a new one delivered this morning. He did the calibrations and installed the unit about an hour prior to takeoff."

With a spoonful of chicken stew halfway to his mouth Broughton said, "Surely not a coincidence."

"No. And early on the day it was discovered to be malfunctioning, there was a one-hour stretch of the security tape which is a replay from the previous day. Slick work, too. The bump was barely visible to the naked eye, but it popped when I ran a scanner through the program."

"We're dealing with someone who has better-than-average electronic skills," said Alex.

"More like exceptional. Meyers systems are very secure."

"Someone wanted…" She stopped, and frowned. "What did they want?"

"Ryder. Apparently the kid has some kind of connection to a person this unsub was working for or friends with."

Watching Alex pick at the bowl of stew instead of eating it, Broughton was reminded of what Consuelo shared with him about her need to eat regularly, if not constantly. Since recovering from the drugs rendering her unable to move only months earlier, she often became hypoglycemic.

Regular protein was the best defense, but if her blood sugar was getting low, she wouldn't feel like eating, and that's when sugar would be the best remedy.

He dug one of the bomb cookies out and cut it in half. "These things are a perfect mix of protein and sugar, and I've been dying to try one, but was warned they're dynamite." He passed half to Alex. "Share with me." *Your blood sugar is tanking. Eat it now.*

She flicked a glance at him and took a bite. "Mmmm."

"Meyers wouldn't have taken the kid on without doing an in-depth background on him. I'm surprised nothing showed up then," said Broughton.

"He was in foster care for the past few years, and those records are harder than others to get into," said Grace.

Broughton's hope for a simple conclusion was gone. "He could have been on his own a lot, or in dozens of different homes." And, as Broughton knew from experience, a teen without parents was ripe for trouble. Hadn't he found it, even though his grandparents were there for him?

Broughton could have easily been taken in by gangs looking for recruits, could have made a bundle as a mule. But having lost his parents because of the crime world, he resisted the draw of belonging and instead enlisted in the Marines.

"Angie's the one who had up-close contact with Ryder, so maybe she can shed some light," said Alex, who, along with Grace, already had better color.

"Speaking of, we should get ready for pickup."

"You guys get any useful footage?" asked Logan.

"Data from four cameras was forwarded to HQ." And he was itching to see the footage. The unsub had to be on it, because there was only one road into the airport. But what if he—hell, they—came in by air? "Shit."

"What?" all three of them asked at the same time.

"What if the unsub came in by air?"

"No worries," said Logan. "James has record of

all air traffic, plus six days' worth of footage from every camera on the grounds, as well as everything from this building."

"Sounds like all the bases are covered." So why did he feel like he'd missed something when he was outside with Alex? That's what he needed to figure out.

"Something's calling me," he said. "I'll be right back."

When Alex started to rise he waved a hand. "You hang here. I'm just going back to where we were a few minutes ago and should be back in less than fifteen." Angie would be here in twenty.

He closed the door behind him and leaned against it until the sensor light blinked off, then waited for his eyes to fully adjust to the darkness. Took a careful look around.

Moving very slowly, so the sensor wouldn't turn the light back on, he slipped the scanner out of his pocket. It was on auto, which would pick up anything in a twenty-foot radius, but anything farther required direction and a request for data. That was the key he hit now, and pointed the device at the edge of the roof on the hangar next door.

One careful step at a time, he moved between the two buildings, and when he reached the corner he stopped. Now he could see a good portion of the airfield, with dozens of planes tied down for the night, and ten or more private hangars, all buttoned up tight.

Broughton's gut said it was the building straight across, and he ran with it. Pointed the handheld, and, sure enough, the red light blinked.

Might just be a private security camera, but he didn't think so. It had a sensor pointed across the runway, right at the Meyers hangar.

He quickly slipped back inside, told the others, then they headed across together, and were able to pluck a tiny camera and sensor from the peak of the ten-foot roof. Good thing Alex had long arms and was pretty light for her height. She was able to stand on his shoulders and reach the cam.

#

Once Alex slipped the tiny camera into her pocket, she was in a bit of a pickle, because she wasn't sure how the heck to get down. Like mountain climbing, going up was the easy part.

Logically, from a standing position on Broughton's shoulders, with his hands wrapped around her ankles, the best way off, was to shift and drop straight down the front of him. He could break her fall by grabbing her in a hug before she hit the ground.

But…

No point being self-conscious, because the dismount was not going to be graceful, no matter which way they did it. Best to get it over with quickly.

"Crouch down, and Logan and I will grab your hands for a balance point, then just hop," said Broughton.

No point overthinking. She did as instructed, and got it over with. Landed—surprisingly—on both feet. And right on cue, they heard the whup, whup of a helo.

Grace, Alex, and Logan went right to the Steed

when it landed, while Broughton ran back to the hangar for the coolers.

Alex pulled on her helmet. “Hey, Angie. If you haven’t had a chance to eat, there’s lots of food. Wraps, cookies, coffee.”

“I grabbed a bite when I fueled up. Caught an hour’s sleep, too, because we’re not done yet. I’m legal to fly until eight am, so we’re going to do some recon.”

Broughton stuffed the coolers in the hold behind the seats and shoved the snack tin at Alex.

In some ways it was nice that he was concerned about her, but if he was going to turn mother hen and start watching everything she ate, and counting hours between snacks like she was supposed to, she would have to hurt him. She dug out a candy bar, stuffed it in her pocket and stowed the container under her seat.

No way was she going to slip again today. Once was enough. The candy was full of nuts and sugar, and she could nibble on it for the next few hours and keep herself in order.

When they reached cruising altitude, Angie said, “The area in the official search zone is everything from the airport to the practice grounds, and thirty miles beyond. We’re going outside of that and to the east based on a gut feeling at HQ, unless this group is picking up something different.”

When no one spoke, she said, “Then we go east. The complicating factor it that we’ll be over cattle country, and every damn operation has an airstrip and lots of aircraft on the ground. The one we’re looking for is white with a navy blue M painted on the top of the fuselage, which helps, but is also easily covered by a tarp or blanket, so I'll have to go in close on anything suspicious."

Interior walls slid aside to reveal observation windows, as did a small portion of the floor.

"Night vision overhead," he said, and she reached up to unhook a set of goggles obviously designed to fit over the helmets, and after adjusting the strap, slipped hers down to hang around her neck, ready for use when the time came.

Alex had put in the required time in the simulator with night vision, but done nothing real…yet. Her heart bumped a bit harder, and she consciously brought it back to a normal rate—an exercise she'd excelled at. Biofeedback was apparently her forte.

Was it because of the weeks of drug-induced paralysis? Probably not entirely. Control had always been her thing, and working with thoroughbreds, especially with mares and foals, she'd learned early to keep her own system at a quiet, calm level in order to get optimum cooperation from the equines—a skill she'd learned as a kid tagging around after her mom. Heck, there were photos of her as a baby, in a stroller parked in front of the stall her mom was mucking out.

Horses were as close as she'd ever gotten to having siblings, and she simply understood them. Never had to think about it. Knew every move they were going to make even before they made it. Perhaps she'd been a horse in a previous life.

And there again came the physical control. Horses were prey animals. They had to be aware of everything around them, be prepared to fight or flee, and for most horses, flight was most often the choice. The one she preferred herself.

"We'll be into fresh, unsearched territory in about ten minutes," said Angie. "Here's how it's going to go."

Alex slid the goggles into place and closed her eyes to listen.

"Besides a view visible to you on the screen behind me, the Steed's cameras will be transmitting to HQ, and they have a satellite map showing our progress using GPS. James is on our radio frequency and will hear everything we say. If you spot something, say it out loud, and with any directions needed for him to put a mark on the map and determine if it is something to investigate further."

"Do we say our seat position?" asked Alex.

"Nope, he's got that, so if you call out "UD, white, ten o'clock," he will mark an unidentified white object at the ten o'clock position, from your seat behind me. Logan and Grace are both on the right, so one of them will monitor the floor view."

"It's hard on the neck," said Logan. "Let's spell off, thirty-minute intervals. I'll start."

"Let James know when you switch."

Alex dug out her candy bar and broke off a bite, then hit the mute button on her helmet. She stuffed the snack up through the soft cushioning and into her mouth. Savored the caramel and salty peanuts. Damn, now she could use a good swig of water, but—

Grace touched her shoulder. Passed her a water

bottle with a matching metal straw, and Alex noted she and Logan each had one too. With a grateful thumbs-up, she was happy to sip the coolness.

"T minus one," said Angie, and Alex swung her focus to the ground below. Let her eyes adjust to the roll of the land, the bulge of small hills and the depressions where lakes and ponds had been. This area was very dry, almost barren from her sky view. But how high up were they? Without knowing that, she couldn't say whether what she saw was ground cover, or bushy trees.

When she spotted a narrow dirt road, she finally got a feel for how close to the ground they were, and she'd guess it was no more than two thousand feet.

Silence reigned for a long time, until Logan said, "Unidentified. Gray? At two-thirty."

"Copy." Ah, good. James would acknowledge their transmission. Made it much easier than them saying it twice, as she'd been taught previously.

Another half hour went by and Broughton said, "Approaching airstrip, twelve-thirty."

"Copy. Alex, scan perimeter."

"Copy," she said, and concentrated on the outer edges of her view.

"Hangar-sized buildings, three o'clock. Possible second runway beyond."

"Copy."

And so it went. By the time they returned to the Meyers ranch, they had spotted several dozen places where an aircraft could be hidden, and just as many craft were checked out and eliminated.

Leaving Angie to put the Steed to bed, the

others piled into the waiting SUV and drove to the main house. First stop, war room.

11

Broughton parked at the main entrance, and while Logan, Grace, and Alex headed directly to the war room, he detoured to the kitchen.

Consuelo glanced up from where she was working at the stove. "Long night for your team. Set those on the table for now, and take this with you," she said while adding something to one of the covered dishes on the loaded trolley.

Frown lines formed between her eyes. "You look like hell, and I don't suppose the others look much better after twenty-eight hours without sleep. You'll get some soon, but in the meantime, refuel." She pointed. "Eggs, beans, and rice in the hot dishes, along with peanut butter and banana-stuffed French toast. Oatmeal in the slow cooker, lots of fruit and other stuff on the second shelf."

"Woman of my dreams," he said, planting a kiss on her forehead. She shooed him out of the room with a reminder to plug in when he got there.

"Breakfast from Consuelo," he said wheeling through the doorway, and there were happy sounds from the team.

Broughton half-filled a bowl with oatmeal, topped it with a couple of scoops of blueberries, and splashed milk over the works. With that and French toast, he grabbed a seat at the wide table and dug in.

He was pleased to see Alex had gone for the omelet. A good choice for her, considering. And geez, as beat as he was, maybe he should have loaded up with more protein. Was he getting too old to pull all-nighters? Who the hell knew? Or cared, for that matter.

As soon as they were seated, James began with a recap of what he'd done on his end while they were in the air.

He pointed out areas of interest for further investigation, and then they hashed out the details of sleep breaks and work for later. Everyone was to have at least four hours downtime while he and Julia worked through the aerial footage from the Steed, as well as everything from the airport and surrounding areas.

"Any questions?" As always, James making eye contact with each of them was further invitation, but Broughton shook his head.

Yes, he wanted to ask about Ryder's connection to James, but there was no point right now. It could wait. Had to wait until a full complement of brain cells was back up and running.

"Okay then, get some sleep," said James before leaving the room with his dog glued to his side. And if Swagger was sticking that close, James wasn't as chill as he appeared. Perhaps the lack of sleep put him at risk of his symptoms resurfacing. Good thing their new house was finally finished. The walk up the hill would give him the benefit of exercise and fresh air, and once inside, he could relax completely, because the security system was beyond remarkable—hypervigilance at its finest—and if the technology was taking care of that part, James would be able to rest.

Broughton set his dish on the bottom shelf of the rolling cart and contemplated loading everything back on. There was still a ton of food. "Does this go back to the kitchen, or are we leaving it for the others?"

"For the others. They have a briefing with Julia in about fifteen," said Grace.

Perfect. Broughton stuck the milk jug and pitcher of orange juice in the fridge. "Works for me. I'm done. Catch y'all in four."

Alex followed him right to the door of his room, and he was at a loss for what to say when he realized she was going on by. Hadn't been trying to join him at all. Damn, he really needed sleep if his mind was that far gone.

He stripped off his clothes, and crawled under the covers, grateful for the intense training which had resulted in being able to drop off to sleep almost on command. He set his internal clock for three and a half hours and was out in seconds.

But the one thing training had no control over were his dreams. And searching for a kid he had shit in common with had apparently brought old memories to the surface. Slipped the disk into the slot and set it up to play the moment he surrendered to sleep.

Broughton was a scared kid again. Waking up to a feeling that something was wrong, he crept down the hall to where he heard his mother's frightened voice.

"You're scaring me," she said. "Tell me what it is, dammit!"

"I can't."

"You *have* to."

There was a loud crashing, smashing kind of noise.

"Stop it! Breaking things isn't helping either of us."

"Oh, God." His dad's voice was muffled.

Creeping closer, Broughton was able to see them in the living room. His dad sitting on the edge of the recliner, bent forward with his face in his hands. Shiny bits of whatever had been thrown at the fireplace were strewn on the carpeted floor, and Broughton's mom was crouched in front of his dad with a grip on his arms as though trying to tug his hands away from his face.

"You have to talk to me."

"I can't. Don't you see? I just can't."

"Won't, and you're being a stubborn ass."

"I've done everything they asked, but I can't. Won't do this." His voice was low, muffled.

"Do what?"

He dropped his hands and Broughton was shocked to see red eyes and a face wet with tears. "I can't do it."

He shoved out of the chair, went to stand at the

front window. "There will be an execution tomorrow, and I'm to be part of it."

"They can't expect you—"

"They can! Do."

"I meant your side. Your handler. What did he say?"

"I haven't told him yet, but I know what he'll want, because this will be the last hurdle. I'll be one of them then, and have access to the top. That's what the agency is after."

"What about your own boss with the PD? He gave you the option of joining the special team and going undercover, but he'd never condone this."

"Telling him would break my vow of confidentiality."

"Go to your handler, then. Tell him. Tell him you won't do it. You're not a killer."

"But I promised to do whatever it took to get in. I've done so much I hated, and this is just one more step. There's nothing left of the man I used to be, and if I cross them, they'll come after you and Caleb." He mopped his face with a handkerchief, and his shoulders shook.

They stood together for a long time while his father cried and Broughton's mother kept her arms wrapped around him.

"I'm scared. So fucking scared they'll come here."

Broughton's mom pushed away. Held her husband at arm's length and, from the look on her face, she was going to tear into him for being a coward. "You're *exactly* the man you always were. But tonight you need my help."

She led him back to his chair and made him sit. Then she crouched in front of him again and said, "Here's what you're going to do."

Listening, Broughton fought to reconcile this powerful woman with the giggling one his dad spun around in a circle when he got home the day he was accepted onto the special team.

His father, the strong, capable cop, was reduced to taking orders from a woman who was afraid of snakes and guns.

"You will contact your handler first thing in the morning. Spell it all out, and tell him you won't do it. If that gets you kicked off the team, so be it."

"I should never have joined."

"Bullshit. It was a good job, with a good purpose. But now it's changed. This isn't what you signed on for, and you *won't* continue to play along. Not when lives are being sacrificed in the name of evidence gathering."

"I'm afraid they'll tell me I don't have a choice."

She straightened up and strode away from him, spun back and stared. "Then you'll get your ass back here and we'll bug out." She nodded. "Yes. I'll plan for it. Be packed and ready. Hell, we can go now."

Again, his dad broke down and bawled like a baby.

Broughton didn't want to see any more. Know any more. What he wanted to do was run away. Hide from the mess that used to be his hero, the man who wasn't afraid of anything, anyone. Who spent his life serving and protecting.

Back in his room, he stared out the window into darkness. Wishing he hadn't been a witness. But then it got worse.

The adult Broughton clawed his way out of the dream, and woke up sweating, breathing hard. He shook off the thickness of sleep and the weight of a dream he hadn't had in many, many, years.

He cursed the memories, and wondered what had triggered this shit from his past.

Ryder's situation was nothing like what Broughton went through. Sure, they both lost their parents, but Broughton's hadn't died quick and easy in a plane crash. Hadn't left the world exactly as they were. Hadn't been average citizens doing nothing more than taking a vacation.

He glanced at the clock. Still an hour left to call his own. He could force sleep. But the dream wasn't finished. Hadn't taken him to the end. To the places he'd rather not go, ever again.

He shoved the sheet aside and swung his legs over. Scrubbed his hands over his face. Didn't feel rested or revived. Maybe exercise would be a better remedy for his bone-deep exhaustion.

He took a quick shower and headed for the indoor lap pool, because at this time of day the outdoor one could be crowded with shrieking kids.

Walking the long hallways, he met no one, but arriving at the pool discovered Alex was already there. Long, lean muscles working rhythmically, cutting through the water with minimal disturbance. Funny, she was like that upright too. Graceful and economical, as though displacing no air while she quickly covered ground.

He didn't dive in until she was at the far end. She was sticking close to the right wall, so he'd stay to the left, leaving room for a couple more swimmers if anyone else showed up.

With limited time instead of the two hours he'd prefer, he made good use of the minutes by pushing hard. He lapped Alex a couple of times, and didn't let up when she got out. Didn't want to see her out of the water in that black, body-molding suit. A glimpse was enough to make him want those sexy legs wrapped—

He pushed off his turn and stayed underwater a full lap, pushed off again and came up about halfway, lungs screaming for air. Again, when he turned he stayed under. Kept the pattern going until he was able to go two laps without a breath, then he switched to a nice, easy cooldown routine with a variety of strokes before climbing out.

Alex was long gone, which was good, and a glance at the clock told him he'd pushed past his allotted time. He wrapped a towel around his waist and jogged back to his room, took a quick shower, and arrived in the war room without a minute to spare.

James and Julia were at the head of the table, Logan and Grace on the far side, and Angie had her back to Broughton. No Alex. Hmm. She'd left the pool long before he did. Was she okay? Maybe he should go check on her.

She slipped through the door and dropped into the chair beside him.

"All okay?" asked Angie.

"Yep. But Dhillon wants to stick close to his

charge." She glanced at James. "Asked if he could listen in from the kitchen. He's got Consuelo's laptop open."

James worked the keyboard in front of him. "Dhillon, do you copy?"

"Affirmative," came the kid's voice through the speakers, but he didn't sound like a kid anymore. Funny, Broughton hadn't noticed his voice deepening, but somewhere along the line it had.

"Then we'll get started." James used a laser pointer on the map currently up on the biggest wall screen and said, "We've highlighted these three areas of interest from the flyover, and they are now under surveillance via satellite."

The screen changed to a photo of Ryder. "This, however, is our focus. According to Grace's vision, Ryder was the target, the reason the plane was hijacked, and we can be fairly certain ransom wasn't the objective. Someone who knew, or knows, Ryder is the key to why he was abducted."

A second screen lit with four photos. "This is Sunrise Ranch, and the couple on the right are Dusty and Chase Mathews. They are the mentors who sent Ryder to us.

"They run a unique summer camp program intended to enrich the lives of First Nations children in the foster-care system. First Nations is a Canadian term used in reference to the indigenous people of that country, similar to our use of Native Americans in the US, and foster-care in Canada is as underfunded as it is here, to say the least. The camp offers kids a fun summer experience enriched with opportunities to learn about their heritage—

something they are without in homes with non-First Nations foster parents. Sunrise specializes in making sure these kids know they matter."

James glanced over at Broughton, and the light came on. The niggling connection he had with Ryder suddenly made sense.

"Ryder's father was born and raised on a reservation in Arizona, and had a passion for flying. He got his private license, and then became an aircraft mechanic. He created a lucrative business by providing private ranchers with a much-needed service. Instead of the inconvenience of taking their planes for regular maintenance, he would fly to where the aircraft were, and work on them there."

James pointed to the photo on the bottom right. "Ryder's parents, Dayson and Mae, Thomas." They were no more than late thirties. He had inky black hair cut short and standing straight up, while hers was long, thick, and wavy. Her skin was slightly lighter than his, and where his face had angles, hers had none.

"Because there was no high school close by, Ryder spent his weekdays boarding at the home of a family friend Monday through Friday, and went home on weekends. With him gone all week, his mom started going with her husband when he worked, and that's where we think things might have become complicated. Ryder told Dusty that in the weeks prior to their plane crash, his mom suddenly stopped going on jobs with his dad, and became fearful when Ryder was out of her sight."

James put another set of photos up. "This is the airport closest to where they lived, and where

Ryder's dad had a shop. The boy spent a lot of time there, sweeping up, fueling planes, manning the radio, washing planes, whatever. And this is where he could have crossed paths with a local gang busted for running drug shipments through there a few years back. No telling what he might have seen or heard. Easy enough for a kid to go unnoticed." James shrugged.

Another thread to tug. And if there'd been a bust, there would be records, names, something solid to investigate.

"The four-place aircraft in the photo is the one Ryder's parents were in, on their way to an airshow when they disappeared The plane was never found, and we can speculate all day about whether they're dead or alive, but for our purposes we're going to assume Dayson and Mae are also on our missing list."

Made good sense. And speaking of senses, Broughton's were tingling. He'd bet money the reason Ryder was missing had something to do with the disappearance of his parents.

"To recap, we're actively searching for the aircraft that vanished yesterday with Del and Ryder at the controls. There is a secondary investigation into Ryder's parents, and here's the kicker. At least one member of our psychic family is picking up a connection between Ryder and the people missing from the Houston evacuation center."

What the hell?

"Both teams will continue to work with what they have until paths cross. Julia and I will monitor all incoming data and keep you apprised of anything you need to know."

When James reached for the keyboard, Julia said, "I've got it," and a list of names appeared on one side of the screen.

"Team one. Broughton, Alex, Logan, Grace, Angie, and Dhillon, your focus is Ryder."

A second set of names appeared on the opposite side.

"Team two. Quinn, Rachel, Nathan, and Tyler on the evac center missing persons. Quinn and Rachel will be here or at Haven, and the twins will stay in Florida for the time being. The good news is that many of the missing there have been accounted for, and it looks like our speculation about a connection to the Houston case is unfounded. Once we get confirmation, Nathan and Tyler will come back here."

James took a deep breath. "Questions?" When his gaze met Broughton's, there was a tiny zing of electricity. A message to open a telepathic link, which he did immediately. *What is it?*

Considering putting boots on the ground closer to Sunrise Ranch. I want your gut on whether or not it should be you.

A no-brainer. *I'm all in. Sooner the better.*

"One more thing," said James. "We're top-heavy here, so I want part of team one to relocate to a safe house close to Sunrise Ranch and meet with Ryder's mentors.

Broughton preferred working on a small team, because numbers muddied things, screwed with communications. But sometimes tidy wasn't possible, and this opportunity to at least be away from the crowd suited him just fine.

"Two options. If Logan flies you in, he can stay and also bring you out. If Angie takes you, she'll have to do a drop and return. Takes her out of the mix here, too, so my second choice."

"I should go," said Grace. "What about if the four of us go? Maybe I can tap into something if I'm in an area Ryder was close to, and that leaves Angie here for HQ."

"Works for me," said James. "Sunrise is literally on the other side of the mountain from the safe house, so doable on foot, but better still, use the ATVs."

"Logan, are you fit to fly, or do you need more down time first?"

"I haven't logged any airtime in two days, so I'm legal. Plus I got four solid this morning, so I'm good, and Grace can always land it if I fall asleep."

All eyes swung to Grace, who simply shrugged and said, "Figured it was time I learned to fly. Got my license about six months ago."

12

Trent flew the four of them to Montana, to a private airfield Alex was told was used by Special Forces and various alphabet agencies. Apparently there were dozens of similar setups all around the world. *Who knew?*

This one masqueraded as a billionaire's estate, with a grand mansion nestled into the mountainside. Running across the valley below it was the runway where they had just landed.

"When we turn at the end, take a good look at what's past the pavement," said Broughton, and when Alex did, she was confused by what she saw.

"Is that paint?" she asked.

"Yep. The runway is twice as long as it appears, with half being painted to look like the barren ground surrounding it. Once your eyes and mind adjust to the camouflage, you'll also see it's wider than it looks."

And therefore capable of handling a wide

variety of aircraft.

“See that white barn, and what looks like an indoor arena?”

She did. It was a beautiful setup. The barn was an older structure with a classic hip roof, had runout paddocks for each bright green stall door, and looked like it housed ten or more horses.

“The arena building is where we’re headed for cover. Policy is to never come to a full stop outside except for doing run-ups. Less chance to be captured on satellite surveillance photos that way.”

They taxied through the wide-open end of the huge building, and Trent shut the engines down immediately, but stayed seated while everyone gathered their personal knapsacks and deplaned.

Alex took a good look around the empty space, which dwarfed the jet they arrived in. There was nothing else visible, but her skin crawled with the knowledge that there was something she was missing. A presence she could feel, but not see.

“Psychic energy meltdown,” she muttered, and Broughton touched the back of her neck. “Nothing bad.”

But she hadn’t missed the pained expression that flitted across Logan’s face just before Grace grabbed his hand and held tight. Then she felt it. The hum of electricity in the air. The awareness of a multitude of energy fields.

“I’m not liking this,” she said.

“Come on.” Broughton led them to the rounded corner at the far end, where he tapped the wall and a section of it swung open silently. “We good to go?” he asked Logan and Grace, and they nodded.

Broughton waved toward the plane and gave a double thumbs-up. The engines started. “Get through so we can close the door. Trent needs to turn that buggy around, and we don’t want to be wearing the jet wash.”

With the door firmly closed, Alex took in her surroundings, which were sparse. Wooden walls, concrete stairs with a metal handrail, and tiny sensor lights. She followed Grace and Logan, with Broughton bringing up the rear.

Several flights down they came to a wide-open area that left her at a loss for words. Aircraft filled the space for as far as she could see. Two long rows of them—everything from brightly-painted single engines and sexy little jets to spooky-looking black military helicopters.

Planes stored underground. Why not?

A man with a freaking machine gun stepped out in front of them, and Alex’s heart shot into her throat.

“Password.”

“There isn’t one,” said Broughton. “At least not yet today.”

The man nodded.

“We’re Meyers, and you have a Cessna for us.”

“Affirmative.”

He led the way to a single-engine aircraft. “This do?”

“Extended range, correct?” asked Logan while opening the door on the left and dropping his knapsack behind the seat.

“Correct, with weight restrictions as advised.”

Alex had wondered why they each had to

weigh in with their bags prior to boarding the jet, but hadn't asked for an explanation. As always, patience produced the answer, and now she understood it was to prepare them for this smaller plane. The one Logan was going to fly.

"As soon as you're ready, I'll take you up," said the uniformed man, and he strode away while Logan walked around the plane, checking things, studying, touching.

"Get in," said Logan. "Back seat first.

Broughton and Alex climbed in on the far side and past the front seat, to settle in the ones in the back, and all four bags were stowed in a tiny space behind them, under a net which she was told would prevent them from flying around if there was turbulence or a rough landing—two possibilities she didn't want to think about.

While Logan continued going through his checklist, the soldier came back with a small machine he hooked to the plane to pull it into a white-painted square on the wide metal floor.

When Logan gave him a thumbs-up, a band of light became visible along the ceiling, and after a second Alex figured out what she was seeing. They were in an open-sided elevator, being propelled up through the floor of the hangar above.

The sound of the elevator stopped, and they were pulled forward, toward the opening of the building. The soldier disconnected the tow bar, moved back into the elevator, and disappeared back down into the underground storage area.

"Freaking amazing."

Broughton grinned. "Like the stuff out of

novels or movies, isn't it?"

Grace laughed. "The first time I saw a full-size jet come up out of there I nearly swallowed my tongue."

"Full-size? Seriously?"

"Big enough to hold about thirty people."

"Holy Hannah."

"What you saw today was the tip of the iceberg," said Broughton. "This entire valley is home to dozens of underground tunnels covering an area almost as vast as ETCETERA's headquarters."

Alex had never been to ETC, but heard plenty about the clandestine agency and its work with psychic warriors. She thought warriors was a strong term for the people who used their amazing abilities to save people from crime and misfortune, but it was their word.

After recovering from the drug paralysis and going back to her vet practice, Alex toyed with an offer to work with the pros at ETC, to hone the telepathic skills she had only just discovered. But being an introvert, the thought of living in a sprawling underground world packed with people was just too far out of her comfort zone.

Working with her cousin at a private facility like Paradise was a much better fit, and Grace's promise of space and alone time was all it took to make her decision. One she was still pleased with.

Lost in thought while Logan taxied into position and did his run-up, she was vaguely surprised and instinctively grabbed onto her safety harness when the plane surged forward for takeoff. A much different feeling than in the jet.

As though sensing her slight discomfort, Grace glanced over her shoulder, and just the slightest of smiles had Alex relaxing immediately. Yeah, the woman had skills.

But they were skills developed from the same extra senses Alex inherited from their mutual grandfather, so maybe one day she too would be adept at their use.

#

Landing on a grass strip in the middle of freaking nowhere wasn't exactly the way Alex envisioned their arrival at the safe house. In her head, there had been a lovely paved runway like the one at Meyers, and perhaps a tiny hangar, all located close to a beautiful house made of logs and glass, perched on a knoll overlooking the valley.

She at least had the part about the house right, and the valley, which was, of course, due to Angie's description. What she had made up in her head about the runway was jarred loose by a long, narrow clearing down the middle of the valley—which she got a good look at when Logan did a first pass, down low enough to check for wildlife, and, she was sure, count the freaking daisies.

And now they were somehow balanced on the back wheels with the nose in the air while they bounced and rattled through ruts and over what were surely boulders. Apparently Logan was in no hurry to lower the front end so the third tire could touch the ground. And while the bouncing, rattling and grinding was bad enough, seeing nothing but sky through the windscreen was downright disconcerting, to say the least.

Not that Alex would say anything at all right now. No point reminding everyone she was a rookie.

The nose lowered, but the ride didn't get any smoother, and to Alex's absolute horror, they were aimed right at an enormous tree…which they managed to stop in front of. Logan then turned the craft and headed back the way they'd come.

Breathe, Alex. Broughton's touch on one of the hands she had fisted around the webbing of her safety harness made her jump like a nervous horse. Good grief, she needed to get a grip. And air. She sucked in the recommended breath, and exhaled slowly through her mouth.

The first landing on an unpaved strip is always a bit tough. You'll know what to expect next time.

Like no one could have warned her beforehand? She flexed her fingers and rubbed her palms on the fabric of her jeans.

"Runway could use some maintenance," said Logan.

No shit.

Broughton laughed. "Uh, yeah. Wouldn't hurt."

"Can't do anything with it until just before we leave, though. Don't want anyone spotting the strip from the air, and a swath of fresh dirt screams, look here!"

Logan had a point, but still. "Does this place get used often?" asked Alex.

"Three or four times a year as a retreat," said Grace. "Much less often as a safe house."

"It's so remote, I would think it would be used more frequently."

"When we have someone in protective custody, the practice is to never stay in one place too long, and because of the long, snowy winters here, it's only accessible by helicopter from September through May. Makes it an expensive choice for a short stay."

Alex didn't bother to mention it was September and they were not in a helicopter.

When they rolled to a stop under camouflage netting strung between several trees, Alex was more than glad to climb out. That's when the air hit her. Clean, pure, mountain air, rich with the smell of pine, and of sunshine on dry earth.

"Wow." She inhaled deeply again. "Freaking incredible."

Broughton grinned. "You can get high on the air here."

"No doubt," she said, slinging her knapsack over her shoulder. She'd packed light, as instructed, because the house here was apparently stocked with everything from clothing and footwear to food and electronics.

Broughton and Logan tied down the plane with ropes hooked to what looked like old tires filled with concrete, while Grace led Alex to the house. Perched on a knoll overlooking the valley, built of logs, and with plenty of windows, the structure almost looked like it had grown there naturally.

Crossing a wide patio surrounded by pine trees Grace stopped and pointed. "See that?"

Alex stared, but saw nothing.

"Look at the structure of the top of that tree. See what looks like it could be a nest or something?"

Ah, there it was. "Is that one of the wind turbines?"

"Exactly. It's completely encased, with the moving parts on the inside. The workings of the system are hidden underneath the deck."

With that, she opened the back door of the house and walked in.

Suddenly on full alert, Alex reached for her weapon, but to confirm, said, "It wasn't locked."

"No point. Way out here, if someone wanted in, they'd break in. Easier to leave it unlocked than have to replace a window, or a door that's been knocked down."

"How can you be sure it's safe to go inside?" Would she ever know everything she needed to feel comfortable as a security agent?

Grace held up a small device that looked like the remote Alex used to start her gas fireplace. "The place is rigged with motion sensors, and if any have been triggered, an alarm will sound when I push this green button." She smiled. "Which I did when Logan did the fly-by. We wouldn't have landed if the security had been breached."

Of course. Highly trained security specialists didn't take unnecessary chances. Every risk was calculated. And one day—maybe—it would all come naturally to Alex, and she wouldn't feel like such an outsider. An imposter. Sure, she excelled at marksmanship, and all the other skills she'd been tested on, but she needed to get to the point where it was reflex, and not something she had to think about. Only then would she feel like she was an asset instead of a liability.

For the time being, she was grateful Dhillon had needed her to check one of the kittens. It was nice to not only feel in control for those few minutes, but to be useful again, and not an appendage the team was stuck with.

And oh, boy, time to ditch the pity party. She glanced around the huge room. “What a beautiful place.” Furniture was made of logs. Much skinnier ones than the walls of the house, but bigger than branches. It was all natural, without that phony, high-gloss look she didn’t like. Fabrics appeared to be hand woven, and the view was to freaking die for.

“Pick a room,” said Grace. “We like the one at the end of the hall. Linens are in sealed containers in each room.”

Alex stuck her head in the first doorway and found an office. The second led to a bedroom with a deep armchair and ottoman in front of a wide window overlooking the valley, and a roomy bathroom.

“This will work for me,” she said, and dropped her knapsack on the floor. She didn’t need anything out of it for now, and had been taught to not unpack, because you never knew when you might have to grab your bag and make a run for it.

She ripped the plastic off the huge bin of supplies and made up the bed, took a pair of towels into the bathroom, then wandered out to the kitchen. Seemed like she was endlessly eating these days, but she was determined not to have any issues with her blood sugar, and it had been eight hours since her last meal. What she wouldn't do for one of Consuelo's signature chicken potpies right now.

13

When Broughton encountered a ghostly brush of vaguely familiar energy on his way from the plane to the house, he stopped. Waited for another feather-light stroke. But nothing happened.

Residual energy perhaps? There didn't seem to be any darkness or sinister undertones lurking, so he continued on, thankful to be at the tail end of a long day.

He opened the door, and his senses were lambasted by the rich scent of chili. Logan came in the door behind him and sniffed the air like a hungry hound. "Something smells good…and that's almost scary."

"Hey," said Grace "Even I can open cans and stir. And turns out Alex makes a mean pot of rice."

"Works for me," said Broughton, lifting the lid off the pot. "Smells awesome. Ha, but then so would the ass end out of a skunk about now."

Grace shooed him away from the food. "Took you guys a long time. Everything okay out there?"

"Did some recon. Looks like hikers have passed through in the past few days."

"Passed through?"

"Stopped a few times and turned around. Perhaps taking photos, or worried a bear was following them. Tracks suggest two men. Size twelve or thirteen boots, but not heavy on their feet."

"If they took photos, what would they show?"

"Seemed to be pointed at the area where the camo-netting is stored, and then a long view of the valley from the far end of the runway," said Logan.

"Either of you picking up anything unusual?" Broughton asked.

Alex frowned, then said, "I was bothered by the door being unlocked when we arrived, until Grace explained about the security sensors, then I was good."

When he glanced back at the pot on the stove Grace laughed and said. "Choose a bedroom, stow your gear, and we'll eat."

He headed down the hall, poking his head through a couple of doorways, and couldn't help but stop at the room Alex had chosen. Her scent was already there, and he could be too if he wasn't such an idiot.

The thought of sliding in beside her warm nakedness not only kicked up his appetite for her, but had him wondering yet again if he dared take a chance.

Nope. With all the complicated situations he ended up in professionally, he needed to keep his life simple.

He tossed his pack into the room beside hers and marched back to the kitchen, where steaming bowls of food were already on the table.

"Grab whatever you're drinking and sit," said Logan, and, since there was no beer, Broughton chose a club soda. "Anyone else?"

"I'll have a cola," said Logan.

"Seriously? With chili?"

Logan raised a single eyebrow. "Am I knocking your choice of *fizzy* water?"

Broughton passed him a cola. "Chili needs beer."

"Amen," said Alex.

They ate in silence until Broughton said, "Damn sight better than MREs."

"A stale cheese sandwich is better than most of those I've tried," said Grace. "But could use some bread to mop up this amazing sauce."

"Hard to believe it came out of cans." Logan and Broughton were both on their second helping.

"And jars," added Alex. "We started with four cans of commercial chili, then opened a few jars of preserves to kick it up a notch. An amazing assortment of food in that pantry, but Grace wouldn't let me toss in the canned peaches. We saved them for dessert instead."

Small mercies. Broughton loved peaches, but putting them in chili would have been an ugly stretch. Still, better than some of the alternatives—like liquid meal replacements.

No matter what flavor he tried, there was a texture thing that made them damn tough to choke down. A peculiar smoothness made him feel like he was trying to drink cooking oil.

"Got a message from James," Grace said. "We're to go west on the mountain trail first thing tomorrow morning. About an hour in there will be an old cabin where Dusty and Chase from Sunrise ranch will meet us."

The strange feeling Broughton put aside earlier, surfaced again. A warning? He would take it as one. "I'll be staying behind."

"But—"

Broughton cut Alex off with a quick lesson in protocol. "Our transportation out of here can't be left unprotected." Not to mention the house and surrounding area. This was their current safe zone, and he would keep it that way. Even though he trusted his team, he wouldn't feel comfortable walking away from here, no matter who was guarding it. And wasn't that odd? He usually had full confidence in Logan and Grace, but that creeping feeling was a game changer.

Fucking annoying game changer, because he couldn't quite put his finger on the problem. Was it his own PTSD slithering back into place? Making him hypervigilant? Vulnerable to the projection of weighty emotions like fear, grief, and anger? Or was it age making him less able to shield himself from the unknown? He slammed the door on that thought.

"Any objections?" he asked.

"I'd like to meet Ryder's people, but will stay if you want us to stick to working in pairs," said Alex.

"You should come along, because from what

Julia told me about Dusty and Chase, there's a good chance you could make a connection. Or at least your horse sense will pick up a nuance or something we can work with." Grace smiled. "You're very gifted at reading silent signals."

"Body language can make or break a vet, and it's not unusual for me to rely more heavily on intuition than on the science of my job."

Grace tipped her head. "On that note, what was wrong with the kitten Dhillon was so worried about?"

"Just an upper respiratory infection. Kind of like a preschooler with a common cold. She should be fine with good supportive care."

So that's why Alex was late for the meeting this morning… Felt like days ago.

Suddenly tired, Broughton glanced around the table. "Three-hour watch shifts work for everyone?"

They nodded.

"Now till eleven, eleven to two, two to five, and five to eight. Pick your poison." He didn't like the idea of Alex sitting in the darkened window with a weapon in her lap. Would rather take her shift since she was too green for this kind of watch, but he didn't know how to pull it off without...

"What about Alex and I doing eight until two together? It's her first watch, and would be a great teaching tool," said Grace, and Broughton could have kissed her feet.

"Works for me. You want the two or the five?" he asked Logan.

"I'll take the two. We're leaving at first light, which puts you on deck from five until we get back.

You'd be looking at around three hours, because the round trip will take two."

That worked. Now if he could find a way to fall asleep while Alex and Grace…he stopped the thought. He was thinking he couldn't be safe with two females at the helm, and that was bullshit. Grace was highly trained, and Alex's lack of training would be eclipsed by her brains and determination.

"I'll clean up in here," he said. Penance for wrong thinking, and a thank-you for them putting a meal in front of him.

Taking his time over the task, he let his mind drift back to the house he'd grown up in. The one he'd pedaled away from dozens of years earlier. His mother was a stickler for fair play. The cook never had to clean up after, and she taught him to cook before he was tall enough to see the back burner of the stove. His dad built a long bench for him to stand on while he stirred the gravy, or the red sauce his mom helped him create. He produced complete meals before he was ten, and still cooked for himself, but didn't enjoy it the same way he did when he was a kid…before his world imploded.

Not going there. Needed to keep his head in the here and now.

When the kitchen duties were finished, Broughton turned off the light, and the entire great room was plunged into darkness. Good. He hated interior illumination. He always felt as if his every move was visible to anyone outside—even though he knew the treatment on the glass made it impossible.

Once his eyes adjusted to the blackness, he crossed to the window. "You ever seen the northern lights, Alex?"

"No." She joined him looking toward the faint yellow light in the sky well past the end of the runway.

"Not as dramatic as the photos I've seen online."

"We're too far south to see vibrant greens and blues, and even the yellow would be more spectacular if we flew north for a couple of hours."

"Definitely not impressive enough to tick it off my bucket list," she said. "I'll make it to Alaska one day to see the northern lights at their strongest."

"Or the Yukon," said Grace. "We have an amazing lodge outside of Whitehorse."

"You have places everywhere, don't you?"

"Pretty much."

"Handy," said Broughton.

"It is."

Conversation wound around the various inns and lodges Grace's father had bought and converted to safe places for people wanting to stay hidden for any number of reasons. They often provided havens for the rich and famous seeking relaxation away from prying eyes and camera lenses.

And several of the locations, such as Paradise, sheltered those rescued from human traffickers. Provision was made for the best possible recovery and reintegration into society, yet some never left, staying instead to help rehabilitate others.

Broughton stopped the memories trying to surface. "I'm going to call it a night," he said, and swung through the kitchen for a bottle of water to take with him.

Logan kissed his wife. “I’m turning in as well.”

#

Grace listened to the footsteps receding. Waited until she heard doors click shut, then said, “Our conversation was difficult for Broughton.”

After a moment, Alex said, “He’s been tense since we got here.”

That was true, but this was more. “The subject of human trafficking is especially hard on those who’ve been there, seen….”

“He talked about his work a bit, back when he was keeping me company. Said he left the FBI to go solo a few years back, and the way he said the word ‘solo’ made it sound more like rogue.”

How much to say? Sharing information about another person was so not Grace’s thing. But as Alex’s trainer, she had a responsibility to make sure she understood the man she was working with.

“He has a talent for extracting people from terrifying situations. For the most part it’s feel-good work, but there were occasions when he had to let a criminal go in order to save the victim. Months later he’d have to pick up more victims, knowing he had been in a position to stop the criminals who harmed them, but had to let them go. That kind of thing can eat at a man’s soul.” Or a woman’s.

Grace, too, suffered because of the ones she couldn’t save…and they haunted her still.

“The man who sat at my bedside just to keep me company wouldn’t do well with letting a perpetrator of evil walk.”

"That would be the same man who brought six girls directly to Paradise instead of leaving them in the hands of the appropriate departments and government agencies."

She would never forget that night. Broughton's voice blasting its way into her head, even though she was telepathically shut down while she wallowed in self-pity, blaming herself for the loss of—

You okay?

Logan never missed. Always knew when she needed him.

I was trying to let Alex know a bit about how Broughton operates. How he doesn't hesitate to break a rule if he thinks it's in the best interests of a victim. It made me think of the night he demanded I meet him at Paradise to take in the girls.

When you were still recovering from your own mission.

I was wallowing.

And shut me out.

That, too. I was short on brain cells for a while.

Have you told Alex what happened? About when we met?

No. I don't want her feeling awkward about her name. And truthfully I'd rather not dredge it all up.

I'm here for you, whichever you choose.

You need to get some sleep.

I will, now I know you're okay.

Their link faded. Grace wanted nothing more than to curl up in his arms and soak in the love he gave so freely. She had wondered, in the beginning, if his way would ever rub off on her, and it hadn't.

Oh, she had learned how to express her love, but for Logan, it was simply his way. Part of who he was.

Unlike her, he could protect his inner self without the walls and armor she wore. People called her aloof, which was better than being called snotty, and she'd been there too.

"Considering we're partnered, is it really okay for me to not stay with him tomorrow?"

"I think it's important for you to come with us."

"Do you have any ideas about what's really going on? Why Ryder was abducted?"

"Logan and I rarely do hands-on anymore, but we're both driven to work this case. It feels big, like every single one of us will be needed."

"Human trafficking seems to be a hot button. Do you think that's what we're up against?"

"I'm getting mixed signals there, but I won't be surprised if it's the underlying motive. Ryder doesn't seem like a good fit, but then again, he has skills, and no family to miss him."

"What about Del? No one seems to be worried about him at all."

Grace sighed. In her vision, it was very clear that the interest was in Ryder—which meant Del would be eliminated, first chance. Given the circumstances, she had little hope Del would still be alive.

#

Alex woke with a start.

She distinctly remembered locking the door and checking the windows when she turned in after their long security shift, but someone was definitely in the room with her now.

She lay very still, working hard to feign sleep, and, keeping her breathing slow and steady, while engaging her senses to search. Found a presence behind her, just inside her door. Unmoving.

Could she reach the weapon on her night stand *and* swing it toward the intruder faster than he could close the space between them? Or would the move make her vulnerable?

Would it be better to roll toward the door as though still sleeping and get a glimpse of what—who—she was up against? But then her weapon would be behind her.

Was she alone? Had the intruder already taken out the others?

Without warning, the incredible tension in her muscles eased, as though her subconscious had decided there was no threat, even though the intruder was still there.

Could it be Broughton?

Still feigning sleep, she rolled over and opened her eyes just a crack.

Nothing. What? With her senses on full alert, there was no way she would have missed the sound of the door.

Her heart rate bumped up again while she sent sensory feelers throughout the room.

Nothing. No one. She sat up. Flicked on the light, but the room stayed dark. She grabbed the flashlight from under her and did a careful perusal of the entire space, got up and checked the bathroom, the closet, and under the bed.

Nothing.

Had she been dreaming? Perhaps. But the light? She headed for the door, planning to test the overhead, but stopped abruptly when she hit a blast of cold air.

From under the door?

She swiftly made for the bathroom again, tried the light there, but it didn't come on. She dragged on pants and a sweater, and with the flashlight in one hand and her gun in the other, she headed for the door. Stopped.

Should she call out telepathically?

She chewed the inside of her cheek. Why wake the others up if it was nothing more than the remnants of a silly dream?

Alex twisted the knob and inched the door open. Cool air and darkness. She checked her watch. Five-thirty. Broughton would be on watch.

Broughton? She waited, but there was no response. With adrenaline coursing through her, it was hard to remember the steps needed to reach someone who was shut down to telepathic communications. It was something she had no practical experience with, only training exercises.

She visualized Broughton, then went inside her own head, strode through the pathways, past open windows and closed doors until she found one with a golden glow. That would be Grace. She continued on until she found the one she was looking for. The light coming from it was minimal. Not the least bit inviting, but she stopped, laid her palms against the surface and felt the warm.

She conjured up a visual of him looking directly at her and sent a wave of energy.

Broughton, I need you. There's something wrong, and I need your help.

Alex repeated this message over and over until she felt the door edge away from her hands.

What's wrong?

I woke up feeling an intruder in my room, but there's no one there, and there's no power.

Where are you?

In the hallway.

Come to the great room.

He certainly didn't sound concerned. Was she being an idiot? Overreacting?

He was sitting in a chair pulled right up to the wide window, with his feet propped on the wide ledge.

Alex slid another chair over and joined him. "Tell me what happened."

He was completely silent while she described the experience in great detail. He didn't nod, or give her an encouraging sound of any kind, but when she finished, he said, "You have good instincts. I need coffee, want some?"

He went to the kitchen, and she heard the flick and swoosh of a burner lighting, then the tinny sound of the old-fashioned coffeepot on the stove.

"The power is off on purpose," he said. "It's a frequently-used tactic, because darkness inside is good defense."

"We already had all the lights out."

"In the kind of darkness we have here, because of the isolated location, one flick of a light switch makes us vulnerable."

She had done exactly that. Reached without

thinking and switched on a light. If the power hadn't been off... Her stomach hit rock bottom, because if that had been a test, she would have failed.

A nasty realization crept under her skin. "It was you in my room. You were testing me."

"How do you take your coffee?"

When she didn't answer, he set two short jars and a spoon on the coffee table he pulled over between their chairs, and that's when she noticed the thin, very thin light of approaching dawn.

"Black." Sweetener or fake milk wouldn't sit well in her belly right now. "How long were you there before I woke up?"

"Seconds."

At least she had decent reaction time. Would he have known she tried to turn on the light if she hadn't told him? Good question.

"Why did it feel like you were still there, even when you weren't?"

"Do you know anything about quantum physics?"

Holy crap. "You can teleport?"

He set two mugs on the table and settled into his chair. "Reality is much different. I can't will myself to be somewhere I'm not, but under certain circumstances, I can remove my physical self from view."

"Invisibility?" This just got wilder by the minute.

"I was still there, but you couldn't see me."

Alex knew the Steed appeared to be invisible because the skin—the outer surface—reflected the surroundings, but human skin couldn't do that, could it?

"The key element is preternatural stillness. The rest is way too complicated to explain."

"If I had walked to the door and reached out to open it, I would have touched you." The blast of cold air. "You did that. Made the air cold to spook me and make me back away."

"It's all part of the package."

She sat back, sipped the slightly bitter coffee. He had been there the whole time. Watching her reaction to the unknown—just as he was now. But this time it wasn't fear threatening to take over. It was indignation and anger.

"In spite of being told I was capable, and had excelled in every area of my training," *almost*, "you felt the need to put me through that as a test."

He sighed and set his cup on the low window ledge, crouched in front of her. "This is new ground for me. I've never worked with someone brand new. At least not since I was a rookie myself. I need to know what you're made of when the chips are down. Needed to see what your reactions will look like."

Broughton tipped his head as though listening, then a slow smile spread across his face. "Watch," he said, pointing to the window.

It only took a moment. An elk. A large bull, as tall from his forehead to the top of his rack as he was from his forehead to the ground. The impressive creature lifted his head as though scenting the air, then moved past the pine trees where the plane was hidden, and slipped out of sight.

"What did you just learn?" asked Broughton.

Without hesitation she said, "He wasn't worried in any way, which should suggest the area is clear of threats. Specifically, there are no threats to the east, where the wind is coming from."

"Good," said Broughton. "Very good. What else?"

"You have very keen senses to be able to pick up his presence through triple glazed glass and thick log walls, and you're masterful at defusing a situation. Handy when I was on the fence, still trying to decide how pissed off I am that you still don't trust me."

"Trust is not personal. There are a great many people I like but would not trust with my life, simply because they aren't equipped to protect me. Mortal trust is earned, Alex, and has absolutely nothing to do with anything else."

"Which means?"

"It doesn't matter if I'm attracted to someone, if I hate them, or if we've just fucked each other blind. Nothing but fact-based trust matters."

Not much she could say to that. Nor could she be offended that he'd felt a need to test her earlier in her room, and now with his words. She'd have to find a way to ditch her feelings and stay completely entrenched in reality. A reality in which the man she was halfway in love with was able to make himself invisible.

And a man who would be glad she wasn't staying behind with him later. She felt the sting, but also surprising relief.

They sat in silence, watching the blackness of night fade completely, and color begin to appear as if a painter was using the light of the rising sun to slowly bring the landscape to life.

#

When Logan and Grace strolled in looking well rested and...hmmm...sated, Alex glanced at Broughton to see one corner of his mouth tip up. Her insides quivered. Dammit, he shouldn't be able to affect her that way. Not after the conversation they just had. She locked down her emotions.

"Coffee's hot," she said.

"But an hour old," added Broughton.

Logan set to making fresh while Grace brought out Mason jars filled with various cereals. Poured a couple of varieties into a bowl and held up a jar. "Anyone else?"

Alex shook her head. Straight carbs were not a good idea for her system. She needed protein, or she'd crash in a couple of hours.

She headed for the kitchen. "Can I get anything for the rest of you?" she asked.

"Eggs and bacon?"

"Ha-ha." She stepped into the pantry and raised her voice. "Fruit, beans, jerky, all kinds of pickled veggies, almonds, oatmeal, granola bars, and—oh, ewww—pickled eggs."

"Pickled eggs?"

Alex held out the jar for Grace to see, and she shook her head. "That's just disgusting."

Logan laughed. "I've eaten them a few times, but usually at a bar after a couple of beers. How about beans and jerky? Or I can make oatmeal if anyone can eat it without milk."

"I like the beans idea," said Alex.

"Ditto," said Broughton.

Logan chopped the jerky up into tiny pieces and tossed it in with the beans Alex dumped into a pot, and twenty minutes later the meal was poured into bowls.

"Wow," said Alex. "Who knew what a difference teriyaki beef could make to a can of beans." The scoop of brown sugar hadn't hurt, either.

"Damn good," said Broughton, and she took that as a high compliment from a man who acted like food was little more than sustenance.

Once they finished and cleaned up the kitchen, Alex filled a small plastic bag with cereal and almonds to take along on their hike. She also stuck some jerky into a bag and stuffed it in another pocket. Smiled to herself. She'd never worn cargo pants until they were given to her as part of her Meyers uniform, and now couldn't imagine doing without them. She loved the gazillion pockets and the soft fabric. Might never go back to jeans.

Logan loaded a pack with a bunch of water bottles, and more of the jerky. "Stuff's addictive, and a good protein source," he said, winking at her. "I hate protein bars."

Alex loved them. Especially the latest ones she'd discovered with chocolate coating. Nothing she couldn't eat if it was dipped in chocolate.

"You got bear spray in that pack?" Broughton asked Logan.

"Yep, but we'll be on the ATVs, so the engine

noise should keep them out of our path."

Alex had never met a bear in the wild, and the idea gave her a bit of a bump. She'd love to see one, but she had utmost respect for their strength, and would never want to put a wild animal in a position where it had to defend itself.

She had zero experience in a wilderness setting, had never been camping or fishing, even as a kid, but was quickly falling in love with the smell of the pines, the crunch of needles underfoot, and the sound of the wind weaving through the trees.

Did she want all that ruined by the roar of engines? Nope, but she didn't want to run into a bear, either. And maybe, when they returned, she could sit on the deck out back and just soak up the atmosphere.

14

Broughton stood in the cover of the trees listening to the four-wheelers climb the mountain trail. Alex had appeared both excited and worried, which was good. Meant she wasn't taking anything too lightly.

Her reaction to his foray into her bedroom this morning impressed him. She hadn't fired at him in anger, or allowed herself to lead with wounded feelings. She handled herself as well as she had at the time of the incident. Yes, she tried to turn on a light, which was a mistake, but it was the only one she made, and considering it was her first encounter with an intruder situation she believed was real, her reactions were spot on.

Would he be comfortable going through a door with her if they didn't know what was on the other side? Not yet. But maybe someday, when she had more mileage under her belt.

He liked her new attitude too, and hoped it

lasted. She remembered her backbone this morning, no longer looking at him like a woman would, but like a partner, and that was going to make all the difference during this mission. He would be able to quit second-guessing everything he said and did. Something to look forward to.

He liked Alex. Hell, in truth he more than liked her. Let her get under his skin while he watched over her all those months ago but couldn't have it getting in his way now. Not with a missing kid needing all his attention.

And he was hoping they'd be able to save Del, too. He could easily be dead already, but Broughton would assume the best and root for the man to survive.

Not that Broughton was an optimist, not by any stretch of the imagination, but to his way of thinking, negative energy could be defeated by positive, so he never, ever wrote off a life until he knew for certain it was gone.

Instead of going back into the house, he started up the same trail the team had used, but when he got to a fork, took the path to the left. The others had stayed right.

Broughton's choice brought him to a lookout. A beautiful spot, with a view of the entire valley, including the lodge and the plane. Or at least the area where he knew the plane was hidden. He could also see the storage shed where the ATVs and fuel were stored.

Cut into the hill, with nothing to see but doors, it wasn't easy to spot, but Broughton knew where to look. Just as he knew where the high-tech wind turbines were mounted in trees. Nothing to see but a cylinder painted to look like bark. Brilliantly hidden in plain sight, as were the storage cells.

The whole setup was something of a miracle. Old wood and brand-new science combined to make it a highly functioning contradiction. Broughton could quite happily hang out here for months if he had the opportunity. His dogs would love it here, too. Lots of room to roam, like they had in New Mexico, and a fireplace to sprawl in front of when it was cold.

Broughton lifted his binoculars to study the chimney. It was huge, as though supporting a massive fireplace, but what was hidden within the structure was a filter system which eliminated particulates, so there was never any visible smoke. He could have used that in New Mexico, on those cold nights when he'd wrapped up in sub-zero sleeping bags, half freezing to death because he didn't dare light a fire and draw attention to his location.

Hiding out there, he loved the solitude, but he was too young to be doing nothing. To have no purpose. When James sent his team to roust Broughton and bring him in on a mission, it was both a blessing and a curse.

And now was not when he should be thinking about it. He glanced at his watch. Forty-five minutes. They should be close by now. Would the people they were meeting be able to give them anything useful? Did they know something the team didn't know?

Logan would get it out of them by fair means

or foul. He had skills. Was able to sense when someone's mind was the most vulnerable, and at that precise moment he would slip inside and gather information as easily as going through a filing cabinet.

Few knew of Logan's abilities, and he rarely used them to the fullest, preferring instead to use what he called his farmer skills. Plant a seed, watch it grow, and make the harvesting quick and simple.

Grace was also far more skilled than she let on. Witnessing her slip ideas into the mind of a stranger was something Broughton would never forget.

Although Grace and Logan were what they laughingly called semi-retired...which meant they cherry-picked their assignments...what few knew about was their participation in the location, rescue, and rehabilitation of minors salvaged from human traffickers.

Weird energy suddenly curled around Broughton again...like a presence, but not. Like a warning without malice. As though information danced around him just beyond reach.

#

Alex needed to have a clear head for this meeting. And thinking about Broughton and his ability to become invisible to the naked eye, not to mention his spying on her, would not be conducive to receiving new information. To being a good observer.

To clear her mind, she concentrated on her surroundings, and was somewhat surprised by the lack of grandeur. The mountain had looked both magnificent and imposing from the house, but once on the trail, she saw nothing but trees and rocks and bunches of grass. Not very impressive at all.

The ground beneath their wheels was littered with cones and dead needles in various shades of brown—similar to the rusty-colored earth—with the only variation being one open meadow where a light wind over dried grass made it look like a pale golden sea.

The trail they followed was a series of small climbs followed by flat stretches along ridges, and dips down into gullies, followed by more climbing.

Remembering to glance behind her repeatedly so she would recognize the trail when they returned, she almost ran up the back of Grace's ATV when it came to a stop. Off to the right, and hidden by tall evergreens, was a very small building made of old weathered logs gone silver with time and a sod roof.

The moment they shut off the machines, the silence of the forest wrapped around them, and the hair on Alex's arms prickled, making her glance over her shoulder.

Grace and Logan stepped off and removed their helmets, and Alex followed suit, hooking it over the handlebar. She was glad they decided to use the cycling helmets instead of the big, blocky motorcycle variety. The smaller ones allowed them better peripheral vision, and since they were out on a wild mountainside, easy access to a three-sixty view was important. That, and they weren't planning to do any fast riding or risk-taking today.

At the comfortably familiar creak of saddle leather, Alex quickly looked past the cabin, and wasn't surprised to see the two people ride into view. A tiny woman on a magnificent black thoroughbred, and a man on a big chestnut that could also be a thoroughbred, but a lack of fluidity in his gait suggested he had many years under his belt.

She nearly laughed out loud. You could take the girl out of Kentucky, but you couldn't get rid of the horsewoman. If she closed her eyes right now, she could describe the horses in great detail, but the riders? Not so much.

She studied them now. Both rode like they were a part of their horse, with light hands and legs that didn't interfere. In faded blue jeans and matching jacket, the woman rode bareback, with her black hair pulled behind her in a braid, or tail—hard to tell from the front, but Alex guessed braid, since that's what she would have done to prevent tangles.

The man swung off his horse with the lean, limber strength of a mountain lion, and loosened the cinch, slipped off the bridle. Hooked it over the saddle horn with his own headgear.

The woman slid gracefully to the ground, and Alex sucked in a hard breath when she saw the scar. A patch of thick black flesh with no hair spread from the mare's shoulder to where a rider's leg would be positioned. And there was more scarring on the fronts of her legs, on her chest, and face. Alex had only seen something similar once, and it was on a horse who had escaped a burning barn.

Oh, the pain this poor mare must have endured.

When the simple bridle—a single strip of leather, a snaffle bit, and a leather loop for reins—was removed, the black dropped her head to nibble grass while the gelding stood in something of a sentry position. Interesting.

"I'm Chase," said the man, offering his hand to Logan, who had stepped forward as their leader. That's when Alex noticed the scar on his face. Probably a burn as well, which would suggest he was with the mare…

"And this is Dusty," he said.

Shaking the offered hands, Logan said, "Pleasure to meet you. I'm impressed by the work you do at Sunrise. I'm Logan." He tipped his head toward the rest of his team. "My wife, Grace, and her cousin Alex."

Cousin. She'd never been introduced that way before, and it felt odd, but she understood Logan's tactics of going with the personal rather than referring to them as a team, or partners

When the handshaking was done, Chase suggested they go inside to talk, and Alex took a quick three-sixty of the area first, just to have a reference image for when she came back out. She would know if anything changed.

A woodstove stood in the center of the single room, with a small wooden table and two chairs on one side and a wide, bench-like platform running the length of the opposite wall.

Dusty swung open the back door and used her helmet to hold it in place. "This will give us a bit more light," she said, and it did make a difference. But would it make their conversation less secure?

As though reading her thoughts—which was quite possible, because she hadn't been blocking—Chase said, "This is a very safe location, and if anyone comes into the area, we will know."

"I don't feel any electronic security," said Logan, surprising Alex that he would give away one of his abilities to virtual strangers. But then perhaps it was his way of showing trust in order to gain trust.

Dusty smiled. "Our system is much older, and basic. You might call it earthy. We are connected to all living things, and with sensitivity at a cellular level, we are privy to a remarkable early warning system."

Chase dragged the table and chairs over by the bench, creating a circle for them to sit.

"What can you tell us about Ryder?" Dusty asked the moment everyone was seated.

"I'm afraid we have no new information," said Logan, and pain flickered across Dusty's face. That's when Alex saw the wisdom in her bright green eyes. This woman might only be in her forties, but she had known hard times, and great pain.

"Do you believe in psychic gifts?" asked Grace.

Dusty's eyes lit with a barely-visible smile and she glanced at her husband. "I believe anything is possible, and we don't always know how it happens." Her head tipped up. "You're gifted?"

Grace nodded. "I was able to tap into the event. It was an abduction." And she went on to tell them, leaving nothing out.

Before they could respond, Logan said, "Ryder became a target because of something or someone he knows. We're hoping you can shed some light on his background. Help us piece together the *why* so we can figure out the where and go in after him. Bring him home."

Dusty nodded. "After the call from James, we did some digging." She held up her hand. "Discreet digging, per his cautionary instructions, and so far we've come up with nothing."

Logan hesitated, and Alex had the impression he was communicating with Grace. Then he said. "We would like to run through things with you, because sometimes we don't even know what we know. You might have seen something completely unremarkable, but put together with other information, it could create a key we can use."

"Understood," said Chase. "We're willing to answer any questions you have, because Ryder is very special to us. From the moment he arrived, we were drawn to his enthusiasm, and to his determination. Unlike some of the children who come our way, he had a solid background, with two parents who loved him for the first fifteen years of his life." Alex heard something unusual in his voice, an oddly intermittent huskiness she didn't think was caused by emotion.

"May I say," said Grace, "your camp for damaged children—"

"They are not damaged," Chase said with quiet conviction. "They are children who have had to struggle harder than some, and not as hard as others. Our camp is for foster kids with First Nations heritage. Most began in loving homes, good, solid homes which came apart due to illness, death, divorce, or addiction. Some have been abused. But others have been in homes with good foster parents who love them and care for them, but have no idea how to address their cultural needs."

"Sunrise," said Dusty, "provides them with a safe place to learn about who they are, what and where they come from, and an opportunity to experience the world as their ancestors knew it. They have the mountains to explore, horses to ride, a vast library of information about First Nations history, culture, and spirituality, and like-minded children and adults…" Her voice trailed off.

"And now I will get off my soapbox." Chase took her hand, and her easy smile returned. "I get caught up."

"I understand your passion," said Grace. "I have a place called Paradise where I provide shelter and rehabilitation for young women rescued from human trafficking. Interesting, isn't it, that horses are also an integral part of my program? My Farley is very like your black mare, although he's a Friesian, and I'm guessing she is a thoroughbred. Something very special about her."

"I'll tell you the story of her amazing survival one day." She glanced around. "But first we need to find Ryder."

Logan nodded. "I have a ton of questions, and some will seem ridiculously redundant, but they're part of a whole, so I'd appreciate if you answer them all, even if you feel like you're repeating yourself."

Dusty sat back on the bench and brought her feet up, crossed her legs. "Fire away."

"Before we get started, how much time do you

have before you'll be missed, and someone might ask questions about where you've been?"

"We have all day. Murray came to babysit the ranch while we're gone, and it's not unusual for us to take off for a full-day ride."

"Does this Murray person know what's going on?"

"Yes," said Chase. "He's a very close friend. Came to work for me about a hundred years ago, or so it seems. Became a friend. Family, really. He's all we have, and we're all he has."

"Okay, as long as he knows not to tell anyone we're here. He can't talk to anyone about what's going on."

"Murray is cool. And the kids won't be around until the weekend."

"Kids?" Logan's eyebrows went up. "I thought the camp was only open in the summer."

"We team-foster," said Dusty. "Six kids who live in town all week while they're going to school come home to us on the weekends." Her expression froze, and she grabbed Chase's arm.

"Tell me none of them are in jeopardy," she demanded, staring at Logan. "Tell me, or I'm gone right now. I'll head straight to town and pull them out of school. I can keep them safe on the ranch."

Grace shook her head. "This doesn't have anything to do with the others, unless they're connected to Ryder's background or his parents."

"Okay. That's okay, then. He only met the kids this past summer."

Chase placed his hand over the one with a death grip on his arm. "Ryder came here in June and stayed through to the first week of September. He had aged out of foster care, and we helped him with the transition. Spent time with him, trying to figure out where he could go to school to learn the trade he's so passionate about. But we also made sure he could still be a kid while he was here, and enjoy all Sunrise has to offer."

"Airplanes," said Dusty. "All he cared about was airplanes, and since he lost his parents in a plane crash, and we weren't certain his obsession was a healthy one, we made sure he was shown plenty of other possibilities."

"But he was dug in," said Chase. "Determined that nothing would sway him from his original goal."

"But he did inhale and master everything else that came his way," added his wife.

"As in?" Logan prodded.

"Horses, climbing, fishing, all of it. Murray showed him how to tie a simple fly, and within days he'd mastered the skill and was not only tackling dozens of different kinds, but creating them at warp speed." The skin around Chase's eyes crinkled as though a smile lurked under the surface.

"And horses. He'd never been on one before he came here, but by the end of the summer he was teaching the new kids how to ride, and he was helping me break a couple of yearlings. A natural talent. Gentle, yet firm, and always careful to end on a good note, even if he had to back up to the previous day's lesson in order for the horse to succeed."

"And he aced survival week," said Dusty. "If

he was dropped in the middle of the wilderness, he could survive for months." Her face lit with a beautiful smile, but before she could speak, Chase did.

"If he can get away from his captors, he'll survive."

But could he get away?

15

Logan's interrogation skills were so slick even Alex—who was tasked with taking notes—found herself listening as if what was being said was a normal conversation. But she had written down all the pertinent details, and should have no trouble adding in the impressions and nuances later…she hoped.

When Logan wound his way to the background of Ryder's parents, the answers continued to come smoothly, easily, and without thought.

"Did he talk about his parents much?"

"Constantly. As in, if there was mention of planes or aviation, he was all about, 'My dad this,' or 'My dad that.'"

"Anything specific come to mind?"

Chase glanced left and upward, searching his memory. "When he was fishing once, and a float plane came in low over the lake, Ryder told the others his dad used to do that when he was scouting a new spot, deciding if it was safe to land, or if the lake was worth checking out on the maps when they got home. Went on about how his dad never made a move without thinking it through, because there was no point in taking stupid chances."

"Was it said defensively?" asked Grace. "Or did he sound like a boy trying to convince *himself* the plane's crash or disappearance at least wasn't his dad's fault?"

"Pride," said Chase without hesitation.

"Anything else that might connect to his background?" Logan was very adept at open-ended questions, using them frequently to encourage unsolicited information.

Dusty nodded slowly. "When I asked him if he'd ever ridden, he said he hadn't, but his mom once told him she used to ride show horses, the kind that did the three things to get a final score. When I asked him if he meant eventing, he said yes, that was the word, and went on to say she wouldn't let him do it because it was too dangerous."

"We can work with that," Grace said. "Look for bad accidents, incidents where a girl was injured."

"You know, even though he was easy with the horses on the ground, he was nervous the first time he climbed on one—so that rings true." Dusty smiled. "But as soon as he made his first lap of the training pen I could see he was hooked, like he had inherent horse sense and knew he was where he belonged." She glanced at her husband. "He was the same way when he learned to fly, wasn't he?"

Chase nodded. "According to his instructor,

from the moment he took the controls he was a natural. Like the plane was simply an extension of himself."

Silence hung for a minute, and Logan finally asked, "Is there anything else you recall about Ryder and his parents?"

Chase and Dusty looked at each other, then Chase said, "Talking about someone not in the room goes against our principles, so you'll have to bear with us. We understand you need information, and we want to help as much as possible, but gossip is diametrically opposed to our ideals, what we live for."

"But," said Dusty, "we also understand your purpose, and will do the best we can to help. Please feel free to prod us unmercifully."

"Your principles are refreshing," said Grace.

Logan leaned forward, braced his elbows on his knees, and let his hands hang between them. "I'm going to be very honest and tell you more than I should, because I trust you to keep this information to yourselves." He touched his fingertips together. "The people who took Ryder did so for a reason. Hijacking a plane and abduction are not something taken on lightly, or by the average individual. Therefore we are making an educated guess that this is connected to organized crime."

"What would they want with a boy?" A frown marred Dusty's beautiful features.

"That's the question of the day, and one we're determined to get to the bottom of while the rest of the team continues searching for him. We need you to share any and every tidbit about Ryder that crosses your mind. I don't want you to censor your thoughts or how you express them. Just let things spill when they come to you. Protecting his rights, his individuality, is off the table while we're in this room."

Dusty took a deep breath and blew it out slowly. "He didn't do well in foster care. Reports on his file were numerous, and ranged from anger issues to being disrespectful to authority figures, or becoming withdrawn. I have to point out, though, that we rarely see a file *without* that kind of information. Kids who lose their parents, their homes, and their safe place in the world, are rarely happy and well-adjusted. Grief and loneliness lead to feeling rejected, or even unworthy and undeserving of happiness."

"Anything specific to Ryder? Unusual in comparison to others?"

"His grades. Most kids begin to fail in school, but he excelled, took extra courses in his spare time, and was glued to his computer, but not for the games or social media."

Alex glanced at Grace and knew instantly they were thinking similar thoughts. "What kind of online courses?"

"Mostly aviation-related."

"Mostly? What else?"

"Genealogy." She shifted in her seat, and Chase gently rubbed her back. "He was interested in the history of his people."

"History is important, and can contain secrets. Things hidden for years, even centuries," said Grace.

"He was very proud of the fact he was born—entered this world—in exactly the same place as his father, grandfather, and great-grandfather."

"I'm guessing you mean on the reservation, not a hospital or nearby town."

"Yes, in Arizona or New Mexico...or maybe Texas? I can't remember which."

Alex felt an edge of excitement. "He wasn't local?"

"No."

"Is that unusual? To have American kids at your camp?"

"No. We're not government funded, which means we don't have their rules to adhere to and can welcome any child who needs our program."

"How do people find out about it?"

"Word of mouth, caseworkers, conferences, a gazillion ways." Ah, so not that big a deal for Ryder to be in at a Canadian camp, and for James to have some connection.

"What about his mother's family?" asked Logan.

"Ryder spent all summer trying to trace her background, but the end result was frustration. Mae's mother died in childbirth, and her father was unknown. She was raised by elders who are now both dead."

Alex wasn't certain if the hum she felt was her own senses coming to full alert, or if she was picking up from the others in the room, but there was suddenly no doubt in her mind that the boy's disappearance had something to do with his mother.

Logan as always, stayed on task. "Marriage

license?"

"Not the legal kind from the state, but Ryder once showed me a single sheet of lined paper with what appeared to be their promises to each other. It was signed by both."

"Dated?"

"I don't recall the exact date, but I remember thinking it was over a year before Ryder was born, which meant theirs wasn't a marriage of necessity." Dusty shrugged. "Kids sometimes carry guilt, taking the blame for their parents being forced to marry, so we watch for that kind of detail."

Logan leaned back in his chair as though relaxed. "Did he ever talk about his grandfather, or about the reservation?"

"Not a word, even when I gave him an opening."

"I would like for us to go there, to meet some of the band members. Talk to them, and see if anything pops," said Logan.

Chase nodded. "They would be grateful for any update, and I'm sure more than willing to help any way they could." He unfolded a sheet of paper and took the satellite phone Dusty passed to him.

"Wait," said Logan. "It would be better if we meet in person, and if they don't know I'm coming." When Dusty's eyebrows went up, Logan smiled. "If they know ahead, they'll be thinking things over, and could have preconceived ideas about what kind of information we're looking for."

#

When they got back to the lodge, they tucked the machines away and headed for the kitchen, where they found Broughton sitting at the table with aeronautical maps spread out in front of him.

"Coffee's hot," he said, and the aroma was heavenly. They filled mugs and joined him, brought him up to speed on what they'd learned.

"Do you speak their language?" Grace asked Broughton. He had lived on the outer boundary of an Apache reservation for several years while hiding from the FBI and other government agencies.

"I can get by. More importantly, I was welcomed into the community, and learned enough about their culture to be able to communicate on a level which should give me an edge."

"And makes you the point man on this visit," she said. "Now the question is whether you go alone, and if not, who goes with you."

"This needs to be done right," said Alex. "We should all go." She hesitated for only an instant before plowing on. "In vet school, one of the students was, as she said, from a rez in New Mexico, and I got to know her some. Came to understand her unique combination of sadness, resentment, and pride." Alex's emotional load had been similar, but different.

"She was accustomed to being treated like a throw-away person, she said, because the government—among others—regarded her people as similar to the coyotes encroaching on cities. Some felt badly for their loss of habitat, but most were uncomfortable with their presence. Tossed food at them, but wanted them to stay away, out of sight."

She ran her thumb up and down the side of her

cup. "If it was Lacy's family we were approaching, I think they would be astounded if four agents showed up to investigate the disappearance of one of 'theirs.'"

Broughton had a peculiar look on his face. "I agree. All of us arriving on their doorstep will make it obvious how much Ryder matters to us. That *they* matter. And I'll call a friend to meet us, to be sure we approach in a manner respectful of their homes, land, ways."

"Then we're good to go," said Logan.

Broughton nodded. "For the record, I'll be glad to blow this pop stand."

"Something wrong?" Logan was studying in face.

"Can't put my finger on the why, but there's an odd pressure in my chest—and no, I'm not having a heart attack."

Grace leaned forward, and Broughton held up a hand. "Yes, I checked in with Eve. She ran tests remotely and agreed that there's nothing going on with me physically." Eve was the doctor of the Meyers family. But more than that, she was a gifted healer, and researcher of all things physical and metaphysical.

Logan tapped a single fingertip on the table. "Interesting, don't you think, that even though you and I have similar wiring, I'm not picking up anything."

"Which makes me think it's connected to an old case. As though I'm subconsciously recognizing a wavelength." He shook his head. "And I don't like it. From the moment I got up this morning, the growing need to put miles between us and this place grew steadily, and now it's blasting at me like a damn fire alarm."

"Then we'll get the hell gone," said Logan, and he shoved back his chair, gathering the empty cups. "Everyone grab your bags."

"What do we do about the linens?" asked Alex.

"Leave the bedrooms looking like we're coming back."

As though by tacit agreement, silence descended. Everyone would now be in an open and vulnerable state, with their extra senses engaged to pick up anything unusual going on in the area or atmosphere.

Less than ten minutes later, while they made their way to the plane, Alex concentrated on the sounds of the forest, alert for anything off or out of place.

But besides the low-pitched hum of the wind passing through millions of pine needles, there were no other sounds—which wasn't surprising, because the human presence was enough to disturb the natural ebb and flow.

They took their seats while Logan checked the exterior of the plane, and before long he climbed in, still focused on his task. He flicked switches, pushed buttons, brought the engine roaring to life, and soon they were moving across the rough ground—a brutal reminder that takeoff was not going to be a pleasant experience.

At least now—unlike when they landed—she knew about the horrendous bumping and pitching, and she tightened her grip on the shoulder harness while praying for enough speed to get airborne and not end up in a crumpled heap.

With her jaw clenched as tightly as every other muscle in her body, she fought the instinct to close her eyes, and was gobsmacked when the tiny craft leapt into the air and cleared the trees at the end of the valley—the ones she was afraid she was going to get to know up close and personal.

"If you don't let that breath out, you're going to either explode or pass out," Broughton said quietly.

She swung to stare at him while she exhaled with a whoosh.

His smile showed concern, and only a flickering of amusement. "Points for not closing your eyes."

She bit down on a snarky comeback. He wasn't judging, or even teasing her. He was being kind, just like when he sat at her bedside for hours and hours and hours talking about whatever seemed to pop into his head. She had thought him the kindest man alive while she lay there, unable to move anything but her eyes. And she could hear that same soothing concern in his voice now.

Such a conundrum, this man who was suddenly staring out the window as though he had never spoken, as though she wasn't even there. How could he have such a good and generous heart, yet shut down and ignore what they could have together?

Every cell in her body was tuned to him, yet he could close her out in a heartbeat. Memories surfaced of him kissing her sweetly, then putting space between them, holding her away from him until he shook his head and stepped off her front porch.

"The feelings you have for me are because I was the one to pluck you out of a deadly situation."

"But—"

"Alex, I'm not who you think I am. Not that nice guy who sat at your bedside. The guy you're kissing doesn't exist."

He walked away that night, and he was apparently still walking.

When they reached cruising altitude, Grace turned in her seat. "Did the young woman from your college make it through vet school?"

"She did, and went on to work at a track in Florida."

"Long way from home for someone raised in New Mexico."

"She had a plan. Was going to work like a demon, and save until she was able to open a clinic of her own on her family's land. She'd lost a few horses to colic when she was a kid, and wanted to provide a much-needed service. Her dream was to be able to save some kid's horse."

"Did she make it?"

"Back home? I don't know. We didn't stay in touch." Alex shook her head. "Why is that? You spend gazillions of hours with people in school, or at a job, and when life leads you elsewhere, you don't look back."

"Your lives went different directions."

"Not that different. We were both working in the thoroughbred industry. You'd think we could have at least stayed in touch through Christmas cards."

"You still send Christmas cards?"

"Actually, no. But the clinic I was working with did."

"Not the same."

"No, it's not. And to be honest, I've never even bought a Christmas card. Not one. My mom didn't believe in cards of any kind. Said it was a waste of money to sit a card on a shelf for a day or two, then toss it in the trash."

"I think I'd have liked her," said Grace.

Just thinking about her mother missing the opportunity to meet Grace, a niece she'd never even known existed, hurt Alex's heart too much. She couldn't think about it. "She hated cut flowers too."

"Flowers? Why? Allergies?"

"No. She called it murderous wastefulness. Hated that a flower's lifespan was so drastically shortened by cutting it and sticking it in a vase. She'd rather have a live flower in a pot than a single stem of anything in water."

"You must miss her terribly."

She closed her eyes and leaned her head against the back of her seat. Swallowed to dislodge the lump forming in the back of her throat. "I miss her messy hair, baggy shirts, and overcooked pork chops. I miss eating tasteless carrots and peas every night of the week because they came frozen and cheap, and veggies were important." They were best mixed in with the mashed potatoes—the kind that came in a box and cooked up in less than ten minutes.

"There was always a spoon in the sugar bowl, and a butter knife perched on the edge of the sink.

She cleaned out the fridge on January first every year and tried to remember to wash the bedsheets on Saturday mornings. If she forgot, they waited until the next weekend." Alex took over laundry when she was about eight.

Alex smiled. "When I had a bad day, I got extra mac and cheese for supper, and once a week we went out for a burger."

"Sounds like your mom was very real."

"She didn't sweat the small stuff, but she found ways to manage our lives and look after the important little things. She made sure I had two weeks' worth of socks and underwear, so even if she forgot to do laundry, we never had to put on dirty ones." Alex always had two pairs of jeans. One for school and one for the barn.

"Dinner was usually a mess because of the horses and chores and stuff, and we ate on the fly, but she believed in breakfast. Got up early every single morning to make porridge, and we always sat down and ate together before our day started." For a couple of years after her mom's death Alex wasn't able to sit at that kitchen table in the morning...or any other time. And even now, with the first taste of hot cereal came the sound of her mom's voice, rusty from sleep.

"Oatmeal was a staple in our house too," said Broughton.

Jarred back to the here and now, Alex's eyes popped open, and once again she saw kindness in his.

16

They landed on a dirt strip and taxied toward a single garage-like building where a tall man stood with his back to the sun, feet apart, and his face shadowed by a wide-brimmed hat.

"Your friend is rather formidable-looking," said Grace.

"He likes to think so."

"Right outta the movies," said Alex when they came to a stop just a few feet away.

Broughton frowned. Stared at her. "He's no movie star." Although his friend had worked on many movies, watching over the rights and the integrity of Native Americans and how they were portrayed. And Link had great fun playing the part, slipping into the expected stereotype as he was doing now.

"Weathered face, chiseled features, and the posture of a warrior. A perfect cinematic image. All he needs is a horse, a few feathers…and I don't mean that disrespectfully. Just that he embodies a certain romantic image and could make a killing."

"Seriously?" Broughton bit his lip. He supposed it served him right. He'd pushed her away, and now she was lusting after his friend. His very unmarried friend who loved women of all shapes and sizes. Not that Broughton was any different. Should he warn Alex? Tell her his buddy was a love 'em and leave 'em kinda hound dog?

No point. If she showed interest, Link would be the first to tell her what he was about, because he had class, and principles.

The instant they drew to a stop, Broughton was out, and Link met him halfway for a full-on hug. None of that one-armed, back-thumping stuff, and although they didn't *need* to speak out loud, they did, for the benefit of the others.

"Feels like forever since," said Broughton.

"Long time, but not."

"Lincoln Scott, these are my friends, Logan, Grace, and Alexandra."

"Nice to meet you, but odd to think of Caleb having friends."

Broughton laughed. When he'd lived near and under the protection of Link and his brothers, he never had a visitor, and of course never left the property. His dogs were all he had, and he liked it that way. People complicated a person's life. "These three are special, and we're also working together."

"So you have no choice," Link said to the others. "Understandable." A smile suddenly lit his face. "You're a lucky man, Caleb. Come on." He led them to a battered truck. "Crew cab was the best I could do on short notice."

"You didn't want to squeeze us into one of your toys? Link collects sports cars. Restores old MGs."

"My father had a weakness for two-seaters," said Grace. "So I've driven a few. Nothing quite like it."

"Especially on the narrow roads of France and Italy," said Link.

"Europe? Who knew?" Broughton grinned. "Don't tell me you did the college kid thing."

"Nope. I got picked up by a team. Worked my ass off for a few years and got to do some maintenance runs."

Conversation wound around cars while the truck bounced and ground its way over unpaved roads. When a collection of buildings came into sight, Link asked, "Now where?"

"Follow the main road until it splits, then stay left. When we reach the string of houses, it will be third on the left.

As they parked in front of a single story house of pale gray, Grace said to Link, "I'm glad you know him so we're not going in cold."

"We've never met, but he will know who I am because of the work I do with many of the Nations, assisting in various areas. They all know to call on me to help out."

"Link's an attorney, among other things," said Broughton.

"But Ryder's family didn't reach out to you when he went missing?"

"No. Caleb's call was the first I heard of it." And from the look on his face, it wasn't sitting very well. Link liked to think he had a finger on the pulse of all things Native American. He fought hard for his people.

With Link and Grace in the lead, they approached the front door, and when it opened, an old man with a dark, weathered face stared at them for a half a beat, then said, "I knew you would come."

He stepped back, holding the door wide. "Welcome."

He led them to a kitchen which seemed to own the house, spilling over into another room lined with old couches and a few end tables. Bright blankets covered every chair, and a wide swath of colored fabric ran down the middle of a huge, heavy, wooden table.

Alex brushed the glossy surface with her fingertips. "This is beautiful."

"Hand-crafted from a California redwood."

"Exquisite workmanship."

"It came from a hunting lodge up north. My son often flew hunters in, and got to know the owner, the man who created this table. He left it to Dayson."

His expression sobered so quickly, it was as though the smile had never been. "Please, sit, and tell me how I can help you find my grandson."

Broughton made the introductions and explained that Link was there to ensure the interests of Ryder's family were protected.

The old man nodded but said nothing.

"We suspect Ryder's abduction connects to his mother, and we need to know more about her background. Since she has no living kin, we're asking for your help."

The old man was looking straight ahead, but it was obvious his gaze was turned inward. They waited while he seemed to gather his thoughts.

"I wondered. Always wondered why no one came looking for her when she was first here. And when they vanished a few years ago, I wondered again. Now I'm certain they never looked for her back then because they knew."

"Knew what?" Logan's voice was low and compelling, and drew a sharp glance from the old man.

"Your tactics are wasted on me, and unnecessary. I intend to tell you everything I know."

"Respectfully acknowledged," said Logan. "Not often we deal with others as gifted as we are, or those willing to expose secrets long kept."

He nodded. "Late one night, Dayson was returning from a job at a ranch some distance away, and his dog suddenly began to bark. Thinking the critter needed to pee, Day stopped the truck and let him out."

The old man got up and began making coffee while continuing his monologue.

"Dog ran off and didn't come back no matter how much Day called—and he was usually an obedient creature. When the howling started, Day grabbed a flashlight and headed out among the scrub, found him with what looked like a corpse."

He set mugs in the middle of the table.

"She was naked. Half frozen—damn cold out here at night—but he found a pulse. The hospital in town was two hours away, and he didn't want her dying on the way, so he brought her home, to our healer."

He continued the simple tasks while he talked, adding a sugar bowl, spoons, and a jar of powdered creamer to the table.

"She had been beaten and raped. Left for dead, or for the coyotes to finish off. Took some time to get her warmed up and awake, and then she begged us not to call the law. Refused to ever say her name, or what had happened to her. Our people are not big on the law, or on making anyone do something they don't want to do. She was taken in by elders who had lost a daughter years earlier. She took their name, and before long, she married my son and had his name too."

He stood in front of the coffee maker, watching the last drops descend. "She never left the reservation. Not until Ryder went off to high school and didn't come home on weeknights. That's when Dayson talked her into going on a few jobs with him, and she seemed happy. Until…"

Broughton fought the impulse to sit forward, to urge the old man to get to it more quickly, while tension descended on the group, as if they all knew they were about to hit the motherlode.

"Don't know what happened. She stopped going with Day and mostly stayed in her house alone. Didn't talk to anyone for a month or two, but gradually started to relax again. Seemed herself.

Started going with Day once or twice a week. And then one day they didn't come home. Hadn't got where they were going, either."

His hand shook when he set the coffee pot on a thick mat beside the mugs. "Please," he said, and gestured for them to help themselves. He went to the window and stared out at the wide expanse.

"My son loved his home almost as much as he loved the sky. But he would have given it all up to save his family."

From the looks on the other faces, Broughton knew he wasn't the only one to feel the tingling of revelation, but waiting wasn't working.

"What do you think happened?"

"I think Mae saw someone she recognized. Someone connected to her being left for dead all those years ago."

Everyone nodded.

"But there's more," said Broughton.

"There is. Before they disappeared, Day was troubled, torn, said things. He went up into the mountains a couple of times—what he used to do to think. Came back the last time, and I knew from what he said, his decision was made."

"What did he say?"

"Talked about Ryder's future, how he would one day fly all around the world, pilot the kind of aircraft Day only dreamed of. Talked about the possible training programs he could aim for. Talked about the Air Force, the school in Texas, and one in Canada. Reasonable talk if the boy hadn't just started high school."

"He was making sure you knew what they

wanted?"

He nodded. "Talked about making sure Ryder worked toward a scholarship of some kind if he was to go private and not Air Force."

"He was planning on the boy growing up without him?"

"He came to say goodbye to me that day. I asked him if he was going away for long, and he said probably. Asked me to look after his boy."

"What about Mae?"

"He said she was going with him because she needed to get away, said it just like that. And they were going to take in an airshow, have a bit of a vacation. I guess that was so we wouldn't look for them right away."

"Why do you think he made them disappear?"

"He had to protect his family by making the world believe Mae was gone. Ryder would be safe then. Couldn't be used as a tool against them."

"And yet…" said Grace.

"It wasn't enough," the old man agreed.

"You think your son and Mae are alive."

"I believe that."

Broughton heard something in his voice. "Do you know where they could be?"

"Anywhere." His glance encompassed the group. "We stand together, protect each other, and even strangers from vastly different backgrounds. Mae was not born one of us, but she was deeply tanned, and they would blend."

"But would stand out elsewhere."

"Exactly."

"You've never tried to find them?"

"If I made that effort, it could get out that I don't believe they died in a crash, and then others would search for them."

"Understood. But if you had spoken with someone like Link, he'd have kept an eye out for them," said Logan.

"How could I take such a risk with the boy's life? My son trusted me to protect his child by getting him away from where he could be found and used as a pawn, and that is what I did."

Broughton leaned forward. "But now all bets are off."

"Exactly."

"Then we start at the beginning. We need the date Dayson found Mae. From there we'll try to figure out how she ended up waiting for death that night."

He reeled off a date from almost twenty years earlier. "I have a friend who saves papers, and after Mae had been here for a few weeks I visited and went through a stack of them looking for anything about her being missing. I was afraid there was family who needed to know she was safe, but there was nothing."

"We can search databases now, and try to make connections," said Logan. "Your son had a home. Possessions. There could be a clue."

"It's gone."

"Burned?"

"Not the house—it's made of concrete blocks—but the contents. Anything that couldn't be used by someone else, I burned."

Grace's chin tipped up. "You saved nothing for

yourself, or for Ryder? No mementos?"

The old man's smile came slowly. "Dayson is in my mind, my heart."

"If I could touch something of his, I might be able to connect with him," she said. "Something of Mae's would be even better."

The old man's smile widened. "You speak with those still in this world."

"I can only reach those seeking help."

Without another word he left the room. They glanced at each other but waited in silence. He returned, dragging what looked like a typical army duffle. He set it on a chair and pulled out a small woven blanket. Passed it to Grace and her eyes went wide the moment she touched it.

"Ohhh, my." She met his gaze. "Mae was the weaver, the creator of this beauty."

"Exactly right," he said. "And here there could be important information." He folded back the opening of the bag to expose a collection of binders. "Dayson kept good records."

Hallelujah. "He kept paper on his jobs?"

"Until the last few years. You'll find the last ones on this." He handed Broughton a memory stick. "You can take it all, but I want it back after."

Not after they were found, or after they had picked it all apart, recorded information, just, after.

"Absolutely."

From a pocket he produced a wide, heavily engraved, silver bracelet with one large piece of turquoise. He rubbed the stone with loving fingertips. "Dayson always wore this. Always. But he gave it to me the day before he left. Said Ryder should have it one day." He sighed. "I was afraid of it being recognized, so the boy doesn't even know I have it."

"A wise decision," said Broughton.

The old man handed it to him. "If anything will connect you to him, it will be this."

A warm hum started in his hand, worked its way up his arm. Made Broughton think of tall grass swaying as wind passed over it.

There was no more information to be gathered here, but Broughton didn't want to leave. This was his first time on a reservation since he'd learned of his own Native heritage. "It is peaceful here. Makes me want to linger when we need to be going, getting on with the searching."

The old man smiled and nodded. "Good energy is hard to leave until your well has been replenished." He stared into Broughton's eyes. "The trouble you were feeling around you is coming from the inside. Something yours alone, and unfinished for a very long time. You put others' needs before your own, but soon you will have to finish."

Shaken by what felt like the truth banging on a closed door, Broughton maintained. Showed nothing on the outside. Kept his walls intact.

"Like my son, you will have to face what you don't want to know. What will change everything." The old man glanced at the others. "You are good friends, but you have your own to deal with, and you may not be able to support this man in the way you would like. Take what is available, possible, and know it is all. Be content with that." He frowned. "Roots go deep with all of you, and spread in unexpected directions. I hope my grandson is found quickly so you can complete your own personal quests and grow in the direction you need to go."

He rose. "You are good people, and I am glad you have come into my life, because this bond will never be broken. It's time to leave, but you will always be welcome back." He turned to Link. "Thank you."

As a group they followed him to the door, Broughton last to go through it. "I don't understand our connection," he said. "But I value it. Thank you."

"I look forward to meeting again. Some time. Somewhere." The old man opened his arms, and Broughton stepped into them. Feeling oddly safe. Comfortable for the first time in days.

Halfway to the car, Logan called back, "Dayson and Mae's house, could we look at it?"

The old man tipped his head toward the east. "Last one on this side."

"No one else has moved in?"

"It is empty. Completely empty. Their belongings were dispersed among the others and what was left was burned. The door is unlocked if you want to go in. I will not."

"Thanks again," said Logan. "We'll keep you informed."

"And we'll do everything in our power to bring your family back to you," added Grace.

They left him there, and drove nearly a half mile to the last house on the right. Link stayed in the car. Alex and Broughton waited on the porch, and the other two went inside.

About five minutes passed before the door opened. “Come on in,” said Logan. “We’re not getting anything much. Maybe if we pool our strength it will help Grace make a connection.

They joined hands, cleared their minds, and waited. Waited. Broughton’s thoughts slipped in, wove around the silver and turquoise he had stuffed in his pocket. The vibration was still there, but he’d already grown used to it, as though he’d adjusted to its tone. Or was it cadence?

He shook his head, and a small sound from Grace had him focusing quickly. She let go of Logan and Alex. Held a hand out to Broughton. “Give me the bracelet. And I want the blanket too.”

Alex scooted out to the car to get it.

Grace sat cross-legged in the middle of the room with the bracelet in one hand and the blanket in the other. She closed her eyes and let her head tip back.

Seconds became minutes, then tears slid down Grace’s cheeks. Dripped off her chin. “So afraid.” She opened her eyes. “She was so terribly afraid for her son. Wanted to take him with them, but Dayson said he’d be safe here as long as they were gone. It broke her heart, but she agreed. Wanted her son to have a normal life, and where they were going it wouldn’t be possible. Even if they were lucky enough to stay in one place, it was no way for a bright young man to grow up.”

Grace swiped at her tears, pulled a tissue from her pocket and blew her nose. “We can go now.”

Logan helped her up, into his arms, and, moved

by the depth of understanding between them, Broughton couldn't resist draping an arm across Alex's shoulders.

17

The weight of sorrow and the brightness of love swirled in the empty house, clinging together, then separating like a murmuration of birds, bending, swaying, and molding in a dance designed to surprise and delight.

Drawn to stay, yet determined to leave, Alex allowed Broughton to lead her out. Away from something she would never forget. Yes, she'd seen the connection between Logan and Grace many times, but this was the first time the feelings had slipped inside her, warmed and comforted her. Chased away the emotional anguish of people forced to give up everything they knew and loved.

And they *had* been forced. Alex had no doubt now that she'd also experienced the darkness of Mae's fear. Fear because the men who hurt her so very long ago were men with powerful connections, and if they ever found out she was alive and could identify them, they would come after her. Do whatever it took to find her. End her. And everyone she might have told.

"You picked up stuff in there too," said Broughton, and she was disappointed in her inability to hide her feelings. She'd kept her expression neutral, and the tears she shed had been internal only.

"So much sadness." Why didn't she want to say what she knew?

"Almost overwhelming," he said. "Have to admit that shielding and only seeing through their eyes is preferable to experiencing what a target is going through."

Target. Such a cold word. "Does it get easier with time? I mean to refer to the people you're searching for as targets? Does that help to keep your distance, to think of it as work, a job?"

They were standing beside the truck. Warm wind filled with fine dust and the scent of sage also carried both promise and despair. This part of the reservation had newer houses, but there were a few of the others left. The ones with broken walls and windows. Without doors. So many lives had begun and ended on this piece of earth. As had hopes and dreams.

"It *is* my job."

She glanced at him. "I'm sorry for that."

She climbed up to the back seat and stared off into the distance, wondering about the people still, and trying to ignore the small ache in her chest. She'd fallen in love with a man who would not acknowledge his own heart.

#

James Meyers stood in his usual spot at the

head of the huge table in the war room. A formidable figure until you noticed the way his left hand rubbed his dog's head. He waited until everyone was seated and then dove in.

"Still nothing coming up on Mae," he said. "No missing person reports for anyone matching her description. And that's going back six months from the date you gave me."

Grace tapped the table with a fingertip. "She was very young, and they had her for a long time. She was one of many. Held captive, trained."

Alex's stomach went sour. She knew human trafficking existed, but it was like something seen on television, not in real life.

"Define very young," said James.

"While she was weaving the blanket, memories of the bad times slipped in constantly, and she pushed them away with images of Dayson and Ryder for the most part, but there were a few of her on horseback, riding over jumps, and the children she was competing against were in the range of ten to twelve."

"Any impression of how old she was when she escaped?"

"Between fifteen and eighteen would be my guess. But again, guessing."

While James input the information, Alex studied Grace, who had seen and felt far more than Alex had of Mae's life in captivity.

How did one live with that kind of vision?

Picking up the swirling feelings of past inhabitants of the reservation had been almost more than Alex could bear.

"That narrows it down to several thousand possibilities, even if we only look at stranger abductions," said James, looking thoughtful, and a question rolling around in Alex's head had to be asked.

"How many children a year?"

"Missing person reports top out at around four hundred thousand," said Grace. "Those actually attributed to being taken by a stranger are in the range of a hundred. Human traffickers target runaways, and those most vulnerable."

Grace didn't ever talk about the children she rescued over the years, but Logan—with his wife's blessing—filled Alex in. Grace had saved several hundred women and children from huge trafficking rings. And worked tirelessly to help law enforcement put an end to many of the groups by taking out their leaders.

"I'm narrowing now by age and gender, and using what Grace was able to observe," said James, with his fingers flying over the keyboard.

If she had been reported missing. And even if they found out who she was, would the information help them find her now, or help them identify who took her then? Would they get any closer to finding Ryder?

One thing Grace drilled into her from day one was the importance of details, and in this case, maybe a detail from the past would help them unlock the mystery of today.

"Better," said James. "Here you have them." He pointed at the big wall screen, which was now lit with hundreds of tiny photos. "Five hundred and forty-six."

"Looks like we have our work cut out for us," said Broughton.

James glanced at the wall clock. "The other teams will work on this while you catch some down time. Back here at oh seven hundred."

Which gave them eight hours, and Alex was more than ready for sleep.

Or at least her body was. After flipping and flopping around in her bed for about an hour, with the events of the day dancing around in her head, she got up and took a long, hot shower. Felt better, but now she was hungry.

She should have forced herself to eat before she came to bed, but she'd been so body weary, legs leaden, back humming with exhaustion.

She glanced down at her boxers and tank. Did she dare to scoot to the kitchen like this? Who was she going to run into at two in the morning? The others working on the research maybe? She pulled on an oversized flannel shirt and considered her reflection in the mirror. She was covered neck to mid-thigh. Good enough.

But when she pushed through the kitchen door and found Broughton sitting at the table, she wasn't sure she'd made a wise choice. Something about the way he kept his eyes locked with hers, as though trying not to look down, would have made her laugh if she hadn't seen the heat in his gaze.

She swallowed hard.

"Chicken stew in the slow cooker," he said.

"Oh. Well. Thanks, but I just wanted a cup of tea," she said, plugging in the kettle. "And maybe a cookie."

She lifted the lid on the first of three ceramic cookie jars and the scent wafted out. Peanut butter and chocolate. Yum. She grabbed one, bit in, then opened the next jar. The sweet, earthy smell of coconut assailed her nostrils, and she loved macaroons. What the heck.

A cookie in each hand, her gaze went to the third container, and Broughton laughed. "Go for it."

"The sugar will probably keep me awake."

"Not to mention the tea."

She shook her head. "Consuelo has the decaf kind."

By the time her tea was ready the cookies were gone, and she wasn't sure if she'd been that hungry, or if it was the nerves jumping because of Broughton's hot gaze.

She added milk to the cup, then sat across from him. Sipped.

"Did you swim?" he asked.

Confused by the question, she frowned, and he said, "Your hair is wet."

"Ah. Long, hot shower. Couldn't sleep. Then I was even more wide awake and needed food, so I'm here." She hesitated. "And I really want another cookie."

"Then have one."

"My blood sugar will tank big time in about an hour."

"And then you'll be able to sleep."

"But not good for the body." She needed a bit of protein, and wondered what he'd think of one of her guilty pleasures.

She went to the fridge and found what she needed. Spread a nice layer of cream cheese on a sugar cookie, and sat back down, studiously keeping her focus on the cookie while she nibbled slowly.

"That is seriously twisted," he said.

"Don't knock it if you've never tried it." She smiled and held it out to him. "Be brave, just a little taste." She made the mistake of looking into his eyes, and now she was trapped. Couldn't look away.

He took her hand. Guided it to his mouth and took a bite. Didn't let go of her hand while he chewed. Swallowed.

"I want more," he said and without letting go of her, got up, moved around the table and drew her from her chair. "I want this," he said, and his mouth settled over hers.

Alex was lost in the taste, and it had nothing to do with cookies. His mouth was hard, yet not. And she raised up on tiptoe to get closer, take them both deeper into that place where nothing lived but sensation.

Her hand curled around the back of his neck and her breasts pressed against his wide chest. When his arm came behind her waist, she arched into him, lost herself, until Broughton wrenched his mouth away from hers and buried his face in her hair, his breathing ragged.

Alex's heart was pounding against his, and she, too, struggled to get her breathing back under control. Seconds ticked by and Broughton made no move to let her go.

"Does this mean you liked the cookie?" she asked.

He lifted his face from her hair, stared into her eyes, and she was shocked at how raw he looked. Almost afraid. She touched his cheek. "Are you okay?"

Indecision flickered, and just when she was certain he was going to lean in for another kiss, he shook his head. "I can't do this."

"Do what?"

"Be with you." His slid his hands into her hair. Stared into her eyes. "You will break me, and I can't be broken. I already want you too much." He pressed his mouth against her forehead, and then he was gone.

She watched the door swing back and forth until it stilled. Understood more than she wanted to, and whispered, "You're already broken. That's the problem, and you don't even know it."

#

To say Alex was surprised to not only fall asleep, but stay in a dreamless state for hours, was a huge understatement. And she woke feeling refreshed. Even spunky. And craving cookies for breakfast.

Skirting thoughts of cookies and kisses, she opted to skip the kitchen and begin her day in the war room instead. She could grab a protein bar there. But the smell of bacon hit her smack in the face when she opened the door.

The sideboard at the back of the room was set with covered warming dishes and boxes of cereal. Consuelo knew her people and provided for their eclectic tastes.

Alex spooned oatmeal from a slow cooker and topped it with brown sugar and fresh berries. Poured a tall glass of milk over ice, then settled in beside Grace and Logan, the only other occupants in the room. When she entered it was apparent they were having a telepathic conversation, but now Grace leaned over and touched Alex's hand.

"Good morning."

Alex grinned. "It really is."

Logan's eyebrows went up. "Somebody got a good night's sleep."

"Yep. Feeling very refreshed and ready to tackle whatever lands on our plate today."

The door opened, and Broughton came in.

"You, on the other hand," said Logan, "didn't fare as well."

Broughton slanted him a look and grunted. Filled a plate with bacon, an omelet, and toast. He looked like he hadn't had any sleep at all, and while that was sad, it didn't affect Alex's good mood. Good grief, she couldn't be gloating because thinking of her might have kept him awake all night…could she?

Nope, she wasn't that small. Wasn't. But neither was she upset to know she did at least affect him in some way. And that kiss… Her toes curled in her boots, and she flicked a glance at him. Was seared by a look she couldn't interpret. Was glad James came in then and distracted her. All of them.

"Good news," said James, and Alex waited, spoon halfway to her mouth. "We've narrowed the possibilities down to eighty-seven. Bad news, eighty-seven from thirty-two states, and eighty-seven cities."

Alex set the spoon back in the bowl. The odds of finding a connection seemed insurmountable.

"More good news. Liz and Galen are on board, and if Mae was reported missing during the five years Liz worked for ETC, there is a good chance she's at least seen, if not worked the file."

"They were going to work remotely as usual, but given that some of us have connected with Mae and her son in various ways, we're hoping it will help Liz find a clue to Mae's identity and that of her captors. If we can get a location, which is something Liz excels at, we'll be able to investigate those known to operate in that area."

Alex hadn't met Liz, but had heard about her unique gift for finding missing children. She was somehow able to connect with them empathically and follow the energy to where they were. Her husband, Galen, was a pilot and a telepath, and Alex had heard he was able to steal information from other people's minds through a very special interrogation technique.

Angie had laughingly told her Galen could seduce a woman with no more than the lightest touch of his hand, and once under his spell, she would tell him all her darkest secrets. When Alex said, "Seriously?" Angie had sobered and said, "Oh, yeah. The man is scary good at getting women naked and making sure they think it's their idea."

As though conjured up by her thoughts, Angie slipped into the room, grabbed a piece of bacon, and joined the group at the table.

"It will also be good to add another pilot to the mix," said James. "Now you've all had a chance to sleep on yesterday's developments, anything pop? Make you curious?"

"How did Ryder come to be at Sunrise?" asked Broughton.

Logan held up a finger. "According to Chase, the boy had heard about their camp for foster kids and sent a resume for a summer job."

"Pretty ballsy," said Angie. "But after meeting and talking to him myself, I'm not surprised. Kid oozes self-confidence. Reminded me of Dhillon in the way he so comfortably communicated with an adult he'd never met before."

Alex thought of herself at the same age, determined to get to vet school. "Sounds like he was very focused, too. Driven to finance his future in flying."

Broughton nodded. "And he got connected to you, James, through someone at Sunrise, correct?"

James nodded. "Murray is tight with the couple who own Sunrise. Takes small groups to his place at a private lake and teaches them to fish. Was impressed with Ryder and approached me about mentoring. I interviewed the boy remotely and did the paperwork. Details of travel and everything else were handled by Murray. I just signed the check and assigned Del as a contact."

"You haven't met Ryder?" The instant flash of regret on James's face made Alex wish she'd kept her mouth shut. Like the man didn't have enough on his shoulders.

"I was away, and when I got back, there…" his

words trailed off. "No. Regretfully, I've never met Ryder."

"You did an amazing thing," said Broughton. "Giving a complete stranger a chance at a future otherwise far beyond his reach."

"Thank you. But today Ryder needs more than an open wallet."

"Hearing Chase and Dusty talk about him made me hopeful," said Grace. "And after meeting his grandfather, I'm convinced we're on the right track to rescuing him." She glanced around the room. "My experience in their empty house was unlike anything I've had before. I believe I connected with Mae as a child. When she was captive." She took a deep breath and Logan touched the back of her neck.

"Through her eyes I saw outbuildings and a generator, so I'm guessing they were off the grid."

"What else did you see?" asked Broughton, and Grace closed her eyes. "Glimpses. It was like a rapid-fire slide show, but that night I dreamed of everything else. Did I fill in the gaps myself? I don't think so, but I can't be certain."

"Can you tell us?"

"Yes."

"Will you let me record it?" asked Angie, and when Grace sent her a sharp glance, she added, "Not audio. Never audio, Grace. I know better. But my fingers are good for a hundred words a minute."

Grace nodded. "That'll work." She rested her elbows on the table and put her face in her hands. Fingertips bracing her forehead, thumbs on her jawline, and eyes closed again, she took a long, deep breath and held it for what seemed like minutes, then exhaled slowly through her mouth.

“She was one of a dozen kept in a large building. An outbuilding like a barn or shop, but with mattresses on the floor. There were other small, cabin-like buildings where she was taken and cleaned and dressed before going to the house where men were waiting. It was on the way there that she passed the noisy shed with a fuel tank outside of it. My take was generator. After, when she was taken back to the shed, she walked past a long structure I would call a carport. There was a roof, and no sides, and it had many vehicles parked under it. Big black SUVs, mostly. I tried to see the plates, but she wasn’t looking in that direction. There were no fences, just wide-open land with scrubby bushes and tufts of grass more gray than green. And everything was dust-coated.

“There was a big padlock on the door where she went in. She stared at it, and at the hand with the key that opened it. She moved it with her mind, made it slip from his grasp, and he let go of her to pick it up. That’s when she took off running.”

“That’s how she got away?” Angie asked.

“But he was right on her heels. She couldn’t see where she was going and stumbled, fell, and he had her. Out there in the blackness, he pounded her with his fists, put his boots to her, and with a final flick of his knife across her throat, muttered, ‘Coyote bait.’ And left her there.

“She clamped a hand to her throat, and when she could no longer hear his footsteps, she got to her feet and headed the opposite direction. Didn’t stop. Just kept on going farther and farther from the light of the buildings. In the morning she huddled under a low bush and slept, and that night she continued on toward where the sun rose each morning. On the third night she faltered fell, got up, and fell again. Over and over.

"When she woke up, she was safe. Warm. And an old man was spooning bits of liquid into her mouth. She swallowed and her throat burned. Words didn't make sense, but the hands were gentle and the voice encouraging."

Grace raised her face. Blinked. "She survived."

Alex's heart hurt for the child who had suffered such horror, and for the woman who had channeled the experience. She went to the fridge at the back of the room and poured a glass of orange juice. Brought it to Grace and was thanked with a wan smile.

Logan's hand was wrapped around the back of Grace's neck as though he was helping hold her upright—and Alex knew it was entirely possible. One thing she had learned while training was that Grace was always weakened by a psychic encounter. And the subject matter of this one would have kicked her while she was down. Would have seared her on the inside.

Alex grabbed a plate of cookies from the sideboard and set it in the middle of the table, within Grace and Logan's reach. "Sugar, ya know?"

James was busy with his keyboard, as was Angie. A satellite map was up on the big screen with a star in the middle, indicating the reservation where Dayson and Mae lived.

"An hour's drive away when he found her, right?" James made a circle around the star.

"And a two-and-a-half day hike, in the dark." He added another circle outside the first.

"Somewhere on or close to this bigger circle, we'll find the place she was held." He looked up. "Angie, fire up the Steed. Broughton and Alex go as lookouts, Logan and Grace, your call. Work here or go with them."

"I have to go," said Grace. "It will be empty, but the child might be there again. Might show me more. I have to go."

"What can we do to make it easier for you?" asked Alex.

Grace smiled. "Be there. Be open."

That she could do. "I'll get supplies, too," she said.

Angie pushed back her chair. "Liftoff in twenty," she said, and headed out, cell phone to her ear. "Matthias. Change of plans."

18

On her way to meet Broughton after grabbing her sunglasses and weapon, Alex was intercepted by Consuelo, who handed her the trusty cooler bag.

"More food? Consuelo, we just had breakfast, and I have the pocket full of candies you already gave me."

"It's food, and it's all I can offer to help while you go out there trying to find the innocent. Angie has the cold drinks."

Consuelo laid a hand to Alex's cheek. "There will be lots of wild energy flying around today. Take care of each other out there."

Alex surprised herself by leaning down and planting a kiss on Consuelo's cheek. "We'll be okay. And thanks for looking after us."

Broughton was waiting for her when she stepped outside. "Can I take that?" he asked.

"I'm good."

"Ride or walk?"

"We're probably going to be sitting for hours, so let's walk."

It was early still, so the air wasn't rudely hot, but halfway to the helipad Alex could feel the prickle of sweat under her shirt and muttered, "This ain't Kentucky."

Broughton laughed. "You could slow down."

"Oh, well." She'd always been a super-fast walker. It was natural, and slowing wasn't, but she did slow. "I never learned how to stroll."

"I like your walk. You look like someone with a destination. Somewhere to go, something to do."

Her heart skipped a beat, and she wanted to slap herself. "I like your walk" wasn't exactly a declaration of love, so she needed to dial back. Again.

"Places to go, people to see, my mother used to say." Alex moved the bag to her other shoulder. "I'm impatient mostly."

"Me too. Give me the damn bag."

She frowned. "Why?"

"It's heavy."

"I'm perfectly capable of carrying a heavy bag, and I certainly don't need a man to carry it for me."

"It's not a matter of need, Alex. It would be easier for me to carry it than you. I'm proportionately bigger than you, and that has nothing to do with being male or female."

"Do you really think it would make sense for me to take a bag from Angie and carry it just because I'm about a foot taller than she is?"

"Well, sure."

"Bullshit. If she was struggling and unable, I'd

offer. But otherwise, I'd leave her be because I don't have testicles."

He stopped. And when she turned to see what he was doing, he was staring at her. "What?"

"I fucking hate that you're right. But my daddy raised me to be a gentleman. To help a lady. And I don't think that's wrong."

"It's not, if the lady wants help. If she doesn't and you persist, it's insulting."

"So noted."

#

With the Steed's exceptional speed, they were at the search site in less than ninety minutes, and twenty minutes in they found what they were looking for. Or what was left of it. Outbuildings were nothing more than charred scars on the ground, and the house had been leveled with some kind of heavy machinery. Aged bricks and cement blocks were spread over a wide area, with bits of wooden door and window frames twisted among the wreckage.

Grace walked through the rubble, stopping occasionally, while Logan hovered close by. Alex and Broughton went in opposite directions, searching the perimeter for something, anything, that might be useful. A clue, evidence for use if the perpetrators were ever found.

A quick movement caught Alex's attention, and she wheeled to see Logan rush to Grace, who was on her knees. Alex froze. Watched Grace reach for Logan's hand.

She was asking him for help, for strength, and Alex could lend her own power to the mix. She joined them. Held out her hand, and Logan took it. Nodded. Held on.

When Broughton came to her side, she grabbed his hand too. The three of them would power Grace's vision while Angie watched from the helicopter. She was their control. Would be there to pull them all out if need be, because who knew where Grace was taking them? Her previous vision was through the eyes of a child who had been an adult for nearly twenty years.

Power thrummed through Alex, heated her hands, and her arms vibrated with the extraordinary energy. Air stilled, and the light thinned. The world was now faded and gray, and there were men. Half a dozen men, shouting over the roar of the machine. Sharp, snapping noises jarred like gunfire as the house was mowed down, and the acrid smell of burning plastic scorched the lining of her nostrils.

"More fuel!" someone shouted, and then with a whoosh, flames shot into the sky where a tiny building stood only moments before. Two men stood silently watching.

"Two-two-seven. Told ya months ago she was going to be trouble. Bitch cost us a good setup."

"You're sure she's dead?"

"Found that bloody shirt all ripped and chewed. Coyotes had a feast."

"Why we burning things up, then?"

"Because the boss never saw the body and he's paranoid. Fucking pansy lit out of here within minutes of finding out she ran. Gave the orders to wipe this place clean and took off like the sheriff was on his tail."

The other guy laughed. "Casey was our best fucking customer. He'll be bummed. Won't be happy about having to drive an extra hour each way."

More laughing. "Maybe he'll start using one of them copters when he wants to kiddy-bang."

Light filtered in slowly. The smoke cleared, and the images faded away. Alex blinked. Holy Hannah, she'd been right there, witnessing a scene from the past, like a proverbial fly on the wall. Coolness slipped over her, took the heat from her hands, the vibration from her arms.

At some point they had all ended up sitting in the dirt. Except Grace, who was still on her knees.

"Broughton," said Logan, then cleared his throat. "Move around and take Grace's other hand to complete the circle."

Once he did, Alex felt her own power dip. Dim. And she imagined it was going to Grace, to bolster her. She could call out to Angie, and get the bag of snacks, but eating or drinking would require letting go of hands, and for now they needed to hang on. Replenish Grace this way first.

She let out a deep sigh, and sank down, plunked her butt in the dirt. "Wow."

"You okay?" asked Logan.

"Depleted. But okay. Did you see any of that?"

"The destruction of the area?"

"Yeah."

Grace glanced at the others. "You guys?"

"Yep," said Alex, and Broughton nodded.

"I'm going to contact James through Julia. See if we can go on from here, try to find the other site."

"Nearly twenty years ago," said Alex. "Would they still be there?"

"Mae saw something or someone who scared her into running again, and it happened when she was on a day job with Dayson." A job there seemed to be no record of, no matter where or how Meyers searched.

"Let her know about the sheriff, too. Best we know if he's still around."

"I'm good now." Grace let go of Broughton and Logan. "Need a minute." She got up slowly and wobbled to the Steed.

Logan expelled a long breath, and Broughton said, "Watching what she goes through has to suck for you."

"Fucking A."

"Musta been hard, learning when to step in and when to leave her alone."

"Only hard part was the bruises she left when I screwed up."

Broughton's eyebrows shot up, and Alex nearly laughed out loud. "Logan's exaggerating about the bruises. Grace is very nonviolent."

"On the outside. Tough as nails, though. Battered myself bloody against her attitude, beliefs, and stubbornness. Lots of bouncing off walls and tripping on hazards. But today she charted new territory by dragging all of us along in her vision. Perfect example of gifts expanding."

"You've never been inside one of her visions?"

"Not a scene like that. Usually I get the slide show-type images. What about you?" he asked Broughton. "You've ridden shotgun on plenty of missions. You ever had an experience like today?"

"Only once, but it was more of a prequel. A premonition, I suppose. Nothing I could do to change the outcome. Even when I was living it weeks later and knew how it would unfold. Not a damn thing I could do differently."

#

Grace sat in the open doorway of the Steed and leaned in to pluck a soda from the cooler. Popped the top and guzzled.

"Any luck?" asked Angie.

"And then some. I need to update HQ."

Angie lifted Grace's helmet from her seat and held it out. "Here, use the embedded mic, and I'll switch the radio for you."

"Thanks, but I'm going to go through Julia. Safer until we know who we're dealing with."

Angie grinned. "Good point. Since Kelton and Rollins, no amount of security seems good enough."

The sugar started working right away, and Grace's legs were losing that rubbery feeling, and her thoughts were already less tangled.

She focused inward, on the pathway to her aunt. *Julia?*

Grace.

You were waiting, ready.

When it began, you were broadcasting hard.

Oh no, what if—

I wrapped you up. Full protection, and I was the only one besides the four of you on the inside. I took notes for James, and he's scanning satellite footage now, looking for their next location, even though he doesn't think they would stay in one place for more than a year or so. Although having a sheriff in their pocket makes a difference.

If that sheriff is still in charge.

He's checking on that too.

Grace stared at the broken and scattered bricks. *Wait. I can't imagine they'd be setting up shop on reservation land, and in this area, that narrows down the possibilities.*

Drastically. That's why James thinks he can find them. There was the slightest hesitation before she asked, *How are you holding up?*

Getting my strength back. Probably at about eighty percent so far. She rifled the snack bag for a wedge of creamy cheese and a cookie, alternating bites between the two. The first time she'd seen Alex make the same combo she'd been appalled, but when challenged, she tried it and was instantly hooked.

She finished her soda and dug out an iced tea. Caffeine would be the perfect way to round out her power snack.

James has some coordinates for Angie.

Hang on. Angie was sitting in the pilot seat, her back to Grace. "Coordinates incoming. You got a pen?"

She held up a hand. "Affirmative. Standing by."

Fire away.

Julia rattled off numbers, and Grace repeated them aloud, then Angie repeated them back, and Grace did the same. Seemed a bit like overkill, but erring on the side of caution worked. Kept people alive, and often found the missing.

When they were done, and she'd been updated on the sheriff, Grace said goodbye to her aunt and called in the others. "Time to get back into search mode. Julia went on that last ride with us and updated James. He's now given Angie some places to check out."

"Perfect," said Alex. "What about Casey?"

"Retired about two months before Dayson and Mae went missing."

Alex was frowning. "I don't like the timing."

"Yeah. I felt that all-too-familiar click in my head when Julia told me."

Grace had dealt with law enforcement gone bad. Didn't like it. Too many eyes and ears. Too much inside information. And who knew how many hands were involved, how many turned a blind eye? This could turn into a total shitshow, and would it get them any closer to finding Ryder? Maybe. And that maybe was what drove her.

You okay?

She took Logan's hand. *I'm good.*

Your hand is warm. Your energy level must be getting back to normal.

Ninety percent and climbing.

He kissed her softly. *Use me for the last ten.*

Grace smiled. *Nah, I've got this. I'll use you later, when I can get you naked.*

#

The first location turned out to be an abandoned homestead with an outhouse, a small barn, a chicken coop, and no bad vibes. When they landed at the second, there was much of the same, but they still did a full search for any kind of clue to the previous residents.

Broughton watched Alex boldly touch doorknobs, window ledges, and even an old metal bedframe, and he'd been ready to catch her, or at least support her if she got a sensory blast.

But nothing happened, and while he felt relieved, there was a niggling disappointment. Had he wanted an opportunity to "rescue" her? And wouldn't that be every color of wrong…and irritating?

He shook it off and climbed back into the Steed. Strapped into the front seat.

"Ready?" Angie's voice came through the headsets built into their helmets. They each answered, and the helo lifted off the ground, slid forward, and picked up speed, swooping higher, then levelling out.

"Now what?" he asked.

"James just found one more area for us to check out. Said he saw movement near one of the buildings," Grace told the group. "We're headed there now and need to be ready for action. Weapons drawn prior to landing."

"The invisibility and soundlessness of the Steed will give us the element of surprise," said Broughton, "But means we have to keep our helmets on, so peripheral vision will be compromised." They could use auxiliary ear plugs, but then they wouldn't be able to hear each other. This way was better. "Makes formation important for the first sweep. I'll take the left rear. Logan go front right. Alex in front of me, Grace behind Logan."

"Copy," said Logan. "Are you familiar with this approach, Alex?"

"Affirmative. Keep my view front and left, you'll be front and right."

"Correct. Broughton and Grace have our sixes."

"Where we're headed is right on the edge of reservation land," said Angie.

"Pretty desolate-looking," said Alex. And she wasn't wrong. The land "given" to indigenous people was what the government of the times had no use for. It wasn't fertile, or rich in any way. It held no appeal for settlers, and wasn't suited to raising cattle. A no-man's-land.

But those who owned it now cherished it as all that was left of their heritage. They could make the corn grow, and made use of the resources. Marketed the natural beauty. Put on eco tours, and started power farms. Did what they needed to do to survive while they fought to keep their young from moving away, drawn to wealth and promises of an end to the boredom in their dusty valley.

Dwellings in this area but outside the reservation raised a red flag. There was no good reason to settle out here unless there was something you were hiding from. A large percentage of those living purposely off the grid did so to maintain their anonymity. They worked hard to stay under the radar.

As Broughton had while he was hiding from the FBI and a few other agencies. But when he left, he torched his place. There was no evidence left behind. Nothing to connect to him.

If the satellite had picked up movement, but James hadn't been able to get a handle on the what or who, Broughton suspected it was probably wildlife. He glanced out the side window. Couldn't imagine much living on its own out there. Rodents? Coyotes? Not much else.

"Touchdown in ten," said Angie, and Broughton lowered his shoulders, flexed his fingers, turned his head from side to side to loosen his neck muscles, then slipped from his seat and into the back so they would all use the same door. Drew his weapon from the holster strapped to his chest.

They got into position. Logan with one hand on the door latch, Alex beside him, Grace behind them. Broughton took up his positon behind Alex.

"Wait for my count," said Angie.

Broughton rested a hand on Alex's back.

"You'll have a house at twelve o'clock, and outbuildings at two and four. Stand by."

Broughton drew a long, slow breath.

"In three, two, one, go."

The door slid back, and they were on the ground as one. Moving quickly, but with purpose. They cleared a ramshackle shed, which could have been the original residence, then the hollow shell of a barn. Nothing but dust and a pile of tumbleweed.

There was no electricity in the air. No blip of energy to suggest there were any humans around, but they stayed in formation and moved on to the house. The door was ajar, and Logan gave it a kick to widen the opening.

A flurry of movement set reflex into motion, and before the thought had even crossed his mind,

Broughton had taken aim.

"No!" Alex stopped herself half a step out of formation. Held. "Don't shoot. It's only a cat."

A very small and not very brave tabby peered at them from behind the leg of an old wooden chair.

"Finish the sweep," Logan instructed, and they quickly ascertained the three-room abode was free of anything threatening. Although the cat did hiss a time or two.

"Poor thing's half starved," said Grace.

Alex was on her knees, talking to it. She pulled a lump from her vest pocket and unwrapped a cookie. Dropped a piece on the floor near the feline, and they all watched it snick forward and gobble up the offering.

"We can't leave it here. Someone already left him to die, and he survived. We have to take him with us," said Alex.

"Give me your helmet," said Grace. "I'll take it to the helo and get something you can put him in."

"She hasn't caught him yet," said Broughton.

"Oh, she will."

While Logan did a closer examination of the other two rooms, Broughton studied the kitchen—and Alex. He was impressed with how easily she slipped into animal communication. He could do that with dogs, but other animals didn't respond to him.

Logan said, "Let's leave her to it and take another look outside. See what we can pick up."

"I should come with you," said Alex.

"We've got it. You stay here."

"You find anything?" asked Broughton, after

carefully closing the door so the cat couldn't escape.

"Someone lived here for a very long time, and didn't move away."

That piqued his interest. "Tell me."

"Blankets on the bed shoved back like someone just got out of it with every intention of returning, but dust-covered, so not recently. A pair of pants and a shirt draped over the back of a chair. Again, layered with dust."

"There was a mug on the kitchen floor, near the door," said Broughton, "and a sugar bowl not far from it. My guess they were on the table or the sideboard, and the cat moved them while trying to get the dregs of anything in them."

"Cats eat sugar?"

Broughton shrugged. "I've heard they will eat twigs and rocks if they're starving, so sugar would seem likely."

"Good point."

"If the missing human died outside, the coyotes would have dealt with the remains."

"We'll do a walk around."

Grace passed them, cooler in hand. "You pick up anything?"

"Not inside. We're going to do a walk around now."

"Don't shoot any cats." She grinned and went inside.

"Smart-ass." He shook his head. "I hadn't sensed anything, but an empty building, and then the damned thing moved. Caught me flat-footed."

"I was reaching," said Logan. "You were

faster." He stopped, and lifted his chin. Looked like a wolf searching for a scent. "East."

"I agree. Something tugging."

Logan bore left, Broughton right, and with about twenty feet between them, they slowly worked their way through the scrub until they found a gravesite with several markers. A family had buried their dead here over fifty years ago.

They doubled back, covered more ground on the way just in case, but found nothing, and the women were all waiting at the helicopter when they got back.

"Where's your new friend?" asked Logan.

"In the Cabinet of Silence. He'll be safe there." Protected from the internal noise of the Steed. Broughton's dogs rode there the day Meyers brought him in from exile.

He glanced around the spartan homestead. What he had for those two years was even less than this. A one-room cabin, but less exposed. In an area where there were hills and trees. He wasn't sure if he'd have done as well in a location like this one, where there was nothing as far as the eye could see.

"Why would anyone homestead here?" he asked. "Was it this bleak a hundred years ago?"

"Some people love the wide-open spaces. Big sky, they call it," said Angie. "Everyone strapped in?"

They were soon airborne and sliding over the barren landscape. "The gravesite you found," said Alex. "Was it a whole family? Children? What were the dates?"

Broughton frowned. "All dead over forty years

ago, and I didn't look at the names, ages." It hadn't occurred to him. Wasn't relevant to the case. Why would she care?

"Maybe they were pioneers. Homesteaders come from the east, seeking a new life, a place of their own. The furniture in that house was all handmade, and quite rough except for the sideboard. It must have come on a wagon. A family heirloom, perhaps. What stories it could tell."

Broughton's frown deepened. Why did she care? People long dead. A piece of wood hauled across the country in a wagon. So what? A person couldn't get sentimental about things, histories, family stories. They had no substance. Nothing you could wrap your hands around.

19

"Another whole day and we're no closer to finding Ryder," said Alex, and Broughton heard the frustration in her voice.

"We've covered ground that needed covering, eliminated several angles, and now we know for sure where Mae came from."

"We do?"

"The vision," said Grace.

"But it wasn't through her eyes like the other one."

"No, but it was the part of her still there that let me in. Gave me the connection."

"Oh. The how's and why's of psychic energy are so over my head," Alex said. "I'd been hoping we would bust open a human trafficking ring and rescue someone today. Anyone. But that was just a far-fetched dream. And really? I didn't have a clue what to expect. Or about how human trafficking, or selling, or abuse, or whatever the hell it's called, even works, you know? It's like something that's hung in the periphery of my mind, knowing horrible things happen, but not really understanding anything like the logistics, the mechanics."

She heaved a sigh. "This mission began as a search for people missing from Houston. Then the plane vanished, and we switched to searching for Ryder. Then we got to Mae and her history, and now we're nose to the ground after human traffickers. I understand the path we've taken, but my scientific vet brain needs more information. I'm used to researching what I don't know, or what I don't understand. Finding other vets who have encountered whatever the problem is, and picking their brains for clues to help with my case."

"Human trafficking, put simply," said Broughton, "is the buying and selling of human beings. But that much you know already. In the world of organized crime, it is second in profitability only to drug trafficking, and encompasses any and all barter and trade of human beings for any purpose."

"The operation we had a glimpse of today technically sold blocks of time with children for sex," said Grace. "The children were imprisoned, and completely dependent on their keepers for basic survival. For those taken at a very young age, it would not occur to them to run away, because life there was all they knew."

"I suppose it's a contradiction to wish there had been someone there today, someone we could have saved, but it was better that there was no one. I shouldn't be disappointed the place was deserted."

"If James thought there was any chance of finding life there, the team would have included a great deal of law enforcement, and a doctor," said Broughton.

"However," said Grace, in her teachable moment tone, "James is only right ninety-nine point nine percent of the time, so just in case that ever happens and you find yourself doing a fast switch from recon to rescue, there are a few things you need to know."

More than a few, but Broughton would hear Grace out before adding anything.

"Things can get real messy real fast. Children often don't trust the rescuers. Might even fight them because of conditioning. Teaching them to fear people in uniform makes darn certain they'll never consider going to the law for help. Unless they are totally shut down, they will be defensive—imagine trying to free a mountain lion from a leg-hold trap. He's not going to believe you're trying to help him."

"On the other end of the spectrum," said Logan, "are those who are simply cold, hungry, and grateful to be saved from the hell they've been living."

Images flashed in Broughton's mind, and he shut them down. "As for the adults in charge, they are well armed, and will fight to the death. So shoot first and ask questions later."

The sucked-in breath had to be Alex, and he wasn't sorry. She needed to know he was capable—more than capable—of taking a life without remorse.

"If," Logan cut into the uncomfortable silence. "If James had been wrong, we would have done what had to be done."

How many times had Broughton walked in blind? Not all that many, because he was good, but there had been a couple, and he refused to back out once he knew what was inside. There were two kids in this world who should have been on an entirely different plane, like the others who were piled against the wall. But he refused to leave without them. Clawed at broken bricks until the opening was big enough to get them through, and took two bullets on the way out. Running, running, and the copter wasn't there when he got to the clearing. Small arms knocked his communicator—

"Broughton?" Logan's voice was low. "What's going on?"

Shit. He slowed his heartrate. Eased back in his seat. "Sorry, remembering a few of those missions we've refused to abort at the last minute. Pumped me for a sec." And dammit, he knew better than to let his emotions have free rein to plunge him into flashback territory.

"Later," said Logan, "we might have to share a few of those stories for reference, and also, now we know the twist, we need to bring Alex up to speed on some of the directions this one could go."

How fucked up was the world if abducting and enslaving humans was called a "twist?" He did a mental head shake. He needed to get a grip. Because it *was* a twist in their case. They could be almost positive Ryder's abduction was related to Mae being a captive many years earlier.

The burning question was, what would the abductors do with the kid? Yes, they took him so they could find his mother, but he had skills, was trainable, could be brainwashed into joining the group while he remained a prisoner. Or he could be exploited sexually. Hell, they'd already had him for how many days?

Broughton shuddered. He hated the "investigation" part of the job. Much preferred action. Getting the job done.

Extractions were his crack.

#

Alex was quiet for the rest of the trip back to the ranch because there was little to say. She learned a lot today, was still processing most of it, and the hardest part was keeping her own feelings out of the mix. She knew what it felt like to be abducted, to be at the mercy of others. Strangers. And to be completely, utterly helpless. At least they hadn't touched her in a sexual way—not that she hadn't seen the idea flicker in the eyes of one of her abductors.

Finding children so horribly abused would be hard, but she had no doubt she could handle it. In her job she saw plenty of awful, and knew how to compartmentalize and move on. She also knew such behavior put her at risk of compassion fatigue—something blamed for the suicide rate among veterinarians being higher than that of war veterans. A damned scary statistic.

Luckily her clients were the kind who could afford the best of care for their horses, and abused neither the equines nor the vet staff. It didn't make it any easier to lose a patient, but at least her hands were never tied, and she was free to do whatever was necessary to save a creature in her care.

And when euthanasia was the only choice left, it was easier. She'd known going in that there would be days when she had to take a life, and she didn't like it, never would, but she could deal.

Broughton had taken lives too, but in a different way, and for different reasons, and that put a queasy feeling in her stomach. Not because of what he had done, but the lack of remorse in his voice when he spoke of it earlier. His tone said he did it and was glad. Would do it again in a heartbeat.

The Broughton she met months earlier, the one who helped her get through the horrors and logistics of full body paralysis, had treated her with kindness, and had genuinely cared about her and her needs. And from the beginning, when he lifted her helpless body into his arms, she knew there was a hard edge in him. Hell, that was likely why she was so attracted, because soft men never appealed to her. She was one of the stupid females ridiculously drawn to bad boys. And look how well that worked out for her.

She was very glad she no longer had an abusive and controlling boyfriend, but she would never have wished him dead. That was on him, because besides being a bad boy, he made bad decisions.

He was the kind of man Broughton would have put a bullet in. He really was. Her stomach went from a bit queasy to roiling. If Broughton ever took the plunge with her and tried to have a relationship, would he become controlling? He'd fussed about her blood sugar. Told her where to sit in the Steed, where she was to be in the formation.

But he was her partner, and her senior. Her trainer of sorts.

"Alex." His voice was sharp.

He was standing in the open doorway. How had she not known they were landing? That Grace and Logan had already gotten out?

"Are you okay?"

She pulled off her helmet. "Yep."

Removing his own helmet, he studied her face, looking, she supposed, for signs of a problem. "We need to get a move on. Meeting in the war room."

She slid the empty cooler toward the cabinet. "If you'll shut the door, I can get the cat."

He surprised and then annoyed her just a bit by hopping in before sliding the door into place.

"Pretend you're a statue, and he should be okay." She hoped. "And don't look at him. Eye contact is perceived as a threat."

She sat on the floor and tugged off her jacket. Cracked open the cabinet door. "Hey, buddy." With her hands inside the sleeves, and groping for the cat, she was surprised to feel him right there, leaning into her. She'd had visions of crawling in after him—which was totally doable because the space was designed to fit a full-sized human.

With said feline safely transferred to the cooler bag, she leaned back on her hands. "Way easier than expected."

"Can he breathe in there?"

She bit her lip. Stuck two fingers through the

opening at the end of the zipper. “It’s not done up all the way. And I’ll have him out in less than ten minutes.” A tick in the good column because he’d been concerned, but it didn’t take away from the fact he thought she was stupid enough to suffocate the poor animal.

“Ready?” he asked.

“Yeah,” she said, and stayed sitting—easier to then simply slide out and take the cat with her. But when he didn’t open the door, she glanced up.

“It was a reflex question. I know you wouldn’t hurt him.”

“Mind reading without permission?”

“Nope, it was written all over your face.” His face lit with a smile. “You’d make a lousy poker player.” He opened the door.

One day she’d make him eat those words because, in fact, she was good. Very good. And bluffing was her thing.

The others were waiting for them in Angie’s SUV, and the ride up to the big house was quick.

“I’m just going to take this guy to my room, then I’ll catch up.” She swung into the kitchen.

“Hey, Consuelo.” She had cookie dough rolled out on the wide island and was cutting it into star shapes.

“Ball game tomorrow,” she said. “Just dump that on the counter by the sink and I’ll unpack it later.”

Alex laughed. “Not a good idea.” And as though on cue, a sad meow came from the bag. “I picked up a passenger. Was hoping to grab some food and set him up in my room.”

Consuelo nodded. “Pantry, back left corner for all things critter-related. Help yourself.”

Alex was impressed. There was everything from a stack of litter boxes to toys and beds of every shape and size. Also a good selection of canned food and dry for cats, and an even bigger selection for dogs. “I guess you get all kinds of visitors here.”

“Raised ten kids in this house, and they were always bringing something home. Still doin’ it, plus the next generation has already started. What’s the story here?” she asked.

“Found him at an abandoned homestead. Looks like he’s been on his own for a while… and he loves your sugar cookies.”

Consuelo grinned. “Makes him smart, and a keeper. You setting him up in your bathroom to start?”

“Yep, smaller space and all, until I get to know him. Then we’ll see where he wants to live. Might want to stay outdoors, or in-out as he pleases once he’s settled and gets to know all the dogs. Odd to have none in here right now.” There was a double dog bed in the corner, and a water dish, but no occupant today.

“Boys came home this morning, Puck and Stick are glued to them. Chance is with Dhillon, and Swagger is with James in the war room.”

“Reminds me, I’d better run. Need to get to the debrief.” She dropped a small bag of litter, a couple of dishes, and a can of cat food into the litter pan, slung the cooler strap over her shoulder and headed for her room.

"Sorry, this is going to be a dump and run," she said to the cat when she let him out in her bathroom. "But you've got all you need for now."

She put food and water in one corner of the room and the litter at the other. Pulled a towel off the shelf and set it down as a bed. "I'll be back as fast as I can."

He stared up at her as though she was his last friend in the world, and she dropped her jacket on top of the towel. "Here, this is the promise I'll be back." He immediately sat in the middle of it and she gave him a thumbs-up, then took off.

She raced down the hall, sailed into the war room, and dropped into the only empty chair.

James rose to his feet. "We'll get started."

They had waited for her. A tiny glow lit somewhere near her heart.

20

Grace usually skipped this kind of debrief, because, for one, it was just a rehash of the day's events, and two, there were too many people. Granted, the room was spacious, and physical crowding wasn't an issue, but the minds, the tangle of thoughts, threatened to overwhelm. She glanced at the twins. Why the hell weren't they blocking?

Julia, I'm going to have to leave before my head explodes.

Hang on, I'll add to your protection web, and I'll shut down the boys.

The pressure suddenly eased, thank God. She took a swallow from the giant glass of ice water in front of her, and Logan rested his arm across the back of her chair. Touched her shoulder. *You okay?*

I am now. Julia shut the twins down and strengthened my protective shell.

One of these days I'm going to master that trick so I can help you.

I'm not sure if it can be mastered like a skill. I think it's a particular gift. Kelton and Julia were the only people able to do it for me.

I should have shut down the guys. They're pretty pumped about something tonight, busting to share. Maybe once they do—

"Grace?"

Dammit, she hated getting caught.

"Sorry, your question?"

"Your vision of the breakup where the operation was. Do you have anything to add to the report?"

"No."

"Did you see the people involved clearly enough to identify them?"

"Yes, as will those who shared my vision. Is there an update on Sheriff Casey?"

"He's in the wind."

"For how long?"

"Packed up and moved away when he retired. No forwarding address. Some say he bought himself a lake up north so he could fish his days away, other say he went to Florida."

"He either spread cover stories, or they're just making shit up," said Broughton.

"Agreed." James pointed to the screen where a map of the area was displayed. He used a laser pointer to circle a collection of colored dots. "Here are the places you checked out today, the town, the sheriff's home, the reservation, and where Mae was found. When I zoom out," which he did, sliding the map so the areas they had been to were now on the bottom left, "you can also see the last known location for the missing planes. Ryder's and Dayson's were both slightly northeast."

"Makes me think we're on the right track, even though we never really found anything today."

"You eliminated possibilities, and that's huge. Means we've cleared the whole southwest area."

"I'm liking the northeast quarter for our next run," said Broughton, and the instant hum of his energy was almost visible, making Grace even more grateful for the extra protection. "How soon can we go out? What about a night search?"

Angie nodded. "I could do the run on my own, and transmit back to HQ so the team could stay here and work from the wall screens. Bigger view and all."

"I could go with you, ya know, to run the comps and cams," said Dhillon.

"Objections?" James asked Angie, and she shook her head.

"As long as it works for the team."

Grace nodded, happy to stay on the ground, because something about the helo's movement while watching the search screens made her nauseous.

"Works for me," said Alex.

All eyes turned to Broughton, and his struggle was nearly palpable. He wanted to be out there, able to tell Angie to set down if there was any shot at doing a rescue. He was a hands-on kind of man, and sitting in this room wasn't a good fit for him. But neither was mentoring a rookie, and he was doing okay in that role. So far.

He drummed his fingers on the table for a

second. "Total recon, with no option to set down?"

"That bird stays in the air," said James, even though everyone in the room knew nothing was ever written in stone.

"You can still come with us and give Dhillon a hand."

"I could probably teach you a thing or two while we're out there," said the teen, and Broughton shifted, pinned him with a teasing look.

"Ya think so?"

"I wrote some software. Helped with the encryption of the files we—"

Angie laughed. "And so it begins."

"Dhillon." James drew the boy's attention back to the head of the table. "You'll be expected to submit a written report within an hour of landing."

"Frosted," he said, rubbing his hands together and wriggling in his seat, and Grace was reminded of the day not so long ago when he shot up a tree in pursuit of his kitten—still very much a kid, and needing work in the area of impulse control. A few hours in Broughton's company would be good for him, and just maybe hanging out with the teen would help the man lighten up.

Grace decided it would also be a great opportunity for Alex. She could work the search screens here at base and do so without Broughton hanging over her, double-checking her work. Not that he hadn't been an excellent teacher so far, but, whether Alex realized it or not, he was crowding her with his intensity.

With the entire Meyers group gathered, the debrief covered each team's day, and it took time.

Those still working on finding the Houston hurricane missing had made little forward progress, but had, through the process of elimination, been able to narrow their focus.

When the twins were asked for their report, the air in the room almost crackled with their excitement. The two youngest Meyers siblings were a handsome pair who possessed many psychic gifts and an incredible zest for life—not unlike the big black dogs at their sides.

In spite of being in their mid-twenties, Nathan and Tyler were often referred to as the boys, but watching them now, Grace saw men. Confident, polished young men, who were comfortable in their own skins and very confident of their abilities.

Nathan's expression suggested he knew a secret—or had found the keys to the universe—and the brightness of expectation vibrated along the edges of Grace's protective shield.

"We spent a ton of time searching for a few dozen people deemed missing after the hurricane in Florida because, as the textbooks say, those suffering economic hardship and lack of a social safety net after a natural disaster are often at risk to human traffickers."

"The good news," said Tyler, "is that every person we went in there to find is safe and accounted for."

Nathan grinned. "But there's better news. During the search process, we also looked for the traffickers—the dirty, slimy predators—and we found them too. A whole shit-load of the bottom-feeders. The street drones who recruit, coerce, and sometimes even kidnap their victims." His anger and disgust floated beneath the surface of his excitement. Tempered it ever so slightly.

"Then we scored," said Tyler. "Got information on the organizations they're working for. Dope on the big guys in charge."

"Holy crap," said Dhillon, earning a poke of his mother's elbow, after which he muttered, "Oops."

"And..." said Nathan with yet another level of excitement in his voice. One that suggested he was about to drop a bombshell. "...we found a connection to your missing kid."

As though controlled by a puppeteer, everyone in the room leaned forward.

Broughton looked ready to burst, or at least tell the boys to get on with it, and James wore an expression of anticipation mixed with pride. He had to already know what they found.

Julia's face gave away nothing, but love and pride shone in her eyes.

"The hurricane, in this case, worked in the opposite way. Up until the storm hit, there was a farm in a remote area which operated like a tiny nation. It was worked by people who were smuggled in from Third World countries—people whose passports had been taken, and who had no idea there was a way out. And there was a brothel of sorts being run on the same property."

"While searching, and talking to people we met on the street, we came across Lana, a young woman who had only been captive at the property for about a year, and still had her wits about her when the storm hit. Their captors, the people in charge, took shelter in the basement of the main house, and left behind everyone else to fend for themselves."

Grace's stomach churned, because more than once she'd gone into similar places and helped bring out girls and women too broken to even care that they had been rescued.

"We charmed Lana into talking to us," said Tyler. The pair were skilled at getting women to trust them, and Grace was certain there was often magic involved, but the twins never admitted what tactics they used.

"Once we'd gathered all the info, we slipped in and paid a visit to the farm…under the cover of night. We put the 'staff'—for lack of a better word—back in their shelter, and made sure they had no memory of coming out after the storm. Then we gathered up all the people who worked for them—foreign nationals with no paperwork—and the young men and women, who were all runaways scooped up from the streets, and got them to safety."

"A fallen tree blocked the doorway to the basement where the staff took shelter, and," he glanced at his watch, "they should be able to dig their way out soon. We made sure they had a week's worth of water, just in case they're really slow, and we left a camera in place so we'll know exactly when they get free."

Grace held a hand out to Nathan for a high five, and when his hit hers, she held on. "Well done." She loved when others thought the way she did.

"We have a team in place to pick them up as soon as they find their own way out. Then they'll be kept for dispatch to local law enforcement once Del and Ryder and his parents are found. Meanwhile, we've used all the info we harvested from them, and that's where we stumbled onto the connection to your case."

Stumbled was an interesting word, suggesting clumsiness, but the twins were smart and sure-footed, whether in the physical world or the metaphysical one. Many of their powers were known by the family, but there was no doubt they had more.

The only other person she knew with the same kind of talent for extracting information was Galen, but his technique included seduction, and Grace would bet that wasn't what the boys used on the staff at the farm. But then again…

Grace rarely spoke during a briefing, avoided the appearance of being part of the team because she was just an add-on, and preferred it that way. But information wasn't forthcoming, so she asked, "How many made up this staff? Males only?"

"Seven men. All white. Ages ranging from twenty-five to fifty. They receive orders and bookings from an email account we haven't been able to trace. Yet. We cloned their laptop and left it looking untouched. Most of their workers are Mexican nationals who believed they were coming into America legally. They paid a princely sum to have their paperwork fast-tracked, and of the seventeen we pulled out, three are doctors, one a dentist, and all have some form of higher education. They arrived at the departure point—where they were to meet and ride together to the airport—with luggage and passports in hand. Their passports and papers were taken, they were loaded into the back of a truck, and they woke up at the farm, sick, some barely alive, with no knowledge of how they got there. They weren't even certain they were in America."

Grace wasn't surprised, but it saddened her that this kind of thing still happened, and on a regular basis. A huge percentage of America's food was planted and tended by people who were prisoners of circumstance who came to this country seeking freedom and ended up with the complete opposite. Some of them were absolutely innocent, others not so much, but the bottom line was that they were humans being used as slaves.

"Where are they now?" asked Broughton.

"Happily on their way home to Mexico, with funding and ongoing support from a Meyers benefactor."

"The girls and women?"

"All but two chose to go to a private facility for recovery. From there they will have access to training programs and endless support. Lana and her friend Demi both love animals and the outdoors, and opted to fly home with us and move in to Haven."

Grace recognized the look on Nathan's face and grimaced. There was something between him and the girl.

"How old are they?"

"Lana is twenty-four, going on eighty. She was fifteen when she ran away from an abusive home. Demi is only eighteen, but even after three years at the farm as a sex worker, she said she'd rather stay than go home. Said at least there they only had to deal with the men three nights a week."

Grace shuddered. Unfortunately her ability to see in the minds of others, and to experience what they did, meant she fully understood Demi's plight. She rubbed at the pain in her chest.

Silence stretched until James said, "Tell us about the connection."

"Lana is a bit of a techy, and light-fingered. She was also good at being well-mannered and earning privileges. Over the past year she not only managed to steal two smartphones from johns, but rigged her own listening device, which she placed in the office when she was cleaning."

Warning bells went off in Grace's head. If Lana was as smart and devious as they said, she could be using this situation to aid the other side, not thwart them. Nathan appeared to be smitten, and that was not a good thing. But one glance at James and she knew he was already on it. Good. She'd keep her own counsel. And keep her eyes open.

"She came up with information about a big operation. Turned out some woman they thought was dead wasn't, but they couldn't find her, so they went after her son. They planned to get him and an airplane at the same time. Then they would wait for the woman to contact them. One of the group asked how the hell that would work and was told the woman would know who had her boy and how to make contact with them."

"What are the chances?" asked Tyler. "A crazy coincidence."

"Too slick," said Broughton. "Way too easy. Something has to be off. I'd like to talk to this Lana."

"Why? You think she's snowing us? How could she know about Ryder and his mom?"

"She could have mined it. Dug it out of your head."

"I'd have known. Besides, she told us this three days ago, and far as I've heard, you didn't know anything about Ryder's mom at that point, so how could we?"

"Point to you." Broughton shook his head. "I just hate when the pieces fit together too easily."

James nodded. "I'm with you. Suspicious as hell. Where exactly did you meet Lana?"

"We heard from someone at the last shelter left in town that there was an abandoned roadhouse just off the main highway where many of the homeless had made camp. That's where she was, along with the rest of the people who escaped the farm."

"You said she had information about the group, their higher-ups?"

Nathan nodded. "And a possible location where they could be holding Ryder."

"Here," said James, circling the top right corner of the map. "Hidden by a phony roof over it. Looks like a small slope, not even a hill, on the satellite cameras. Very similar to what we use."

He hesitated. "Tentative plan, Broughton and I go in tomorrow night. But we stay on our toes and flexible in the meantime. Ready to go."

"How confident are you that it's not a trap?" asked Grace, and all attention swung her way.

21

Alex sucked in a breath. She loved that Grace told it like it was, but still wasn't all that comfortable with anyone speaking out in a way that might offend someone else.

But, life and death. When it came to a life or death situation, hurt feelings didn't get a vote.

Did Grace really think the boys had been duped, set up for a fall, or, worse still, by someone wanting to take down Meyers? Alex agreed the coincidence seemed suspicious, but she'd reached a point in her life where she believed the universe often put things right where they needed to be. And in this case it could be as simple as that. Or not. Who knew?

Scary to think of James and Broughton walking into a trap, being met with guns blazing, or by those who would take them prisoner and use them as bargaining chips. Broughton looked too tough for anyone to take down, especially the way he was sitting with his back straight and his shoulders low and fluid. She'd bet his feet were flat on the floor and just slightly behind his center of gravity. He was always ready to spring into action.

Might as well have the word "control" stamped on his forehead. Nothing rattled him, caught him off guard. Well, she had once, and the memory warmed her. Backing him into the wall and kissing the stuffing—or stuffiness—out of him was a moment she would never forget.

Too bad he regrouped with lightning speed and kept her at a disadvantage ever since. She caught him off guard once, and it would never happen again. He was too well trained for that, dammit. And how could she want anything else? It was that kind of training keeping him alive when he was working dicey ops, going into sketchy locations like the one he was headed for tonight.

But no. That was tomorrow, wasn't it? Hell, she'd let her mind drift and missed details, and from the sound of it, there was a change of plans. Must have picked it up subconsciously.

Now she listened intently. Broughton and James were going to do a flyover with Angie, all systems—including the latest heat-seeking camera and ground-penetrating radar—in use to identify objects and people. Then if things looked good, they would land.

Dhillon seemed halfway pissed to be cheated out of his little op, but also pumped because he got to stay in the war room for the duration and monitor cameras.

"Alex," said James. "You stay here as well,

because your hand-to-hand skills have not been evaluated. And on this run they could be a make-or-break. Tomorrow you and I go into the gym and get that ticked off for you."

He was good. An excellent leader. He made it clear he wouldn't take her until he checked out her skills, yet he showed her he didn't doubt her ability. She nodded. "I can learn a lot from here as well."

Truth was, she would feel better staying here as an observer, imagining how it would feel to be boots on the ground, and thinking through strategies. From here she could see the whole picture because of the surveillance cameras and the body cams.

"Matt refueled for me as soon as I landed, so I'm ready for takeoff in less than ten," said Angie, but James shook his head. "Give us thirty." He glanced at Dhillon. "Where's Chance?"

"Left him with Dad and the cat. Stupid dog's in love with her."

"Swagger could use some exercise while I'm gone. I'll leave you to take care of that."

"Got it, Gramps."

The sound of breath suddenly sucked into several sets of lungs was quickly followed by silence. Stillness. Dhillon's eyes rounded, and James blinked. Once.

"You'd best come home with me to check on your critters, then you can come back up with Matt after I take off," said Angie. She got to the door and turned back. "Now, Dhillon." And the kid who had seemed frozen for a couple of beats suddenly darted across the room and down the hall. Angie closed the door quietly, and there was a collective exhale.

"He cracks me up," said Nathan. "Oomph." He rubbed his side where Broughton's elbow had made sharp contact. "What?"

"I'll run you up to get your gear," Julia told her husband. Their home sat on a knoll about a half mile away.

"Kid's got a smart mouth," said James.

"Takes after his mother, and she takes after you," said Julia.

He turned his head and stared at his wife for a moment, until an uncharacteristic grin bloomed. "Because you're the queen of stoic?"

This hint of playfulness between them was something Alex had never seen before, and it made her sort of warm inside, but a bit uncomfortable too. Like she was nosing in on something private.

"Mom's the best smart-mouth in town," said Nathan. "Omph." He glared at Broughton. "Now what? Not like she doesn't know it."

"Broughton. The Steed in thirty," said James, heading for the door with Julia's hand in his.

"The rest of you back here in thirty," she said, and if they'd been younger, Alex might have thought somebody was about to get lucky. Halfway out of her chair, she froze. Why did she think they were too old to be having a quickie before James headed out?

She had to stifle a grin. Chemistry sparkled between the two of them like champagne in a tall glass. They were definitely going to have sex.

The room emptied quickly, and Alex headed off to check on her new roommate. Found him curled in a tight ball behind the toilet. “Hey, buddy.” He stretched out a front leg, spread his toes wide, and yawned hugely, then got slowly to his feet and came to her.

She rubbed his head, and he leaned against her legs. “Awww, were you lonely? Maybe you could come with me tonight and hang out in the war room.” She opened cupboards, searching for a bin or a box she could use to make him a bed. Something she could cover so he’d feel safe. But she came up empty, gave him some more food, and stroked his back for a minute while he ate.

“I’ll find something and get you set up,” she said, backing out and sliding the door closed. And a scream shot up her throat when a hand touched her shoulder. She spun around.

“What the hell?”

Broughton stood with his hands in the air. Not sure if it was a gesture of surrender or simply showing he was unarmed, but it was the look on his face that captured her attention.

“Sorry. Knew better. Just wanted to make sure you were okay with being stood down.”

She chewed the inside of her check while she sorted through how to respond. It was about time she delivered some Grace-style honesty.

“One half of me appreciates you caring enough to come and talk to me.” His face relaxed a bit. “Don’t get comfortable,” she said, and his jaw tightened.

“The other half of me is pissed because you thought you needed to check up on how I’m handling a solid decision made by my leader.

Seriously? If you'd been partnered with one of the other agents, would this be happening right now?"

He backed up a step. Shook his head. "Damned if I do, and damned if I don't. You're a hard woman to figure out, Alex."

"Oh, fuck that. I'm about as straightforward as you'll ever find. As for being stood down? Pfft. Big deal. James doesn't know I wouldn't be a liability, so he can't in good conscience give me that assignment. Tomorrow he'll test me, and then he'll know I can more than hold my own. Period. Tonight I'll pull my weight in the war room."

He nodded. "Good."

She plucked a candy from her pocket, unwrapped it, and popped it in her mouth. "And as for watching me like a freaking hawk, waiting for my blood sugar to tank? Stop it. I'm good, I'm handled. So back off."

He did. Literally. Latched onto the door knob. "I have to go. But when I get back, you and I are going to have to work some shit out."

He was gone before she could even think, *seriously?*

She raked her fingers through her hair. Work some shit out? Yeah. She could get on board with that. It was time he treated her like a capable human being, and not like the fragile woman she was when he met her.

He *was* amazing when they met. Carried her to safety, guarded her, and throat-punched one of the guys…she wouldn't let her mind go back to when she had felt so helpless at the hands of strangers who didn't care whether she lived or died.

Broughton, on the other hand, was caring and gentle and considerate of her every need.

And that was the problem. She didn't need or want that from him now. She was whole. Well. And capable of looking out for herself, *and* doing the job. Yes, she had a wobbly moment back whenever, but it wouldn't happen again. Consuelo had set her up with about ten pounds of wrapped candies to keep in her pockets, and she could carry enough to get her through several days. She was good.

#

Broughton was relegated to the back seat of the Steed. Not his favorite spot, but James was the lead on this op. Back seat would run the search tools while front seat watched screens and called out coordinates. Headquarters would be getting their live feed, with comments typed into the program by James while he assessed the area in question.

The project went smoothly, and they were soon convinced that even though there was a jeep parked at the side of the house, there was no one there. Phase two was initiated.

The Steed's skids barely grazed the earth while the two men jumped out. They crouched low and started the long run across open ground, pelted by the sand and debris kicked up by the helo lifting quickly back into the blackness of the night sky.

Skirting the jeep, they were quickly at the front door, one on each side, prepared to sweep.

Three, two, one. James eased the door open, slipped in and took the right, Broughton went left, and in less than sixty seconds they cleared the entire building.

"Base, Air Two."

"Base, go ahead, Air Two."

"All clear, secondary search underway." Which they already knew, because both men wore cameras and the video was being transmitted to the war room—base for this op. But still, they followed procedure.

Worked the kitchen first, used a search wand, which checked for any kind of spyware or other electronic devices, plus picked up fingerprints and transmitted them electronically to base.

They checked every Mason jar in the pantry for hidden messages, then moved on to the bedroom and bathroom. Found enough clothing to suggest someone lived there on a regular basis. A shaving kit in the bathroom gave weight to that theory, and pulling back a patch of duct tape on the underside of the dresser revealed two fifty-dollar bills. Emergency fund?

In the bathroom, Broughton went through the shaving kit. Noted everything down to the number of new blades and the brand of shaving cream.

James carefully sifted through papers in the desk but came up with little. Most notably, there was a blank, dust-free space on the surface which suggested a laptop normally sat there.

A shed out back held a generator, four empty jerry cans, three large jugs of water, and a small propane tank. And there was a heavy metal ring with a length of chain and a padlock embedded in the concrete floor.

This was what they were looking for. James ran the wand over the links, got a couple of beeps, and stopped to lift the partial fingerprints.

Broughton's instincts were telling him to examine the wall near the chain, and when he crouched down, he was drawn to what looked like scratches, and turned out to be words. Del + Ryder, and yesterday's date.

James.

"Base, Air Three," said Broughton.

"Go ahead, Air Three."

"Are you picking up this visual clearly?"

"Affirmative. Names and date."

Only missed them by a matter of hours, dammit.

"Air Two and Three, Base."

"Go ahead," said James.

"Vehicle exiting the highway, fifteen miles away."

"Copy. Air One?"

"Air One copies, and coming in hot. Two minutes ETA."

"Negative. Air One, stage for level one extraction."

Broughton didn't feel it, but there was a chance Ryder and/or Del were in the approaching car.

"Copy, Level One, Ex."

"Air One, update at five miles out."

"Copy, update at five miles."

For now they had the power. They knew someone was inbound, but that person or persons had no idea their space had been infiltrated. Broughton and James would incapacitate and interrogate, and if Ryder and Del were with them, it would be a grab and go.

"Air Two, target at five miles."

"Copy." Showtime. Broughton took up a position close to the back door, and James went around to cover the front.

Broughton flicked a mental switch and his senses opened wide.

Engine sound came first, through the open flap of his helmet, then a sweep of headlights illuminated the bleakly barren ground.

When the car stopped beside the jeep, Broughton moved to where he had a clear view just before the driver climbed out and wrenched open the back door.

"Enough!"

"Not nearly," came a quiet voice with an edge of strength.

"Shut the fuck up!" He dove in swinging, and there was the unmistakable sound of a fist meeting flesh. "Fuck." He reared back, shaking his hand.

"You're just fucking lucky they wouldn't let me gag you," he growled out. "Don't know why they give a fuck if you die from lack of air or whatever."

"You need to think about what you're doing, how it will affect your position. If you don't follow what they said, you might be out of a job. The car and jeep are theirs too, right? I'd think about that if I were you."

"Shut the fuck up!" The driver slammed the door. "Nobody said I couldn't leave your ass out here for the night," he snarled while he headed for the house, booted feet thudding on hard-packed ground.

James was already at the car. *Keep him in sight and get us a ride.*

Broughton shot into position outside the kitchen window "Air One, contact."

"Copy. Ninety seconds." Although Angie would be hovering directly overhead, she was at about ten thousand feet. Way high to get a good view, and not have downwash giving away her presence.

If James could make it look like Del escaped, the guy in the house would likely spend all day tomorrow looking for him before contacting his superior, because clearly the guy currently sucking down a room temp beer was at the bottom of the food chain.

He tossed the can in the sink, then headed for the back door.

Broughton flattened against the building, put up a shield of energy which made him almost as invisible as the Steed, sucked in a breath, and held it while the idiot stomped outside, whipped out his dick and took a leak.

Steam billowed, and there was a loud belch exactly when Angie started her countdown…making the scene that much more comical. "Ten, nine, eight…"

Broughton slid along the wall and reached the corner about the same time as the guy went inside.

Where are you? James must be at the helo.

On my way. And he was. Closing the vent on his helmet while sprinting to the Steed. He slid the door shut behind him and strapped in while they went airborne.

Anything I need to know?

Nope.

Broughton offered his hand to the man in the seat beside him. “I’m Broughton.”

“Del. Thanks.”

“Talk to us Del. Where’s the kid? What’s going on?”

“I haven’t seen Ryder since yesterday morning. I was blindfolded in the right seat while the kid flew us from here to somewhere about an hour away. Boy’s got guts. Played a bit, tried to make like there was a problem with the plane so they’d take the hood off me, but they didn’t fall for it.”

“How many?”

“Two. The one who’s been with us since the beginning, and the one who brought me back tonight.”

“How long was the trip back?”

“The last leg started just after sunset, but we’d been on the move since first light.”

“Were you able to see anything familiar?”

He held up a piece of black fabric. “Wore this from the time we left here.”

“No food or water?”

He put his hand inside the hood and poked a finger through a small hole. “Just enough for a water bottle.”

Broughton dug in the emergency supply kit for a protein bar. “Not much, but it might help. If you break it in chunks you can get it through the bottom of your helmet.”

“Thanks.” Del made short work of breaking the bar and shoving pieces up and into his mouth.

"Need water? It's a bit trickier."

"Hang on, I can switch now," said Angie, and a green light on the floor indicated they were no longer in noise absorption mode.

"You can pull off the helmet now for a drink, but put it back on right away in case things change." One never knew, and Angie needed to be free to switch back if necessary.

Del guzzled the entire bottle of water, then slid the helmet into place. "Thanks."

"If you're up to it, we need to have details about your capture, and everything since then," said James.

"I'm good," said Dell.

"You don't mind being recorded, of course?" James was a master at wording things to get the response he wanted.

Dell waved a hand. "Whatever." Then he launched into a long narrative, one full of events and descriptions which left Broughton's teeth on edge and a niggling worry in his mind. Ryder was smart but had no mileage on him, so any move he might try was likely to backfire on him, and that was a huge problem.

And it didn't sound as though there had been any contact with Dayson and Mae yet, and that was problematic as well. Meant they were either unaware of what was going on, or knew, and were working a plan of their own—which could put them on a collision path with the Meyers team, and potentially screw things up royally.

"Does Ryder know what these guys are after?" asked Broughton.

"He told me the other night that he believes his parents are alive, and he's being used to pull them in. Seemed a bit of a stretch at first, but I kept thinking about it, and then heard bits and pieces that made it sound like the kid was right."

"You think they know what they're doing?"

"The underlings? The two who dealt with us were bottom-feeders. Can't imagine anyone above them sharing information." He hesitated. "Can't believe we couldn't get away from them." He shrugged. "I had a couple of prime opportunities, but couldn't leave the kid."

"Then they separated you."

"Yeah, mostly. I think the idiot pair thought they were going to be able to ditch me once the kid was delivered. But the instruction was to keep me alive and well in case they needed me to fly the plane. The guy who brought me back desperately wanted to kill me."

"You worked him on the drive."

Del held up a thumb. "Was hoping he'd dump me in a ditch along the way, or at least leave me in the car for the night, like he did. Figured I could make a run for it, so thanks, saved me from a cold night and a lot of miles on foot."

He shrugged again. "But I survived three tours in 'Nam and wasn't exactly young then, either. Figured I could do a couple of New Mexico nights okay."

Broughton was a good judge of age, and would have put this guy in his early seventies if he didn't know he was eighty-five. At a glance he had the posture of an athlete, with squared shoulders and muscular arms. Yeah, a night out on his own would be no big deal.

"Did Ryder say anything about his parents?" asked James. "Or about anything else interesting?"

Del shook his head. "Kid was pretty quiet. Mostly pissed that he was going to be forced to fly illegally, and maybe ferry drugs or arms. I didn't have the heart to tell him it could be a helluva lot worse. What could I say? No point in scaring him senseless. Wasn't like being prepared for the worst would help him get through the now."

Broughton passed him another bottle of water, mostly because he wanted to see his face, the expressions hidden by the helmet.

There was a tremor visible, barely visible when he raised the bottle to his mouth, and his expression was grim.

"What do you think is going to happen to him? What didn't you tell him?"

He recapped the bottle and pulled his helmet on, clearly well aware that he needed to speak into the microphone so all of them could hear his response. As a pilot he was used to that kind of closed communication system.

"Ryder told me everything he saw. In the big house where we were taken, there was a long hallway, and all the doors leading off of it were padlocked. And when they left us, we were chained to big rings set into the floor on either side of the bed…"

Silence stretched for a minute or two while they waited for him to say more, and finally, after a huge sigh, he did. "They were fully prepared to confine human beings, which makes me certain they're traffickers. And most probably selling sex with their captives, right there behind those locked doors." He ran a hand around the back of his neck.

"I told the kid to do whatever they told him. Fly wherever they wanted him to fly, and not make waves."

"That way they'd keep him out of their sex trade?"

"Hopefully. I figured he'd be safe for a week or so, and by that time I'd be able to get help and get him out of there. He was set up to fly to Florida tomorrow. Short hops, low altitude, private strips the whole way."

"So no opportunities to slip off a runway or clip a wing on the side of a hangar or anything else to stop him from flying the next leg and bring in law enforcement, or at least federal investigators," said Angie.

"Exactly. I told him to keep his eyes open for an opportunity, but not to take any big chances. He'd have to be careful in the beginning so they'd get confident about him, and then he could head in to land at a regulated airport, or fake an engine problem and put down on a highway...or something…problem is, all those moves endanger innocent people."

"Some would only think of the lives potentially being saved."

"As long as he thinks this is about running drugs and weapons, he won't do anything stupid. But if he figures out what they're really up to, all bets will be off."

Could they count on him to not do something rash? Hell, at eighteen, if Broughton had been a pilot, he would have landed a plane on a busy California freeway, no problem. No sense of mortality at that age. Or was it a death wish? He and Ryder had both lost their parents before the age of sixteen. Broughton had become reckless and driven in his quest to right the wrongs in the world.

Was Ryder's life similar? Did he have that same feeling of disconnect that dogged Broughton? Or was everything in his life colored by the deeply hidden, guarded belief that his parents' death was staged?

22

Alex's attempt to study the faces of the men entering the war room was severely hampered by the bump of her heart when Broughton caught her stare and raised an eyebrow ever so slightly.

What the hell was that? Playfulness? A question? Not the freaking time or place.

She shook it off, continued with her assessment, but there was nothing to be learned from their expressions, and none looked any the worse for wear. Even the older man they'd extracted from a hostage-like situation appeared to be in good health.

But when his eyes met hers, she saw a boatload of stress, or strain, or worry, or possibly a combination of all three.

"Del Bowdril, meet the team. You know most of them, I think," said James.

The man's gaze tracked from person to person, and there was a nod of recognition for each until

Alex. "Saw you with this group the other day, but I don't know your name."

"Alex. Alexandra."

"You look like Grace."

"She's my cousin."

He nodded.

James then proceeded to update the team, and they were soon looking at the wall map, trying to estimate Ryder's flight path to a location in Florida.

"I know vets who work the horse farms in that area if it's any help," said Alex.

"Thanks. We'll keep that in our back pocket, but for now we'll stick with our own contacts. The farm we already know about is here," he said, making a circle with the pointer. "And I'm betting the strip isn't far away."

He switched to a satellite photo of where they picked up Del.

"See anything special about this area?"

Alex studied it carefully, as did the others, but no one spoke up.

James smiled. "Doesn't look like a good place to land a small jet, does it? But, in fact, this is five thousand feet of concrete runway." He zoomed in, and Alex still saw nothing but a desert-like landscape, complete with cacti, scrub, and boulders of various sizes.

"What you're looking at is a very large painting."

"Holy crap," said Nathan. "The bad guys are stealing the good guys' ideas. That sucks."

"Couldn't believe my eyes when we landed," said Del. "Was ready to take control and pull up before Ryder started a soft field landing, but when you get down close, you can see it's flat. Just a 3-D painting of rocks and bushes and humps of dirt on smooth-as-silk concrete."

"The hole in its effectiveness is the concrete holds heat evenly, which makes it stand out when using infrared technology. We've found a work-around, so the question now is, have they? We'll have to wait and see." He shrugged.

"Now, according to the flight plan Ryder was working on when Del last saw him, he will be leaving an unknown location at eight am, and arriving in Florida at six pm. That gives us plenty of time to find him, as long as they really were stupid enough to let Del know what was in the works."

"I convinced them he was too green a pilot to be making a cross-country plan by himself. That he'd need me to confirm his fuel calculations so they didn't all end up in a heap in some field, or trying to land on a busy highway."

"Then let's rescue him based on you being far smarter than they are," said Grace, with a hint of something odd in her voice which made Alex focus on her—which was foolish, because Grace was a master at subterfuge, and nothing ever showed.

A tingling began at the base of Alex's neck, and she took care to keep her own expression neutral while she glanced from face to face. No one else seemed to be affected.

Should she? Her gut said yes. She slipped inside the corridors of her mind, pushed open a small window, and a breeze blew in, making the filmy curtains flutter, but no Grace. Alex closed the window and moved on to the next, and the next, and found no one trying to connect with her.

But the tingling didn't let up, and had to be some kind of warning, but of what? She opened her senses wide while still trying to pay attention to the detailed plans for using another agency to do thermal imaging around the Florida farm.

Her training included a ton of information about the kind of technology they were talking about, but she had no field experience. Nothing to add.

Swagger had come in with James and lay beside his master's chair, but now was sitting up, leaning against James's legs, his attention completely centered on the man he took care of.

Alex wasn't the only one feeling something was off. Or was she simply picking up on the dog's concern?

Swagger was able to sense when James was having a bad time and distract him, break his thought pattern, pull him back to the present if the past was threatening to grab him by the throat. Perhaps it was just the presence of a stranger. Her glance flicked from the dog to the newcomer, and she was startled to find Del staring at her. Had she possessed the ability, she'd have lifted an eyebrow in question. Instead, she stared back for as long as she could, but when he didn't break contact, she finally did, and couldn't help but rub the back of her neck.

When she looked up, again, it was Broughton staring at her, and she wanted him to know about her odd feeling. To hell with protocol. She used her inner voice to prod at his mind.

Something off.

Off? His response was so fast she wondered if he'd already been listening to her thoughts.

Tingling at the back of my neck, and Del was staring at me, hard, like I'm a puzzle he needs to solve.

You're one helluva puzzle.

Seriously?

Sorry. Probably just curiosity, since he's known everyone else for years.

Okay. She thought it was more than that, but she needed to focus on the op now James was moving on from the Florida portion of the plan to what would happen here.

The team was split into three groups, and rotation would be three-hour stretches beginning at five am. Alex wasn't on until eight, with Grace, Logan, and Broughton.

Good. Hours before she'd have to deal with him again. Sleep was calling, and she was happy to answer.

Arriving in her room she found the cat stretched out on her bed.

"Well, don't you look comfortable." She was glad she'd released him from the bathroom earlier. "You're just the kind of nonjudgmental bedfellow I need tonight."

"Ouch."

Alex spun to find Broughton leaning on the door she was certain she had locked. "You did that invisible thing again, and I don't like it."

He shrugged started across the room. "I didn't

think you would let me in."

"You were right."

"We need to talk."

"Ha-ha. You need to talk, but I don't feel like listening. I want you to leave."

"No."

She marched past him, determined to open the door and shoo him out, but he grabbed her by the arm, and she froze.

"Don't." She made no effort to pull away. Couldn't. Her heart pounded against her ribs and echoed in her ears, drowning out the sound of his voice while she stared at his moving mouth.

The past hammered at her mind, snapshots flickered in her memory, and then he took her by both shoulders and shook her. It wasn't much at first, but grew, and grew until the world went dark and sparkles filled her vision. She wrenched away, staggering backwards, and landed on the edge of the bed with angry words and bits of images swirling in her mind.

She bent double so her head was between her knees, and took a huge gulp of air. Another. Another. Barely letting one out before drawing the next one in. She forced her breathing to slow until the prickling in her hands and feet began to fade.

The cat rubbed against her side, and she sat up, pulling him into her lap. He reared to bump his forehead under her chin, and she snuggled him in close before glancing at Broughton, who was right where she'd left him.

Alex took the cat with her to an armchair near

the window. His purring anchored her while she worked on slowing her heart rate from a frantic gallop to a more sedate pace.

Broughton sat in the chair across from her. "Who hurt you, Alexandra?"

She sighed. Hated that he knew. "Old news."

"Obviously it still affects you, and that makes me want to gut the bastard, one organ at a time."

"Too late."

"It's never too late."

"Um, cremation makes you wrong on that one."

He shoved at his hair. "He's dead?"

"They have rules about cooking live people."

He rubbed his hands over his face.

"Tell me the story."

"No."

"I've never met a woman so comfortable with that word."

"It's one of my favorites."

"No shit. Why won't you tell me?"

"It's ancient history I'd rather not revisit."

"But a reaction like the one I just saw suggests it's not forgotten."

"PTSD is real. I have it. So do you. I have my triggers, you have yours. Refrain from grabbing me forcefully and trying to control me, and I doubt we'll ever have a problem."

"I want to know."

"Are you prepared to tell me about some of the horrendous shit you've been through? About your PTSD?"

"There's no need—"

"Exactly. So back off. I'm fine. And let me add

that if a man had grabbed you the way you just did me, you might have swung first, asked questions later. Next time that's what I'll do." If she wasn't frozen in the spot by a flashback of terror. "You don't get to manhandle me just because..." She clamped her mouth shut on the rest of the sentence.

No point putting it into words. Just wasn't necessary.

Broughton straightened. "Even with that off the table, we still need to talk."

"About what?"

"About what's happening between us."

"Or not. I think we both clearly stated our positions. Point one. I want a relationship. You don't. No discussion necessary. Point two. We have to work together as partners without letting our feelings get in the way. Agreed."

Broughton stretched his legs out in front of him, crossed one booted foot over the other, and closed his eyes. Was he going to take a nap, right here in the middle of their conversation?

But they weren't having a conversation, were they?

"You need to go to your own room now and get some sleep."

"You're right. Right about that and everything else." He opened one eye. "Does that make you feel better?"

Why did she suddenly feel laughter bubbling up inside of her? Wasn't she still pissed at him for scaring her? For everything?

He still stared at her with one bright blue eye, looking like some kind of cartoon character, and a strangled laugh escaped her.

Now his eyebrow went up and she laughed again. Recognized the slightly out-of-control feeling that came just before she had the kind of laughing fit that got her kicked out of class when she was in high school. The kind of laughter that felt incredibly good, and left her completely exhausted. Even a bit lightheaded—like she needed to go there again today.

He was watching her now with both eyes open, and a half smile on his face. "You're about to lose it, aren't you?"

And that's all it took to push her over the edge into uncontrollable laughter. She slapped a hand over her mouth and rocked in the chair. The cat—being a wise feline—deserted her for the middle of the bed to park and watch from there.

Wiping the streaming tears from her cheeks and catching her breath as she regained control, she caught sight of the indignant look on the displaced feline's face and was suddenly at it again, bent double with laugh cramps in her belly and an inability to breathe.

When the torrent finally slowed again, with her breath only hitching now and again, it was over, and she sat back with what had to be a silly grin on her face.

"Interesting," he said, and she fought to maintain her sober façade. "You do that often?"

She shrugged. "Not so often as an adult, but I guess I had steam to let off."

"Gotta say it's easier to take than a crying jag, or raging in anger. You do cold and measured too well. Yelling would be a complete waste of energy."

"Cold and measured?" Not words she ever wanted a man to say about her. At least not a man she thought she was in love with. She shut down that thought. *Not going there.*

"You need to leave so I can get some sleep. I know we don't start until eight, but I'm beat and need a few solid hours."

"I could keep you company…" he smiled and got to his feet. "Just kidding. Well, unless you're interested…"

She stared hard at him.

"Which clearly you aren't." He stopped at the door. "Good-night kiss is out of the question?"

"Out."

But when he was gone, she wished she'd said yes, because she longed for the taste of him again.

"Not going to happen," she told the cat.

#

Broughton tossed back a swallow of whiskey, and wished it was the burn of Alex on his lips instead. But it would have the opposite effect. Wasn't often he resorted to booze to help him fall asleep, but now and again it was useful. Pissed him off when a doctor offered him prescription help with sleep, suggesting that his heritage made alcohol a bad choice.

Didn't anyone ever do their homework? It was appalling to think a doctor would believe something based on stereotyping. Oh sure, there was empirical data, but from what Broughton learned years earlier, the studies were flawed. Seriously flawed.

Had alcohol killed his father? Or had living on the streets killed him? Yes, the two went together, but his father wasn't homeless because of the booze, and that was something Broughton would never, ever forget.

In spite of the shot of whiskey, he lay awake for a very long time, wishing he could hear Alex breathing next to him, feel the heat of her at his side. He wanted to roll over and draw her against him, hold her there to keep her safe. To keep them both safe from the demons of the dark.

Good memories tickled the edges of his mind like soft fingertips, bad memories had nails to scrape and gouge.

In self-defense he used a ritual taught to him by his grandmother when he was just a boy, feeling abandoned by his parents.

He flopped over on his back and lay with his palms up and open, concentrating on moving energy up from the center of his being, then down his arms to pool in his hands. Once the intensity of power built until it could no longer be contained, he began a silent chant, directing the energy to his list of people—always in the same order.

First to his parents, who were long dead, he sent love, and gratitude for what they gave him, how they sacrificed for him.

Then he chanted silently to the list of living, wishing each and every person whose face appeared on the screen of his memory health, love, courage, and happiness. There were people who had only once crossed his path, and others with a long history of knowing him. It included his grandparents, the entire cast of Meyers, Ryder and his family, and Alex.

He was drifting off to sleep with a smile on his face and her image in his mind when there was a loud knock on his door, and he shot out of bed. Pants on and weapon in hand in mere seconds, he called out, “What is it?”

“War room in ten. Be ready to roll.”

Unable to identify the voice for sure, he jerked open the door. Nathan was marching away.

“What’s up?”

The young man glanced back but never broke stride. “Trouble.” And he was gone.

He and his twin had been on duty for the night, and nothing about this op lent itself to a sudden change of plans, so Broughton couldn’t figure out what might have happened. And that annoyed him.

Ready to roll meant he was about to hit the field and only had minutes to prepare. This was his normal, and steps came without thought. He stripped, washed, brushed, and calculated the time since he’d taken the whisky. All good. He grabbed a roll of fresh clothes from his duffle and dressed. Cargos, shirt, vest, weapon. He stuffed his pockets, laced the boots, grabbed his jacket and gear bag, and headed out.

James and Julia were alone in the war room when he got there, and Angie pounded in moments later, followed almost instantly by Alex. She was wearing exactly the same clothes as he was, but it made her look sexy as hell. What was it about a dead serious-looking woman wearing a shoulder holster that was so damned hot?

James closed the door. "We have reason to believe Ryder is in flight now, headed for Florida."

Broughton maintained eye contact with James, waiting to hear more.

"A low-flying aircraft has been spotted on a similar route to the one Ryder was supposed to be taking several hours from now."

"Spotted?" Alex looked alert, like she'd managed a few hours of sleep while he lay awake thinking about her.

"Using one of the satellite programs Nathan and Tyler developed for a particular government agency. In layman's terms, think radar pointed down from a satellite instead of up from the ground."

"Where?" asked Broughton.

"About halfway between here and Florida, which means it's unlikely the Steed can catch up with him before he reaches his destination, but we'll try just in case his fuel stops are slow. Meantime, Logan and Grace are about to take off in the jet, with Nathan and Tyler along. The hope is for the boys to get them to the right area, where Grace might be able to make a connection with the hostages."

"Wait," said Angie. "The boys freed the girls and the workers from that farm already, so you're saying there are more?"

"Del is suggesting that's the case."

"Del…" Alex murmured, and Broughton watched her face, trying to figure out what she was thinking, but came up empty.

"That group won't be slowing down any. They

would be out recruiting within days, maybe even hours, if the powers above them were pissed about losing what they had."

"That's where Grace's skills are a perfect fit. Newly recruited or grabbed individuals are the easiest to make a connection with, because they're traumatized and sending off waves of fear."

"If Ryder follows what Del says was his flight plan, Logan should have his group within striking distance before Ryder gets there."

Wait. "You know the destination? Found the runway?"

"Not yet, exactly," said James, leaving a helluva lot unsaid while he rubbed Swagger's head. Instead of being down and relaxed, the dog was standing as though prepared to move. Did he sense his master was about to depart? Or was James on edge and Swagger on guard, prepared to help him?

Angie held up a hand. "If there is nothing I need to know before we're in the air, I'd like to go now and get the bird fired up, let Matt know what's going on and shoot Dhillon an email with tomorrow's lessons."

"Go ahead," said James, and Angie shoved out of her chair. Left without a backward glance.

"Alex, you're on this op because we might have to utilize your contacts for cover, and if we pick anyone up with the Steed, I want a female for them."

Broughton wanted to object because she hadn't been cleared yet for this kind of op, but that would be out of line, and the look on Alex's face suggested that if he dared to say anything, she'd geld him.

James flicked a glance at the clock. “Helipad in ten. We’ll finish the briefing in the air.” He dragged his keyboard close, and soon had it rattling.

“Supplies,” said Julia. “Consuelo is packing for you. Stop on the way out.”

“Perfect. I’ll ask her to feed the cat for me in the morning.”

“What about Dhillon? Would you be okay with him doing the cat-sitting?”

“Absolutely.”

“Good. It will help make up for being left behind yet again. Not that Dhillon normally goes on ops, but he was pumped about that surveillance gig.”

Alex slung a small pack over her shoulder, and Broughton followed her to the kitchen, where they found Consuelo with two cold bags stuffed to capacity and a pile of blankets with a carrying strap.

“Sandwiches on the top of the blue bag are for you to eat now,” said Consuelo. “It’s the middle of the night, and all of you need fuel right away, because who knows when you’ll get to eat again. You won’t be in noise-cancelling mode for the first while, so take advantage of having your helmets off.”

Broughton set the blankets on top of one of the coolers.

“I’ve put in lots of protein bars, nuts, and cookies because you might be picking up some damned hungry kids. And the blankets are thin but warm, and will be more comforting than one of those fancy tinfoil things.”

She pressed her mouth into a hard line, and Broughton could feel the emotions she was barely hanging on to. Had to be difficult for a woman who spent her life looking after people, keeping them fed, warm, and well, to even imagine the hunger and chill of those whose freedom had been stolen from them.

"We'll get them out, and we'll bring them to you to fill up with food and love," he promised her.

"Your lips to God's ear." She held out her arms, and with no choice, he stepped into a hug the size of Manhattan.

23

Alex was surprised—yet not—by the softness in Broughton's voice, the gentle way he cupped the older woman's face and planted a kiss on her forehead.

"Go get some sleep. You need energy for when we get back." Alex didn't bother to argue when he stuck his arm though the blanket strap and hefted both bags of food. If he wanted to insist upon being a pack mule, that was his problem. But when they reached the parked vehicles, she took point and selected one of the golf carts. Hopped in and turned the key while he was busy loading the supplies into the back.

He took his place on the passenger side without comment, and never said a word until they were parked in front of Angie's house. The Steed was uncovered, and the doors open.

Broughton lugged the bags to the chopper and Alex followed, staring at his wide shoulders and wondering what it would take to have him regard her as capable—because equal she would never be. He had years of experience. Had seen and done it all, she was sure. What she wanted from him was respect for her training, for her ability to read a situation, and for her physical strength.

She regularly dealt with twelve-hundred-pound stallions, lifted full muck buckets, and tossed around eighty-pound bales of hay. She could stay in a crouch for an hour while suturing a leg wound, or go shoulder-deep inside the birth canal of a mare having contractions. Vets were physically and mentally strong and agile.

"If you're mad at me, you need to leave it at the door," he said quietly.

"Consider it done." She wouldn't—couldn't—ask for what she needed from him. It would have to come naturally. And it would. Of that she was certain, because she'd show him, one way or another, how capable she really was. In the meantime? She did trust him. And that was the main thing.

James arrived then, and Angie came out of the house, climbed in the Steed, and minutes later they were off the ground, headed east.

Broughton passed out the sandwiches and soft drinks, and the briefing began as soon as she and Broughton donned the earbuds James handed them.

The goal was to rescue Ryder and as many others as there might be. Since the aircraft he was flying was a four-seater, and there would have to be at least one armed guard, there was only room for two passengers.

However, without concern for individual safety, and based on weight alone, they could be planning to cram in a lot more.

If that was the case, they'd have to be split between the Steed and the jet. And if they stumbled upon a really large cache of kids, Nathan and Tyler would stay behind to make more room.

Alex wanted to ask about law enforcement or other agencies they would be working with, but without a helmet on, she had no mic.

Glancing at Broughton one seat over, she was surprised to see his eyes closed, and no tension in his body. Had he been anyone else, she would have wondered if he was sleeping. She caught herself staring at his mouth, thinking about the last time it had touched hers, and she quickly looked away.

This was neither the time nor the place for such thoughts. Distractions.

Was that why his eyes were closed? So her presence wouldn't interfere with his concentration? The thought warmed her.

"Alex." Her attention went to James as he detailed what would be expected of her in each possible scenario, depending on how the mission unfolded. Even though there had been no time for testing her abilities himself, he was trusting her, and with every fiber of her being she absorbed her leader's instructions.

This op was about to get very, very real.

#

When James announced they'd be switching to noise-cancelling mode in five minutes, Alex popped a couple of almonds into her mouth and crunched them quickly. Took a long swallow of water, and pulled on her helmet. Concentrated on keeping her heart rate and breathing within normal range. It was way too soon for an adrenaline bump.

"Testing." Alex shot a glance over her shoulder, the direction Angie's voice came from, and was quickly reminded she would be hearing separately from each ear. The earbud in her right was connected to James, and she could only hear the helmet speaker through her left.

"Welcome aboard flight 123, bound for sunny Florida, land of sunshine, oranges, and half the retired population of North America. Does everyone have their helmets in place and their seats in the upright position?"

Alex laughed. "Affirmative."

"Affirmative," said Broughton, and Alex had to fight the reflex to look left again.

"Prepare for descent." She was all business now.

"Update," said James. "Looks like Ryder has yet to depart from his last fuel stop. Could be that was his final destination."

"Makes sense," said Broughton, "for them to set Del and the kid up with misinformation."

"Grace has made contact with one subject. No location yet."

A sudden beat of energy had Alex shooting a glance at Broughton just in time to see him flex his fingers. Then he leaned forward, braced his elbows on his knees and let his hands hang between them.

She'd bet he could be in full flight from that position in little more than a heartbeat. He was powerful in a way that distracted from his physical presence, because his strength was more of an internal thing, a commitment of his being—because he believed.

And she knew this because she felt connected to him at a level that was soul deep. Otherworldly.

Alex had never been a fairy tale kind of girl. Didn't believe in love at first sight or soul mates. She didn't get other women's obsessions with men. Yet here she sat, in the middle of what was about to become a volatile and probably very dangerous situation, feeling like a part of her would be going out the door with him when the helo touched down—even though she was ordered to stay on board.

Broughton and James would do the recon. Alex wasn't to set foot outside, and of course, Angie stayed with the aircraft.

Where they were landing was an unknown, aside from the satellite map up on the screens—one in the control panel, and one on the bulkhead behind Angie. A grass runway with a single hangar, a barn, paddocks, one large, fenced field, a riding ring, and a house.

No horses visible, and although that made Alex curious, it wasn't really noteworthy, because it was a bright, sunny day, and show horses were often only turned out at night so they didn't get sunburned coats.

But there was more. "No sign of the ring being used for riding," she said. "There are small jumps set up, but I can't see from this far out if there are tracks to suggest they've been used."

James's hands went to a keyboard, and the photo was zoomed to show only the riding area.

"No tracks," she said. "Maybe even a bit of grass growing there. Go to the paddocks and field."

The view changed, and it was clear. "Undisturbed. I'd bet there are no horses on the property."

"I've got a live shot now," said James and the screen went back to a wide view of the property. It looked exactly the same until he zoomed in, and she could see what looked like tire tracks down the middle of the runway.

"Incoming? Or outbound?"

"Research department says a plane arrived here an hour ago and nothing left, so it has to be in that hangar. We'll make one pass overhead with all systems and cameras engaged."

A large screen slid down from the ceiling like a garage door and came to life once it was in position in the space between Angie and James, and flush with the bulkhead behind them.

Divided into four quadrants, they had a view of what each camera was picking up and Alex had to squelch a fist-pumping *Yes!*

Thermal imaging showed people inside the house and the barn, and one in the hangar. Would that be Ryder? Unlikely, because there was no guard with him, but then he could be restrained. But he wasn't near a wall. Not that he couldn't be chained to the floor, or simply left there hogtied.

Once they had their data, they went back through the images, mining information.

"Ground is worn like a path from the hangar to

the barn, and there's a tunnel from the barn to the house. Heads up for sensors and booby traps at ground level," said James.

"Agreed," said Broughton. "At least one guard in the barn. They're definitely protecting access to the house."

"Four adults in one room, could be the kitchen. Downstairs there's a guard at the tunnel egress, and the others are smaller, spaced evenly around the perimeter of a large room which suggests a dorm or holding area, and they'll be chained."

Alex was amazed by the technology, and by the skill of the readers. She had only seen a big bunch of people, some sort of superimposed over others. She hadn't understood there was a second floor underneath a house which appeared to be a one-level rancher.

"Bolt cutters," said Angie. "They're on the underside of your seat, Alex. Fastened with Velcro."

Alex bent and groped until she found the edge of the fastener and ripped it open. Expecting a long-handled and slightly awkward tool to drop into her hand, she was surprised by something that looked more like a miniature stun gun. She stared, trying to figure out how it worked.

"All you have to do is slip the U-shaped end around what you want to cut, and squeeze the trigger."

"Cool." Should she be wondering, asking how it worked?

"Stick it in your pocket so it's handy," said Broughton.

Her pocket? As though reading her mind he said, "We each have one already, so you hang on to that one just in case."

Broughton was expecting her to go in with them now?

She slipped it into the right side pocket of her pants and then quickly pulled it out. Switched it to her left hand. Tested the weight, the feel, and skimmed her finger over the outside of the trigger area in a movement similar to what it would take to engage. Then she slipped it to the thigh pocket on her left leg. Much better. Her right hand had to be free for her gun.

"Broughton and I will take out the guards and head upstairs while you release the prisoners and get them into the tunnel. I don't see much cover besides the hangar, Angie."

She was going in. She slipped out of her safety harness, jacket, vest, and shoulder holster. Put them back on, vest first, because, in spite of being comfortably thin, it was bulletproof. Then her holster, and finally the jacket, which was loose enough that it wouldn't hamper reaching for her weapon.

"I'll do two sweeps using downwash to create the illusion of gusting of wind, then settle behind the hangar. They might notice the first pass, but by the third they'll be lulled into complacency. Downwash won't even be noted, and of course, we're fully invisible and soundless, but I'll leave the thermal imaging engaged, just to keep an eye on them."

Two people went to the window at the first pass

and turned away at the second.

Before touching down, Alex rechecked the laces on her boots—again—then touched her fingertips to the top of the zip on her vest, laid a hand over her weapon. She slipped a candy up through the tiny opening in the helmet and crunched it quickly.

Broughton passed her a small black sphere. "Put it in your left ear now so you can pull off your helmet just before we touch down."

"I won't be able to hear Angie."

"You'll have me," said James, and she placed the earplug as instructed. "Stay with Broughton until I eliminate the first two guards."

She glanced at her partner. His eyes met hers, and she nodded. He pointed at her safety harness, then unclipped his own and drew it over his head. She followed suit.

"In ten," said James.

Broughton crouched at the door with one hand wrapped around the handle and the other on the bulkhead. Alex positioned herself behind him.

"Three, two, one, go."

The door slid sideways, and they were on the ground running, following James to the side door of the building. They stayed there, backs against the wall, while James slipped in. Alex took one long, slow breath, let it out.

"Clear."

Broughton pushed inside, and she was right on his heels. There was one plane and a helicopter inside, and a dead guy. According to the Steed's surveillance electronics, there were no cameras in the hangar, but she still did a fast glance-around, searching, just in case. All those training scenarios Grace drilled her with had not been a waste of time.

The tunnel entrance was at the bottom of a set of wooden stairs. She lightened her step, going down them soundlessly in Broughton's equally silent wake.

There they waited. Alex took long, slow breaths, concentrating on achieving optimal oxygenation. Her heart rate was up just enough, and not too much.

"Clear."

Broughton wrenched open the door and ran through the tunnel with Alex close behind. James was waiting with his back to a closed door.

He tipped his chin toward a couple of chairs pulled up to a typical rec-room bar, where someone had recently been playing cards and drinking coffee. "Handled."

She guessed the bodies were behind the bar.

"I told the girls you were coming, Alex," James said, "and they have to go with you to stay safe. We're going up. Activate your mic now."

She touched a button on the collar of her vest and whispered, "Test."

James and Broughton both gave her a thumbs-up, and then James eased the door open for her to slip in, and closed it softly behind her.

Concrete floor. Bare mattresses. Nine girls wearing nothing but oversized white T-shirts and ankle chains attached to rings embedded in the floor.

Alex shook off the horror and the anger. She

had a job to do, and she was fixing a terrible wrong.

"I'm Alex, and I'm getting you out of here." She went to the girl on her immediate left. "What's your name?"

"Jenna."

"Stay really still for me, Jenna." Alex slipped the bolt cutter around the chain on the girl's ankle and with two cuts popped a link. "Stay right here, okay? We all have to leave together or we can't get out safely."

She knelt beside the next mattress, narrowly missing a bucket, and barely noticing it was a crude toilet. "What's your name?"

"Jenna."

It registered somewhere in the back of her mind, but she was too busy releasing the shivering child to think about her having the same name as the first. When the link snapped, she kept hold of the cold foot. Glanced around, but saw nothing. Pulled off her jacket and put it around the girl.

She went to the next.

"What's your name?"

There was no answer and Alex glanced up and into a face consumed with fear. She lowered her voice. "It's okay, little one, I'm going to get you out of here. What's your name?"

"Jenna," she whispered.

Okay, so that was just weird. The cutter engaged. Another one free.

The rest of the girls were equally quiet, and all said their name was Jenna.

Alex shoved at the sick feeling in her gut when she scurried toward the tight little group beside the door. She would not think about what had happened to them. For now, it had to be enough that it would never happen again.

"On our way," she said, for the benefit of her team.

Then she turned to the huddled girls. "When I open this, I'll look around first. If it's okay, you're going to go to the left and out. Just follow the long hallway." Fuck, there was a dead guy at the other end. "But don't go up the stairs. Wait for me to check for safety first."

Three of the girls ran ahead, the rest walked, and one grabbed Alex by the pants leg and held on. The one with her jacket stumbled twice, and Alex finally picked her up, carried her the rest of the way. She was stiff, like rigor had already set in, and Alex had to fight her instincts.

This was neither the time nor the place to stop and console the child. It was more important to get her out of here first. Get them all the hell out. Once the men were back and the Steed was in the air, there would be plenty of time for the rest of it.

The men were silent, and she was hoping it meant all was well, but she feared it was just because their mics were turned off, because otherwise, shouldn't she have heard something? Anything?

Her heart crawled up her throat.

When they were gathered at the base of the steps she said, "We have to stick close together now. Everyone grab hands."

Obediently they did as they were told, and stared up at her.

"Okay, here we go. I'm going to lead." She went up the stairs and circled around the plane so they didn't have to pass the dead guy to get to the side door. She opened it, glanced around.

"You stronger, faster girls go ahead and hop in the helicopter right there so you can help pull the others up."

Three of them raced across the grass and clambered into the Steed. They helped the rest in, and Alex climbed aboard with the last one still in her arms.

One of the older ones was already trying to close the door.

"Wait, we have to wait for the men to come."

"No!"

"The men who brought me here to rescue you. They're good men, and they made it so you could get away," she said, setting her bundle on one of the six seats.

"This is Angie," she said, pointing at the pilot who was watching them. She tapped her ears and pointed at the girls. Angie nodded and leaned back, reaching around the bottom of the bulkhead to open a drawer filled with noise-cancelling headsets.

Alex passed them out. "When we're ready to take off, it will get really noisy in here, so you will have to wear these to protect your ears."

Alex caught Angie's eye again and tapped her earbud, raised her eyebrows. She was getting really worried about James and Broughton. What if they were captured, or injured, or worse? What if the men in the house came out here? Shit.

"Okay, here's the deal, girls. There is food and

water in those bags," she said while digging the stack of blankets out of the cabinet of silence. "I need you to help each other grab a snack, wrap up in a blanket, and strap into a seat so you're ready for takeoff. Some of you can double up. I'm just going to stand outside here and wait for the others. I have to trust that you will be ready to go when I get back in, and you don't have to worry about anything, because Angie is badass, and she's got your back."

Was she supposed to talk to kids that way? Who knew? She was more comfortable dealing with animals, creatures who didn't speak, and who she understood how to comfort.

She slipped around the back of the Steed so the girls couldn't see her, but she still had a clear view of the door. She palmed her weapon. If anyone but Broughton or James stepped out of that building, she was going to shoot first and ask questions later.

"I have the door in my sights, so I suggest telling me if you're coming through," she said, hoping and praying Broughton and James were listening.

Training said aim for the largest target, which was mid body. Three quick shots, and if he didn't go down, aim higher. It was tough to make a head shot, but if they wore body armor, it was the only choice she had.

The air around her was preternaturally still. As though she had stepped outside the real world, into a space between realities. Neither here nor somewhere else.

Alex opened her senses, waiting for something to go bump, or recognition to happen, but there was nothing.

She wanted to peer around the hangar and look at the house, but knew she couldn't do that. What the hell was taking so long? She glanced at her watch. Twenty minutes since they'd hit the ground running. Seemed like so much longer.

"Coming out."

Jerked out of her thoughts, she grinned when something white was waved from the cracked-open doorway. "Don't shoot."

Broughton and James emerged, and although there had been teasing in that voice, their expressions were grim. "Time to get the hell out of Dodge," said James.

Broughton touched Alex's shoulder. It wasn't much more than a brush of his fingertips, but she felt it down to the soles of her feet. Something was wrong.

She climbed into the Steed and smiled at the girls. "We can go now." Nine pairs of eyes stared as Broughton strapped himself into one of the empty seats.

Alex counted heads. The little one she'd carried was lying in the Cabinet of Silence—a compartment that could be sealed to make it soundproof and suitable for transporting children too young for headphones, and animals. A second youngster was with her, and the other seven were crammed into three seats, having managed to fasten themselves in with the safety harnesses. They clearly wanted to be together that way, so it didn't matter that there was a spare seat.

All nine slipped on their headsets.

Alex popped out the black earbud and donned her helmet, asking, “Do the kids have sound in those things?”

“Negative,” said Angie. “Our conversation will be private.”

Alex knew she should wait for James to begin the debrief but couldn’t hold back. “Ryder?”

“Not here.” The Steed lifted off before James continued. “Never was here. Not our plane in the hangar. Looks like it’s a common route, well used by traffickers when they’re moving their product around. Their term, not mine. We accessed their computers and copied everything on them. Ryder wasn’t on their roster for inbounds today, but he is on it for an outbound shipment tomorrow, so the feds are coming in to do cleanup here, and set up for a possible encounter tomorrow just in case we miss him today.”

“Today?”

“Nathan is tracking another aircraft on the exact route Del expected Ryder to be on. It’s about four hours behind us, so there’s time to drop off our charges and get in position.”

Alex glanced at the girls. “They all say their name is Jenna.”

“Whatever they’ve been through,” said James, “they need professional help. We’re taking them to a group who regularly handles this kind of case. They’re a private facility Grace works with, and the girls will get the best possible care.”

She couldn’t imagine what it was like to be them, and she could only hope they would one day be able to have lives that were comfortable. That they would learn there were good people in the world. The kind they could trust and depend on.

"Grace and Logan are doing the transfer. They've left Nathan and Tyler at their target location, and should make it back before Ryder gets there if we miss him."

Feeling him staring at her, Alex turned to look at Broughton, and he winked. She tipped her head in a show of curiosity and although the helmet hid much of his face, she could tell by his eyes he was smiling.

What the heck? If she didn't know better, she'd think he was flirting with her.

"By the way," he said. "Nice job. Handled the kids and the situation like a pro."

Pleasure warmed her as much as surprise did. The man behind *those* words was the one she'd fallen head over heels in love with months ago. The one who—once she was recovered—vanished like smoke on a windy day.

And here she was, letting him get to her again. Nope. Not going there. He didn't want a relationship, and she wanted nothing less.

But wasn't turnabout fair play?

She winked at him before returning her attention to the girls. Dug cookies out of the cooler and passed them around. She crouched to pass snacks to the two in the COS, and when she straightened, a tiny hand wrapped around her ankle.

Alex sat on the floor, and offered her own hand, which was quickly taken between two cold ones. Should she pull the child out and hold her?

"What's our ETA to the meet?"

“Ten minutes,” Angie replied.

Not long enough to bother. Big, brown eyes stared into hers. Oh, what the heck. She slid the child out and into her lap, wrapped the blanket tighter, and held on. The other one gave her a look, and Alex nodded. She usually felt inept and a bit helpless around children, but this was different. They needed, and she was able to provide.

24

Broughton studied the woman currently confusing the hell out of him. She was something his granny would call an enigma, and it was playing havoc with his gut.

His glance took in the rest of the girls. It was rare for him to have trouble staying detached, but what he'd seen in that house and on those computers had lit a fire in him. He only wished he and James hadn't already eliminated the men there, because to be able to keep them alive and torture them for a while would have given him great pleasure.

Dealing them even the tiniest bit of payback might have helped him deal with this sea of troubled faces, because he'd have known he made their tormenters suffer. Instead, these children had months...no, years...ahead of them, tortured by memories, but those responsible had lucked into swift endings.

He had to stop thinking. Get out of his head and back into the now. The op. The forward motion. They would drop the girls with Grace. Then he would go on to find Ryder. Save him from a fate not unlike...

Stop.

Focus.

Look at Alex with the two youngest sleeping in her arms. A pair of brown eyes popped open, stared into his.

I'm not asleep.

Holy shit.

That's swearing.

Broughton rubbed a hand over his face and considered throwing another layer of protection over the word thoughts in his mind...but didn't. She deserved more.

You startled me. Were you listening for long?

You were wishing you did awful things to those men...with your knife.

I'm sorry you saw those private thoughts.

I also wish you could have hurt them the way you wanted to. The way they hurt others.

You're safe now.

What will you do with me?

A lady named Grace is going to take you to a wonderful place where you and the others will be safe and well cared for. Then you'll be able to go home.

No.

No?

I'll just take off again.

You might have other options.

I hated living on the street, but I was safe there, safe until...

Broughton frowned.

How old are you?

Fourteen.

Hey, I'm being honest with you. How old are you really?

Old enough that I don't have to go back. That's fourteen in my home state.

Where you're going, you get to decide where you'll live, no matter what your age. You can stay right there until you're twenty-one if you like, and there are people working there who are just like you, and never wanted to leave.

Really?

Really. How old are you?

Nine.

He lifted an eyebrow.

Honest. I'm really small for my age.

How long were you on the street?

I don't know. A few years, I guess.

Where did you stay? Sleep?

People would take me in sometimes, and I'd stay awhile, but then this dude offered me a place. Said I could have a room all to myself if I was willing to work for it. Keep his friends happy.

Broughton's gut clenched.

What happened?

He gave me a room, just like he said, and some nice clothes, and I got my nails done and my hair dyed, and I partied with his pals and had a lot of fun.

Sex?

I learned to give good head for twenty bucks. Then a guy came and checked me out, handed Marvin a wad of cash, and things got really fucked up after that. Now I'm here in a frosty ride.

What about your family?

Her tone went cold. *I took off the second time my mother tried to sell me to a guy. She was jonesing for a fix, and one of her regulars offered her double to do me instead of her. Lucky for me she decided to haggle and sent me to the bathroom to get prettied up. I went out the window.*

The worst part about her story was that he'd heard similar ones before. Not in person, from the victim, but he knew shit like this happened, and there were so many fucking layers to the horrors of what could happen to a child when the people responsible for their well-being let them down.

What's your name?

Jenna.

Why are you all using the same name?

One of the ladies we were with told us it was a way to stay safe. No one would focus in on one of us if we all had the same name. And then it made us like sisters.

Does everyone hear telepathic voices?

He followed her glance toward the others, and they all nodded.

I think Alexandra should be in on this conversation, then, don't you?

Sure.

He opened the pathway. *Alex, the girls and I were having a conversation and figured you'd like to be in on it.*

Her eyes met his, and he smiled.

Well, hey, everyone. Has Broughton told you about Grace yet?

A bit.

She glanced at the child tucked under her arm. Good. She'd been able to follow the thread back to the source.

Grace is a gifted telepath.

What is a telepath?

Alex smiled. *What you all are. Able to communicate silently. Grace will be taking you to a wonderful place where you can be free of fear. You'll be well fed, and have a warm, safe place to stay, and people you can depend on to protect you, help you get your lives back on track, find your way home.*

Never. Not going back. Ever. And if they try to make me, I'll take off again.

If you don't want to go home, you won't have to. From now on, the things that matter are your safety and your happiness.

The Steed rocked ever so slightly as it touched down, and when Broughton removed his helmet, everyone followed suit.

We've landed, and now you're going to meet Grace and her husband, Logan. They're the best.

When the rotors stopped and Angie gave the all clear, Broughton slid the door open.

Grace and Logan were halfway across the tarmac, the jet behind them.

Hey, you two, meet the Jennas, a group of very special telepaths.

Perfect. But what is a Jenna?

One of nine young ladies who have decided there is safety in all having the same name.

It was a lady who told us. She was a prisoner too, and only with us for a few days before they took her away and she never came back. That was in a different place. A fancy one. She also taught us other stuff, like when they gave us juice it always had drugs in it.

Well it sounds like this lady could use our help too. I'll make sure the team searches for her. What was her name?

Jenna.

Grace laughed. *We're in a bit of a hurry today, so if you're ready for the next leg of your journey, let's get a move on.*

Can we take the cookies with us?

Sure.

And we've got pizza waiting for you. When Logan's voice was added to the mix several startled visibly, but adjusted, and piled out onto the tarmac, except the two in Alex's arms.

Are they injured? Asked Logan. *Shall I carry them?*

Alex looked down at their upturned faces. *Are you good with that?*

They both nodded.

Logan gently lifted the one Broughton had been talking with, and Grace the other, the smallest of the group. When Alex stood to adjust the blanket around her the girl spoke aloud. "Your coat."

"You keep it for now. One day I'll visit, and pick it up then."

As they climbed into the small jet, a tear slid

down Alex's cheek, and Broughton caught it with a fingertip. She shook her head and wiped her eyes.

"We'll take off as soon as you're ready," said Angie, reminding him they needed to get underway again.

"Did you guys pick up that conversation?"

"Affirmative," said Angie.

"Made me want to go back and start over too. Eviscerate the bastards," said James.

"Gotta remember," said Angie, "you just gave those kids the best day of their lives."

Alex sucked it up. She'd done a good job, but that part of the mission was over, and she needed to move on, put her feelings away, just like she used to do in her vet practice. How many times had her heart been ripped out by either the animals or their humans? Too many to count.

She'd learned how to put it aside and move on to the next one needing her help, and that's what she would do now.

Maybe later, when it was all over, she would allow herself to think about the girls and have a good cry, but for now she would simply press on. And she wouldn't think about Broughton's voice in her head either."

"What's the status on Ryder?" she asked.

"He should be landing in about forty minutes. And we'll be there ahead of him by about twenty. Because we have no idea who else is on board, we'll land, get position, and call it as it comes."

"Best case?" asked Broughton, and Alex was certain he would already know, but she appreciated him asking for her benefit. She would love to simply say thanks telepathically, but wasn't certain if she could get a connection with him right now that wouldn't include Angie and James.

"Best case, Ryder, with one person as his guard or handler. We will separate them easily, as soon as they deplane, and hopefully the capture will lead us to others needing our help."

"Jennas," said Alex.

"Exactly. Grace is also going to update us with any mental images she's able to extract from the girls."

"Worst case?" asked Alex.

"Many possibilities. They don't land, or he's surrounded, or he's booby-trapped, or they see us and kill him—which is doubtful, because they could be stranded without a pilot. There's also a chance Ryder won't be on the plane. Anything can happen. Your job is to maintain position until needed, assist when necessary, and be ready to haul ass back to the Steed for a fast takeoff."

"That said, I'll be shut down," said Angie, "and startup takes a full minute, which means you have forty-five seconds to get to the ship once the call is made to get gone."

James set up their screens with aerial photos of where they were headed, and it looked almost the same as where they found the Jennas. A private horse facility with no sign of horses. This one had two barns and no hangar, but there was an indoor arena which was likely used for aircraft.

The flyover with sensors revealed there was no tunnel, no basement, and just one warm body.

"Guard?"

“I can take him,” said Broughton.

“Alive,” James clarified. “We want information, then you can kill him. We’ll save whoever is on the plane for the feds or they’ll start getting antsy. I doubt anyone at this level can identify the people at the top of their food chain, but we can hope.”

“Wind from the north,” said Angie, “and they’ll be landing into it. First touchdown on the south end of the runway.” She did one final pass to stir up a wind, then landed with the arena between them and the house, and just past a fence, which would ensure the other craft wouldn’t run into them while they maintained invisibility.

Broughton had his helmet off and was gone like a bullet, crouched low because the rotors were still moving, and circling the building so he could approach the house from the far side, since it appeared the guard was on the runway side—for now.

“Okay,” James said finally. “Let’s go.”

Alex followed him into the arena, where the ground was packed with tire tracks to confirm planes were often in there. And when they discovered an observation deck along one side of the building, it was decided she would do best hidden up there. She found herself a good spot where she could see between the slats of the railing. Then the waiting began.

“Regroup,” Broughton’s low voice came through her earbud. “Female subject—also named Jenna—was shackled to the wall. Prepare for another passenger. No computers on the premises, will leave it clean for the feds."

"Copy," said Angie.

"Alex, go back to the ship," said James. "Female passenger to be treated with care and suspicion. Could be loyal to whoever is in control of her."

"Copy," said Alex. Her training had included learning about Stockholm syndrome. There was a great deal of interesting material on the subject, which was certainly not cut and dried, but in a nutshell, a victim could develop an emotional bond with the person or persons who have taken away their freedom and physically or psychologically abused them. And the bond can be so strong they might resist rescue, or even harm rescuers.

Alex was being tasked with watching this woman, being intuitive, and keeping everyone safe.

She hot-footed back to the Steed. Grabbed one of the few blankets the girls hadn't taken with them, a bottle of water, and a couple of protein bars.

When Broughton arrived with Jenna—probably the original Jenna—Alex took a good look and saw nothing but relief in the dark brown eyes. Skin as dark as her eyes glistened with a thin sheen of sweat, and the moment she was on board the helo she collapsed into a seat, and doubled over, breathing hard.

Alex laid an arm across her back and was aghast when she felt sharp, protruding shoulder blades and bumpy spine. "Are you okay?"

"Air." More a gasp than a word.

"Oxygen mask," said Angie. "Cabinet beside you, waist level."

Alex popped the tiny door open and the mask fell out. She activated the stream and slipped it over the woman's smooth head. Continued to run a hand over the bony back. "It's okay, you're safe now."

Jenna shook out her hands, as though trying to get feeling back into them.

"Are you tingly, like you're going to pass out?"

"No." She took in a big breath. "Just winded." She exhaled. "Long time since I ran. Even walked." She sat up cautiously. "Used to pace in the beginning. Not anymore."

She leaned back and gawked at the interior of the helicopter. "I'm really out?"

Alex handed her the water. "Yes. We'll get you to safety in just a bit."

"Your friend says you came for a pilot?"

"That's right. He was taken a while back, and we're pretty sure he'll be landing here soon." She ripped the paper off both protein bars, passed one to Jenna, and bit into the other.

"Nobody here in a few weeks. Started wondering if I would die before anyone came back. Thought about cutting off my foot to get out of the chain. Was just trying to figure out how to make something for the bottom of my leg so I could run away…then you guys arrived." She shuddered, and Alex handed her the blanket which she immediately wrapped around her shoulders.

"I'm sure glad you didn't have to do that."

Jenna stared at her. "I was a track star in middle school. Bad enough I couldn't run a hundred yards just now without keeling over. Can't imagine only having one foot."

"What's your name?"

"Jenna."

"What's your real name?"

"How do you know it's not Jenna?"

"We picked up some other prisoners today. Little girls named Jenna."

"Praise the lord. Which ones?"

"Hard to say. Said a woman told them to all call themselves Jenna because it would be safer."

She covered her mouth with her hand, making what she said unintelligible but Alex understood the shaking shoulders, and sat beside her, drew her close, held on to her while she sobbed, but the storm was brief. She mopped her face with the blanket, and Alex passed her tissues for her nose.

"There were nine, did they…" she trailed off, as though afraid to ask, to find out for sure.

"There were still nine."

A shaky hand lifted the bottle, and she drained the rest of the water.

Incoming.

Alex listened intently, and finally heard the engine of a small plane. *Please let it be Ryder, let this work.* She wanted to see what was happening, be there to help, dammit, and this woman was not going to be a problem.

She had an idea. "I have to get you ready for a fast takeoff." She pulled off the blanket, slipped the shoulder harness over her head, and buckled it up really tight. Then she wrapped the blanket around her and tucked it into the back of the seat.

"You okay like this?"

Jenna nodded.

"Angie's going to stay here with you, and she has a gun in case you need to be protected." Or controlled. "I'll be just outside, but you need to stay very quiet, okay?"

She nodded again, and said, "I promise. Please, just don't gag me."

"I promise. Hang tight, and we'll be out of here in just a couple of minutes."

Passenger is safe. I'm going back to position. And she took off at a run.

Take the same place. At least James didn't sound pissed.

She raced up the stairs to the observation landing. She was to be the surprise from above when the plane was brought in here to park, and it was only about a ten-foot drop down into sawdust-like footing, so if she had to go over the side it was totally doable, and her landing could be damn near silent.

What would be hard was staying down and trying to watch through the boards when they pulled inside.

The sound of the plane got louder, and louder, and there it was, skimming over the grass, back wheels on the ground, nose wheel easing down ever so slowly until it was touching, rolling to a stop, turning.

Three souls visible.

Shit. That made Ryder plus two, and the second one could be another prisoner...or not.

She crouched behind the railing.

The plane stopped outside the arena, but the engine wasn't shut down and it just sat there, as though they were waiting for someone, but Alex didn't have a visual from her position.

"Right seat deplaning," came James's voice through the earbud. "White male, fifteen, five ten, blond, black cap, camo T, faded black jeans, black boots. Opening arena gate, getting back in. Ryder left seat, one guard behind is unconfirmed."

Tingling started at the back of her neck, and she didn't hesitate to share. "Something off."

"Copy, stand by."

The plane rolled slowly inside the building and to the far end. The young man got out again and stomped over to a panel on the wall which he shoved aside to access a small ladder, and a hose with a fuel nozzle. A hidden tank for refueling.

He positioned the ladder at the right wing and climbed up. Removed the fuel cap and stuck the nozzle into the tank.

She couldn't see the pilot from her positon, but she wondered why he didn't get out. Dammit, why didn't he need to get out and pee or something? Guys were such camels on a road trip.

She didn't want to chance speaking out loud while the plane was shut down, so used her internal voice. *Should we try to talk to him? Send him a message to get out for a pee?*

Go ahead. Broughton responded, making her wonder where James was.

Ryder, help's coming. Tell them you have to get out to pee.

She waited. Repeated her message a second time, then a third. And finally, she heard low voices. *Come on, Ryder, tell him it's going to stink in there if you can't get out.*

You have him, Alex. Now push. James was back.

Ryder, now! Get out. Now. And walk away from the plane.

She heard the door open. *Walk away, far away, and fall down—now!*

He'd barely hit the ground when Broughton seemed to materialize from nowhere, rushed the plane, and in minutes had the guard out and facedown on the ground beside Ryder who was staying still as the dead.

Alex shot to her feet and trained her weapon on the young man reaching for the back door of the aircraft

Fuel boy's up to something.

Gun's in the plane.

"Don't do it." Her voice came out solid, commanding.

"Shoot him if you have to," said Broughton.

Never taking her eyes off the target, she stalked the length of the platform until she was standing right over the kid. "Easy shot from here, and you probably didn't plan on dying today."

"Talk's cheap, bitch. If you were a man you'd have shot me already. I do pussy, they don't do me."

He dove.

She squeezed the trigger.

And he dropped like a sack of rocks.

25

His howling bounced off the walls and drove her over the side, but she stopped short of where he lay. Studied the blood seeping through to soak the shoulder of his shirt. Nothing stopping him from getting to his feet.

She backed up one step, two, her gun still in her hand, and that's where it was going to stay for now.

Alex?

It's only a shoulder wound. She wanted to glance over at Broughton, but didn't dare take her eyes off of the boy. Hell, he *was* only a boy. But that hadn't stopped him from going for the gun in the plane, and there was no doubt in her mind he would have used it on one or all of them.

She circled him. Reached in for the weapon, felt around on the floor until her fingers closed on the butt and she dragged it out, checked for a bullet in the chamber, ejected the clip. She shoved the gun in the waistband of her pants, at the back, and pulled her vest over it. The clip went in her pocket.

One gun off the floor and now out of commission.

Good work. I'm going to bring this guy around to you.

"Get up."

"Fuck you. Oomph."

"I said, get up."

They rounded the back of the plane, Ryder at Broughton's side, and the guard in front of them. "Right here, on your belly," Broughton told the guard.

"F—"

A quick jerk up on the wrists strapped together and the guy went down on his face. Broughton leaned over. "You're making it much harder than it has to be, pal."

"F—"

"I know, fuck me. Just remember, while I tend to your henchman, here, I could shut you up damned easy with the toe of my boot." He shot a glance at Alex. "Watch him, and feel free to shoot if he moves."

Broughton knelt beside the kid and dragged down the collar of his shirt, then lifted the sleeve. "Went right through. Looks like it's almost done bleeding too, so we'll just leave him for the feds to patch up."

He picked up the kids' head by the hair, got in his face. "Pretty bold move, making that dive while a woman had a gun on you. You should show more respect."

"Pussy oughta know her place."

"Oh, looks to me like she does. What are you doing running with this bunch, kid? Letting them push you around?"

"I'm one of the guys. I got privileges. Black bitch up in the house is mine. Bought and paid for. Gonna make bucks off her fine ass."

Alex's fists clenched. "You slap her around?"

"I tune her when she needs it."

"Give me a minute, would ya? I might be able to fix the pain in his shoulder for him."

Broughton stepped back, and Alex crouched, pulled the fabric to get a good look. "I'm a veterinarian, and I might be able to fix it so you barely feel this."

"Yeah, why don't you kiss it better for me, or better yet," he grabbed at his crotch with his good hand, and she swung so hard and fast she startled them both when her fist plowed into his face. His head jerked, and once again he was a heap on the ground, but this time moaning instead of howling.

And she tried to shake the pain out of her hand.

Chemical ice packs in the Steed when you get back.

Where's James?

He picked up that someone was supposed to be here to meet them, open the gate for the arena when they rolled up. The guy was late, and James intercepted him. Bringing him in here any minute.

When James did, Alex was impressed with the size of the guy walking in front of him. Had to be nearly seven feet tall, because Broughton and James were both over six feet, and this guy towered over both of them.

It took a while to get them well trussed up and attached to tie rings conveniently placed on the walls—fitting that the three of them were now in the positions they put so many innocents in.

Alex, Broughton, and a very quiet Ryder headed for the Steed while James stayed at the arena entrance, watching over their prisoners.

Alex loosened the blanket around Jenna and grabbed a headset for her. Ryder still had his around his neck. "You have to wear ear protection at all times, because the noise in here will be deafening, literally," she told him.

Once they were properly protected, she popped a candy in her mouth and donned her helmet while Angie fired up the helo. Once it was ready, she lifted it off just enough to slide toward the arena, and when a federal agency helicopter landed on the grass runway moments later, James gave it a wave, jogged to the Steed, hopped in, and they lifted off.

Broughton passed Alex a cold pack and she wrapped it around her hand. Who knew it hurt that bad when you punched someone in the face, and why the hell would anyone do it a second time?

Because it feels good... doesn't it?

It's not polite to eavesdrop on someone's thoughts.

It was written all over your face, sunshine.

Sunshine?

Yep, a little ray of. Can't tell you how good it felt to see you deck him, although at first I was worried you might go for his balls—castration being your forte and all.

If only. My plan had been to put a little scare in him, maybe threaten to poke him in the open wound. Of course, I could never do that in good conscience, because of contamination.

To him or you?

Him. She thought about the blood, and the people the kid was running with. *Me too, I guess.*

Try to remember that part.

Yeah. Sex trade, poor medical care. *Got it.* She glanced over at Jenna. How much had the woman been exposed to? Alex had only thought of the psychological aspects of her abuse, and hadn't even considered the possibility of permanent damage to her health.

She'd like to ask Jenna's age, but would have to wait until Angie gave the okay to remove the ear protection. Instead, Alex passed Ryder a protein bar and a bottle of water, then held the cooler up to Jenna. Now she'd eaten the obligatory health snack, she could choose whatever she wanted. Her eyes lit when Alex pointed to the bag of cookies, but she shook her head and tears gleamed in her eyes.

Alex took her hand and put the whole bag in it, and when Jenna's shoulders began to shake, Alex drew her into her arms again.

#

Broughton's heart filled to bursting while he watched her comfort Jenna as she had the little ones. It was a side of Alex he hadn't seen before, or at least not with humans. She showed amazing compassion with animals, but usually stood back with people. He actually felt the emotional distance she put between herself and others, even the Meyers group. Reminded him of his own feelings about people in general. He preferred dogs.

Funny though, now he was thinking about it, they were an awful lot alike. Except for the one fatal difference. She wanted a relationship, and he didn't.

She was sitting there, completely tuned in to a stranger, feeding her cookies and holding her hand. And he was afraid of that, why?

Because it couldn't last. Nothing did. And he wasn't setting himself up for that kind of fall. Been there, done that, didn't need a repeat performance.

Meanwhile, Ryder was staring straight ahead. Broughton waved his hand in front of the kid and he turned his head, but his expression was blank. Too blank.

Hey, Ryder. Nothing. And Broughton wasn't surprised. The kid was pretty shut down. Broughton grabbed the cooler and popped it open, held it out to the boy, whose steady gaze finally flickered. He stared into the container for what seemed like minutes before reaching in. He'd chosen a sandwich. Broughton grabbed a couple of sodas and offered them. Ryder took a cola, and Broughton popped the top on the root beer. Not his fave, but oh, well…. And oh hell, he couldn't drink with the damn helmet on, could he?

"How long until you switch the volume on this rig, Angie?"

"I can do it now. Hang on." There was a faint change in the vibration under his feet, and the red light embedded in the middle of the floor blinked off. The green one on.

He removed his headgear and gestured to Ryder that he could do the same, while Alex looked after Jenna.

"Hey, Ryder, I'm Broughton, and these are Alex and Jenna. Angie and James are front seat."

"I'm responsible for Mr. Meyers's aircraft. I don't know where they took it."

"It's safe there in the arena for now, and they'll get it back after the feds are done with their investigation."

"The one in there wasn't the Meyers plane. I don't know where it is, and it was my responsibility."

"Hey, kid, none of this is your fault."

"I was given an opportunity and I blew it."

"How did you blow it?"

He sighed and looked away.

"Ryder?"

"I asked for it. What happened. I asked for it, and now Del will be dead, and it's my fault." He sounded about to shatter.

Broughton put a degree of command in his voice. "Tell me. All of it, right from the beginning, and leave nothing out."

Ryder's hand shook when he lifted the tin and drank down the rest of his soda, then wrapped up the rest of the sandwich he had stopped eating.

"I figured some stuff out, about my parents, about when they disappeared. I knew my dad wouldn't have crashed. Besides, they'd have been found if they went down where they were headed. That meant they disappeared on purpose. Left me behind on purpose." He sighed.

"Sometimes I thought they just didn't want me, but then I figured out they must have been protecting me, but from what? That's when I started asking questions, and found out my mom wasn't really from the reservation. That I'm not from the clan I was told."

He fiddled with the sandwich wrapping. "Someone hurt my mom when she was just a kid, and she must have stayed on the rez to hide. She was always happy, until one day after she'd been to a job with my dad. She got weird then, kept telling me how much she loved me and stuff, and then just a few weeks later they vanished."

"When exactly did you start putting it all together?"

"When I was at Sunrise, because they got people you can talk to about your heritage and stuff, and they help you research. They want kids to be proud of who they are, and I never really looked like the other kids, ya know? In high school sometimes I'd get called half-breed because my eyes were like yours. Not like everyone else's. Too light, like my skin."

"Must have been hard for you." Broughton remembered the taunts. He'd been too dark, not too light. And he hadn't known about his Native American heritage until Meyers discovered his DNA profile was in the ETC database. Eve had given him the file when they extracted it from the system. His ancestry was an interesting mix of Native American and British.

The Brit blood hadn't been a surprise, because his mother's parents were born in Scotland. He didn't know anything about his father's heritage.

Ryder shrugged. "Naw. Our school was filled with rez kids and Mexicans. Lots of us didn't look like anyone else."

"So what happened after we saw you at the airport that day? You were scheduled for a night flight."

He buried both hands in his hair and scratched his scalp hard. "When I was researching my mom's history, where my dad had worked the week she got weird, and trying to figure out where they might have flown to, I met this guy who seemed to know stuff, and he was all over trying to help me. Said he was going to be a private investigator, but would help me for free so he could get some experience."

He stared down at his boots. "He wanted me to take him out on a flight so he could show me the place he thought my parents had landed the day they vanished. I brought him to the airport with me and told Del I wanted to take him up for an hour, and Del said no. Said Meyers insurance wouldn't cover him. I wasn't allowed to take passengers. My friend was pissed, and I didn't hear from him for a few days, but then he called and asked if I could just smuggle him out on a flight. Said I should keep Del busy while he hopped on the plane, and no harm, no foul."

Ryder shifted in his seat. Crushed the soda can with one hand. "I was stupid. Went along with him, but I was doing a week of night flights, so I told him he'd have to wait a few days. I guess I played right into his hands, and he was there in the plane the night Del and I went up. He made me fly to a place, like a little old farm in a remote area.

"There were other men there, and we were put in a shed. Chained to a wall. We had to fly out in the morning to another hole in the wall. Kept doing that until we got to the fancy place, the one I think my dad took mom to when she saw somebody or something that scared her. They sell people. For sex and other stuff. It's like a business, and they wanted me as a pilot, but if I refused to fly for them, they'd sell me to some big-ass guy from wherever, and he'd make me his bitch."

He stayed silent for so long, just staring at his boots, that Broughton said, "You're right, you did a dumb thing trusting that stranger, but your mistake wasn't intentional. You'll need to eventually forgive yourself so you can move on. We all fuck up. Sometimes it costs us more than other times."

"I was dumb, too," said Jenna in a voice so low he barely heard her. "I fell for a guy who said shit like he loved me, and he wanted me to have nice things, and then he wanted me to go on a trip with him, and…" Her eyes lifted to meet Ryder's gaze. "I ended up chained to the wall in a kitchen for six months. I cooked and cleaned up, and they used me right there on the floor or bent over the counter. But that doesn't make me stupid or bad. I did a dumb thing, and it cost me. Just like you."

Broughton was so humbled by the two of them. He used to call himself a survivor, but these two? They'd nailed it. And they were going to be okay in the end. Sure it would be work, but they'd both get there, he'd put money on it.

"You're a tough and amazing pair," said Alex.

"And not saying the rest of the journey isn't going to have rough patches, but you're over the worst of it, and where you're headed is all good."

"Where are we headed?" asked Ryder.

"To a place where you can heal. Where you'll get all the help you need, and maybe you can help others too."

"Sunrise?"

"No, but you liked it there, didn't you?"

"Really did. Hit it off pretty good with the people who run it, and the guy at the lake. They treated me like a person, not a kid. Talked to me like they cared what I thought, what I said."

"Maybe when you're done rehabbing you can go there for a while. I'll get in touch with them and see what I can set up." Broughton wouldn't mind some time in the mountains. His last trip had been cut short. He could take the kid with him, leave him at the ranch and head east to where the bigger mountains called to him. Be a good place to sort out what to do about Alex. He glanced up to find her watching him. *What?*

She shook her head. Had she heard his thoughts? Of course not. He had all his protection in place. Then why did it feel like she was reading his mind?

26

Alex was too tired for conversation after they dropped Ryder and Jenna off at the rehab center. Grace had still been there, settling the children in, and the girls got very excited when they saw Jenna. Apparently she was the one who told them to all use her name to stay safe, so it would be harder to single one out.

The feel of the brave young woman's bones poking through her skin, and the knowledge in her eyes, would stay with Alex forever, but right now she longed for the oblivion of sleep, and prayed it was something she could find when she was finally able to crawl into bed.

She felt Broughton's gaze on her now and again but didn't look up. Had no defense against him at the moment, and couldn't deal with her own weakness for those amazing dark blue eyes. Eyes which only showed half of his parentage. She'd been listening when he told Ryder that he, too, had

Native American heritage, and it was interesting after that to think about some of his innate qualities that could have come from his DNA. His relationship with the earth—the way he seemed so comfortable in his skin when surrounded by nature. Even the something that drew her to him could be from an ancient ancestry.

But it was too much to think about right now. She slipped another candy in her mouth and silently thanked Consuelo for the supply. They'd been just what she needed to get through the long hours since she had a meal. The homemade protein bars were critical, but the candies were there in between.

With the ranch lights finally below them, James said, "Debrief in ten."

That meant directly to the war room. No stopping to check the cat or to accidently fall into bed and blink out for the rest of the night.

They touched down and went straight to the SUV waiting for them with Matt in the driver's seat. He leaned over and kissed his wife. "Trent will take the bird for fuel and service, then put it to bed for you."

"Perfect. I'm dead on my feet. Well, my ass, really. I've been strapped into that seat for way too many hours."

"And you're stood down for the next forty-eight," said James.

"I'll sleep for the first forty-two."

"Hah," said Matt. "Like you've ever stayed in bed for more than eight or nine."

"What about the weekend at the mountain house?"

"Completely different. You weren't sleeping."

"Uh, father in the back seat," said James.

"Come on, Dad, you know we have sex."

"But I don't want to hear about it."

Silence reigned until they got to the war room, where they were met by Julia. A very startled Julia when James wrapped her in his arms and kissed her with great enthusiasm.

"Dad!"

He turned and grinned at Angie. "Payback."

"Best greeting I've had in days," said Julia, whose husband had obviously filled her in telepathically.

Consuelo broke up the laughter by arriving with a food trolley. "No one leaves this room without hot food in their belly. At least one bowl of either soup, stew, or chili."

She filled bowls and passed them out. Alex loved Consuelo's stew, but her plans for a long sleep didn't include feeling stuffed, so opted for soup. It was steaming hot, and she blew on the surface until Broughton slipped an ice cube into it.

"Old trick my grandmother taught me," he said. "Stir."

She did, and was able to eat the soup right away.

The debrief lasted half an hour, then Julia relayed Grace and Logan's report from the field. "The children are all settled in, and, at Jenna's urging, have given their real names for the records—on the condition they will still be called Jenna for a while at least, and agreeing to be asked about it again in a week. One component of therapy is making decisions for themselves, and learning how to make good ones.

"Six of the girls are runaways, two were kidnapped, and one was sent to America for the opportunity of a fine life among the wealthy." She paused while the contradiction of that sank in.

"As for Jenna and Ryder, they have chosen to stay with the girls for now. Grace is making Paradise available to both of them if and when they are ready to move on, but she thinks Ryder will go to Sunrise instead if it's an option."

"Questions?" asked James.

"Where are Nathan and Tyler?" asked Broughton.

"Still in Florida. They've hooked up with the feds doing the investigation, and are making sure all information we collected is relayed to them. The case will be a bitch to build, but we've given them plenty to work with. And there's a bonus."

James waved a hand toward his wife, and she said, "They went back to the same farm they pulled that bunch out of earlier, just to check it out in case that's where Ryder was flying into. Turns out the place was up and running again, with a full complement of farmworkers."

She hesitated a beat. "Workers who were displaced by the hurricane. The same ones we were searching for. Every one of them has now been located, and we're sponsoring them until they get back on their feet."

"That's incredible," said Alex. "And I'll hang on to it, because as far as the other investigation…" She stopped. No point putting it into words.

Organized crime was making endless billions off of human trafficking, and would be almost impossible to stop.

"The people at the top will be clear already," said Angie. "You can bet on that. And the half dozen dead guys can't exactly talk."

"Actually, their phones are doing the talking, along with their computers. We're getting plenty of incriminating evidence from them," said James. "Anything else?"

Alex nearly held her breath, hoping someone else would say it, but of course that didn't happen, so it was on her. "Del never mentioned Ryder bringing the hijack guy around. About not allowing him to fly with the kid." Which had to be why she got a funny feeling about Del from the moment she met him. He'd been hiding something.

"Julia and I are going to have a sit-down with him in the morning. All he knows so far is that Ryder was picked up and is safe. We'll share details with him tomorrow and get some clarification. And on that note," added James, "you two are off the roster for the next eight. Get some sleep."

No argument from Alex. She made for her room like a heat-seeking missile, and almost managed a smile for the cat sprawled in the middle of her bed. "Hey, buddy."

She shed her clothes, crawled under the covers, and slid into oblivion with the sound of purring close to her ear.

#

Broughton paced his room. Did he dare try to sleep when his brain was refusing to let go of the images, threatening to bring all the children from previous rescues back like a slide show of horrors? He needed his dogs. Just their presence kept the memories at bay.

But he was on his own, wasn't he? Wait. The boys were still in Florida. Maybe…

He made his way to the kitchen, and there they were. Puck and Stick. Two huge, black, fluffy dogs, sitting at attention and staring at him as though to ask why he was waking them up at this ungodly hour.

"Hey, guys." He sat between them on the wide dog bed, and when they leaned in, he dropped an arm around each, and just sat there until his mind settled and the flashes of memory eased off, faded away.

"Thanks." They weren't therapy dogs—his weren't either—but they had a canine awareness that was like nothing else he'd ever encountered, and he felt centered again. He rubbed their heads, then got up to get them a biscuit from the jar on the counter. That's when he spotted the note held in place by a brown coffee mug.

> Broughton.
>
> > Puck and Stick could use some company. Feel free to take them to your room so they don't have to spend the night in the kitchen.
>
> C.

She always knew. Anticipated the needs of all those under her roof. Even though Consuelo came there years ago as hired help, and was not related to anyone by blood, it *was* her roof, because she was mother to them all. She fed them and cared for them as though everyone in her presence was hers. And he loved her like the grandmother who had taken him in as a teenager full of rage, and made a man out of him.

He poured milk and nuked it, drank it down while standing at the sink, and put the mug in the dishwasher. Then he drew a tiny heart under the C, grabbed a couple more biscuits, and headed for his room with the dogs at his heels.

He stopped outside Alex's door and opened his mind to connect with hers, but got nothing. Good. She was asleep. He continued on, dropped his clothes on the floor, and climbed into bed. Lay there for a minute, then snapped his fingers and the dogs leapt up, flopped on either side of him, and he tuned in to their heartbeats. Followed the rhythm toward sleep, and stepped into the darkness without trepidation.

When the dreams came, he was ready for them, beat them back, changed the endings, and slept again, not waking completely until daylight was creeping through the half-closed blinds.

He tried to roll over but was pinned by a hundred or so pounds of canine on the blanket on either side of him. Puck and Stick were apparently planning to sleep in.

"Hey, guys, time to move." They stirred. "As in now." He shoved at them just enough to get their attention. Solemn brown eyes gazed into his. "Consuelo likely has breakfast for you."

Ears tipped forward. "Breakfast." He remembered the biscuits he'd stuck in his pocket.

"I've got treats if you let me up."

The word treats got them moving, and they were soon munching happily and looking for more. "Sorry, guys, that's all I've got."

They went to the door, and when he opened it they sauntered out, apparently done with his company. "Thanks," he said quietly. Best sleep he'd had in a week...or more.

He took a quick shower and headed for the pool, because his body needed exercise, and he needed to think. With the place to himself, he indulged in a shallow racing dive and sprinted two laps before slowing to a good, solid pace he could maintain for an hour or two, not that he would stay that long, but it was his standard workout speed. One he could maintain while his mind went wherever it was needed, and this morning his thoughts turned to Alex, because clearly he wasn't able to shake free of her. To shove her to a back corner of his mind.

Nope, she was there, front and center, demanding his attention, and he had to admit he liked having her there. Her presence was annoying, and, yeah, stirred him up, but was also comfortable. And slipping into her mind...well, that was a temptation damned hard to resist. He got away with it yesterday for the purpose of the op, but didn't dare try now, when he simply wanted to feel closer to her, listen to her thoughts.

The woman had an amazing brain. Always working, looking for patterns, assessing the gestures and expressions of those around her. And she read people as well as she read animals. She'd noticed the deceit in Del long before anyone else did, and sensed the fragile strength of Jenna, the adult one. Had known to hold the children.

She claimed she had no experience with kids, was half afraid of anyone under the age of fifteen, yet she read them well. Instructed when necessary, and asked when it was more appropriate. Earned their trust right from the get-go.

And she had him twisted up like a pretzel because he was trying to resist her. Why? Why not give in and go for it?

Because shit happened. He'd lost everyone important to him, and even when he did everything right when trying to save his dad, it hadn't worked. Took a long time to get over that one, and when the call came years later, announcing his death, Broughton still felt like he'd been pushed off a cliff to fall through empty air for days. Hell, months.

But couldn't it be different with Alex? Probably not. Fresh in his mind was the fear rippling through him only yesterday when she'd been confronted by a guy who was mere inches from grabbing a gun. A gun he meant to kill her with.

Instead, *she* did what needed to be done. And had his six. If he was ever partnered with her again, he wouldn't hesitate to trust her.

And what if? What if they did get something going between them? Would they still work on ops together? Would it be easier? Harder?

Would making her his change how they worked together? Make it complicated? Or could they become like Logan and Grace, a well-oiled machine?

There was an interesting thought. Grace and Logan also disagreed about things and survived. Sometimes she led, other times he did. Logan had told him once that it was having a solid base of shared morals and principals that made it work. And of course, love.

But if Alex and Broughton were together, would he be able to put his foot down about an op to keep her safe?

Not like he could do that now, so argument out the window.

To give his head a break, he flipped over and did the backstroke, concentrating form, optimizing position and buoyancy. He counted strokes, then slipped into an old habit of naming the all the bones in a skeleton, then the muscles, tendons, ligaments, organs.

With his mind finally, blessedly, empty he glanced up at the clock and flipped over to return to a distance-covering crawl.

A sudden environmental flicker told him he was no longer alone, and it only took seconds to recognize Alex's energy.

His heart hummed, and his head screamed a warning. She'd be wearing that sleek black number that looked more like paint than material. Long legs, pretty, tanned skin, and her hair. Wet, it would be straight and look twice as long. Her…

Cones, rods, lens, cornea, vitreous... He recited the components of an eye, then went through a list of ailments as he continued a steady pattern of breathe, two, three, four, breathe, two, three, four.

Hey.

Shit. She wanted him to engage. Bad idea.

Hey. I'm just getting done. I'll catch ya after. Have a good swim. He bypassed the ladders and hefted himself out over the side. Made a beeline for the private shower room. He wasn't ready for a face-to-face with her.

#

Alex was tired of the man's attitude. Maybe it was time to cut bait. Either that or push hard, and she wasn't exactly the pushy type.

The man he was deep inside was the one she wanted. The guy who drew a tiny heart on a note to thank Consuelo. The one who sat with Alex for the days and nights while she lay paralyzed by a mystery drug. The guy who talked her down more than once from a full-blown panic attack when she was freaking out with the fear that she'd never be able to move again.

She wanted the man she'd surprised in the hallway when she kissed the stuffing out of him.

Problem was, he was also the guy who didn't believe she was as capable as any other agent, and who thought he needed to watch over her like some kind of simpleminded kid.

She swam lap after lap, warring with herself over what to do. How to approach the problem of being in love with a man who didn't want her in his life on a permanent basis.

Would she love a one-night stand? A hot and heavy handful of hours in his bed? Oh, yeah. She heated up just thinking about it, but would it be worth the loneliness and longing sure to follow?

Nope.

It was bad enough she had some damned amazing kisses to obsess over. Sex? Him naked on her, in her, surrounding her? His hot flesh in her hands? Her mouth driving him crazy?

She dove, skimmed the bottom, staying down until her lungs were screaming. She surfaced, gulped air, and dove again, not stopping until her mind was clear. Only then did she let her feet drop to the bottom, glad the lap pool was a nice four feet deep end to end. It was time to feed the cat and find some breakfast.

She toweled off and put on her sweats, swung through the kitchen to grab a can of cat food from the pantry. Consuelo was there, cooking breakfast for the masses. At least it seemed like there was an awful lot of bacon on the griddle, and biscuits were in the oven.

"Cereal there if you don't want to wait, or toast," she said.

"I'll be back after my shower, but didn't dare forget this for my buddy, or I'm sure there would be a mutiny. Is there a meeting this morning?"

"Nothing on the schedule. I do this most mornings, so there's lots for the drop-ins and run-throughs. Bacon-stuffed biscuits are the current favorite of many around here."

"Hmm. Sounds good. I'll be back."

Mouth already watering, she scooted off, and popped the top of the can the minute she entered the room. Plopped the whole works in his dish...which she should have cleaned out first, but was afraid he wouldn't wait peacefully. She'd have to get him a fresh dish later. Meanwhile, he was digging in with gusto, and purring at a rocking high decibel level.

Driven by the need for bacon, she showered quickly, and was wearing nothing but a towel when there was a knock on the door. She opened it a crack and peered out.

"Nice," said Broughton. "Consuelo sent me to tell you breakfast is ready."

"I know, I'm on my way."

"Dressed like that?"

"Well, no. But it will only take me a sec."

"I'll wait."

"Seriously?" She shrugged, dug what she needed out of her bag and went back into the bathroom.

"You know," he was right outside the door. "Partners have to be comfortable stripping off in front of each other, or getting dressed, or whatever."

"Partners?"

"We're good together, so James will likely make us a regular pair."

She dragged an oversized orange T-shirt on over her head, then stared at herself in the mirror. *Now he wants us to be partners? Go figure. Just when I'm about to tell James not to pair me with him.*

Why would you do that?

Seriously? You're trespassing. Get out of my head.

No. We need to talk.

About to open the door, she stopped. Leaned on the wall instead. *About what?*

You and me.

We did that already, and it didn't work.

Maybe we'll get it right this time. Come on out here.

I don't think so.

Why?

I'm safer where you can't touch me.

Why?

Oh, come on. You know how I feel about you, and I don't want to give in to chemistry if nothing else is going to work. It's safer for me to keep a door between us so all we do is talk.

You're a tough customer.

I have to be.

Okay, what if I said I was changing my position on...relationships?

I'm listening.

What if I'm not willing to give up wanting you?

Still talking lust. Be more specific.

He heaved out a sigh. *I'm willing to give us a try.*

Still sounded like sex was the item on the table. *Define "us."*

Oh, come on.

Sex isn't enough.

There was pounding on the outer door, and Alex poked her head out in time to see Dhillon in the doorway. "Oh, hey, Alex. James wants you guys in the war room, stat."

"On our way," said Broughton.

"Probably she should get dressed first." The kid grinned and scooted away.

She slammed the bathroom door and stepped into her cargos, decided to switch out the T-shirt, and was surprised to find Broughton still in her room when she emerged. "You're waiting for me?"

"We weren't done talking."

"We are for now. There's business to deal with." She went to the closet and keeping her back to him changed shirts.

Then sitting on the bed she donned socks and boots.

"If we were in a relationship, and called for an op, we'd go together, so I'm testing it for comfort."

She sat back and stared at him. Couldn't read his expression but wasn't surprised when he hauled her to her feet and held her still in front of him. He lifted her chin and stared into her eyes for several beats before lowering his mouth to hers, kissing her in a kind of question she responded to with pent-up frustration. Leaning in, demanding more, and getting what she asked for. Then she backed away abruptly.

"We good?" he asked quietly when she left him flat-footed and headed for the door.

"For now. We'll have to see what happens next." And she fought to slow the pounding of her heart.

27

Broughton followed her into the war room, where James and Julia were waiting.

"There's been a development," said James. "Turns out Ryder's parents are in witness protection—of sorts. I say of sorts, because they're not with one of the official agencies.

"They're working with an undercover group dedicated to ending human trafficking. The group is sanctioned by the government, and well-funded by the same, but invisible to the public.

"When they came in behind us to clean up at the farms, and found out who we pulled out of the last one, wheels were set in motion to let Ryder's parents know, and they want to see him. Give him the option of joining them."

"Kid's scheduled to be in rehab for a few weeks at least. Has a lot to work through," said Broughton.

"The group has been rescuing kids for years. They're equipped to handle Ryder."

Broughton nodded. "So where do we come in?"

"Kid needs a ride, and an escort, and someone he trusts if he decides not to go with them. You have to keep him in sight twenty-four seven, so it will take two of you, and Trent will do the trip in the Steed."

"Where?"

"The mountain safe house. You'll stay there

overnight, and in the morning take him up to the cabin to meet with the folks from Sunrise Ranch."

"Does he know yet?"

"Nope. And they've asked that no one tell him."

"Not sure if I like that," said Broughton. "His recovery is all about getting control back, and then we set him up… Doesn't feel right."

"I had the same argument," said Julia, "But they're afraid he will be angry with them. They're blaming themselves for what he's just gone through. They don't want him to refuse to see them, but he is absolutely free to decide whether or not to join them."

Broughton glanced at Alex. "You okay with that?"

"Yes and no. I can see it both ways." She frowned. "I guess I'd lean toward carrying out the parents' wishes.

"The good news is," said Julia, "you get to make the final call. If the kid isn't dealing with the reunion well, and you think he needs space, time away from them, whatever, you are free to take him back to the house, or even fly out of there."

"I barely know him," said Alex.

"True," Broughton replied. "But we have a unique connection because we rescued him. Sometimes that can be a problem, but in this case it will work in our favor."

"It will be good with Dusty and Chase there as well," said Alex "Their work with fosters probably makes them well-versed in handling custody and parenting situations."

“Actually, they might not be there. They have a couple of mares due to foal in the next couple of days, so their friend Murray, who works with the summer camp kids, will be there instead. Ryder knows him, and they formed a close bond last summer, according to Dusty.”

“I remember them mentioning the mares they rescued from Costa Rica, and being worried about them foaling at this time of year.” said Alex.

Broughton was at a disadvantage, having stayed behind when they headed up the mountain.

“Something was off the last time we were there,” he said.

“We sent a team in after you made your report,” said Julia. “Couldn’t find anything wrong. Not so much as a fingerprint—electronic or otherwise—but that aside, if you’re not comfortable taking Ryder there, we’ll make other arrangements.”

“I’m game as long as we have a Plan B just in case.”

“And C and D,” said James. “Not taking any chances.”

Broughton was good with that, and, thinking back on the unsettling feelings, he still couldn’t put his finger on them. It was as if whatever was poking at him was from a different dimension. And wasn’t that an interesting idea? “It was more a sensation of unease, as though there was something I was missing. Like a ghost poking at me, telling me to look over my shoulder. I felt both an urge to climb that mountain, and a dread of what I might find at the top. A really odd one for me.”

Julia nodded. “I’ve had those moments.”

“You’ll need to be off the ground within the hour, so you get there with plenty of daylight to recon the area, with time to take off again if necessary.” James was making sure they had room to maneuver.

“Julia, will you let Dhillon know my buddy will need him again?”

“Affirmative,” said Julia, and Broughton suddenly saw the similarities she had with Alex. They had the tall, lean physical thing, of course, but it was that air of command, of someone used to being in control, not taking a back seat to anyone. Yet Julia often stepped back to let James take point, or appear to have control. She was a good leader because she wanted those she led to do well. Was happy to sit back and let her team shine. Yet she took no crap.

Broughton glanced at Alex. Meeting her for the first time under such terrible circumstances had put an odd color on who they were to each other. She was helpless, and he cared for her. Helped her cope. Survive. Get through the long days and nights when fear dogged her, and every once in a while he needed to be reminded she wasn’t that weak and vulnerable woman he’d met. She was a strong, vibrant woman who worked hard, and could do anything the other agents could do. More, in some areas. She had protected *him* by shooting a man.

One day he’d like to meet the Argentinean man who stamped three of the strongest women he’d ever met with such powerful personalities, depth of character, and courage.

#

Landing at the mountain safe house was a much pleasanter experience in the Steed. No lumpy, bumpy, runway to contend with, just a gentle touchdown, and for that Alex was grateful.

They'd come in silent, so had to wait until the engine was shut down and the rotors stopped before helmets came off.

"Pretty amazing aircraft," said Ryder. "I'd sure love to work on her. Get a look inside the technology."

"You likely will one day," said Broughton, and Alex wondered. Unless they brought down the organized crime group, the power behind the multi-billion dollar industry, Ryder would always be at risk. He had seen the faces of people in the upper ranks. Could point fingers, even name names. Alex had been shocked when he told them that on the ride in. Equally shocking, the kid seemed no worse for wear once he had a night's sleep. But she knew it was likely all bluff.

Ryder helped Trent set up the portable shelter for the Steed, which had electronic shields so no one could get within a few feet of the barricade without an alarm going off on Trent's wrist unit. Meanwhile, Alex and Broughton went up to the house. Checked the security, did a sweep of every room, both physically and electronically, and the place came up squeaky clean.

"I'm taking the same room as before," she said, needing the familiar.

"I'll do the same."

He tossed his backpack on the bed and headed

for the kitchen. “You hungry?”

She hesitated, and he said, “This is not me trying to manage your blood sugar. I want food, and it was polite to ask you. That’s it.”

She stared while he perused the shelves of the pantry. “I wasn’t going to take issue with you at all.” She sighed. “I wish we could start over.”

He set an armful of jars on the counter and put his hands on her shoulders. “Me too. How about we just do?”

“You think it will be that easy?”

“I think it’s worth the effort, no matter how hard or easy it is.”

“Agreed,” she said, and smiled. “I like not fighting with you.”

He leaned over and planted a quick kiss on her mouth. “Me too.”

“You getting any weird feelings from this place yet?”

“Nope. Not a thing. It feels like whatever was here is gone.”

“Well, that’s a relief. Now if we can just make tomorrow work…”

“I’ve got an idea about that. I think we should go on foot. I figure it will take a couple of hours to get there, but well worth what Ryder will get out of it. He’ll feel more grounded, more connected with Mother Earth.”

“I heard you tell him about your heritage yesterday. Gawd. Was that only yesterday?”

“Yeah, a lot happened in a very short time.”

“You said you only found out through DNA testing.”

"That's true. ETCETERA profiled every person who ever worked for them, and I had a few times. We were led to believe they were collecting data to keep us safe, identify us if we were killed, but the head man was looking for more interesting information, and found it. My dad spoke fluent Spanish, and we lived close to the border, so I believed he was from Mexico. And after he was gone, my grandparents—my mother's parents—were afraid for me, and acted as though he had never existed. Moved us up north." He leaned back against the counter and looked her square in the eye.

"When I was finally an adult, out on my own, I searched for him. Found him on the streets of Vancouver. Dried him out and set him up with an apartment and an allowance, but he wouldn't stay."

Broughton started opening jars, dumping the contents in a big pot.

"What happened to him?" Something had, that much she could read from Broughton's voice.

"Died on the street."

That was it? "You're sure?"

"Claimed his body, buried him beside my mom."

She put a hand on his back. "I'm sorry."

"Me too. He was a cop, an undercover cop, working a big case to take down an organized crime group. He worked his way in, and then they broke him. Made him kill to save my mom and me, and it destroyed him."

He moved away from her to rinse out the jars and cans. "I've killed more than he ever did, and I'm still whole. I wonder what kind of a man that makes me."

Before she could say a word, Trent and Ryder came in, and the moment was lost, but she'd had a glimpse inside the man she was certain she was meant to spend her life with. A glimpse both sad and scary. Was he trying to frighten her off?

If so, it hadn't worked. Only made her more determined to keep him peeling the layers, letting her see inside.

Trent showed Ryder around while Alex did the domestic thing. Set the table, cleaned up behind Broughton while he put together a concoction that was apparently meant to go on rice, as he'd made a huge pot of that too.

He never glanced her way, apparently caught up in his own thoughts, heavy ones she guessed from the expression on his face.

When Trent and Ryder came back, Broughton said, "This shit's ready. Dish up what you want. There's hot sauce on the table. His gaze finally met Alex's, and she nodded. *The boy's awfully quiet.*

No response, and she wasn't surprised he'd shut down. But it hurt just a bit, since they seemed to be making a real connection only minutes earlier. Maybe it was what Grace had warned her about. Telepathy creates a false intimacy. You feel incredibly close to a person when, in fact, all you know about them is language. No different, really, than regular conversation, but it wasn't unlike texting, or messaging, in that there was no nuance to be read.

Fine, then. She'd go the traditional route, and do something she learned when working with feral cats. Push his boundaries.

When dinner was finished, Trent said he and Ryder would wash up, and that was fine with Alex, although… "Why don't you two go to the game room instead and have some fun. Broughton and I will pack this stuff away."

When they disappeared down the hall, Broughton looked at her with a raised eyebrow. "The cook doesn't do cleanup."

"He does tonight. Wash or dry, pick your poison."

"You're kinda bossy."

"I thought Ryder needed some fun, and we were the ones there, pulling him out of that mess, so there's 'stuff' attached to us, you know? He might be able to lighten up a bit more with Trent. They can talk airplanes and stuff."

He nodded. "Good point. I'll wash."

It was nice standing beside him, taking the dripping wet plates as he washed them. Reminded her of fuzzy slippers. A "home" thing, she supposed. Would he be home to her? A place where she could just be?

"Heavy thoughts," he said, handing her a clean mug. "Care to share?"

Really? "Do you live somewhere? I mean have a place?"

"Nothing like your house. I've got a condo in Dallas, but I haven't been in it more than a dozen times."

"I thought when you talked to me, kept me company—back then—you said you had a place in New Mexico."

"Used to." He scrubbed at the bottom of the second pot. "Gone now."

"You didn't know yet that your dad was Native American, but you were living on a reservation?"

"Just outside, actually. I was on the run and needed a place to hide. Met a couple of guys from there, and we hit it off. They helped me build a cabin, and they watched out for me like brothers. That's when I met Link."

"What did they think when you found out they were your kin?"

"I never told them. And I don't know where my dad was from, whether I'm Cree or Apache or Navajo or what. The DNA report just said Native American."

"Why didn't you tell them?" She hung the second dry pot from a hook, and stood back while Broughton wiped the counters, rinsed the sink.

"I didn't feel like blurting out, hey, by the way… Ya know? And I haven't had an opportunity to sit down with any of them."

"Have you explored the history at all?"

"Yeah. Makes me a little crazy."

"All the bad your people have been through?"

"That, and not knowing. A person doesn't have to have related blood in their veins to care. It should have mattered to me, even if I wasn't a descendant." He tossed the cloth into the sink. "It should have mattered, and it didn't. As a human being, I should have fucking cared. But all I did was accept their hospitality, benefit from their friendship. And I have to live with that."

He raked his fingers through his hair. "Sorry,

something about this place puts me off-kilter."

He had made his way across the great room, flicking off the light on his way and was now staring out into the dark. She went to him, took his hand. "Come and sit." He didn't resist, and she led him to a long leather couch.

They sat, and she turned to face him, one leg tucked under her. "Have you considered that maybe this place has connections to your heritage? Perhaps a burial site close by? After meeting Dusty and Chase, I did a bit of research about Sunrise Ranch, and the way they welcome and support the spirituality of all indigenous people. How the ranch was designed using Apache traditions."

She got brave and reached for his hand again. "When I was at that cabin, meeting with them, I felt a lot. Like the presence of the trees, a wolf lurking nearby, and there was life underfoot. What you feel here might be some of that. And maybe it's time you stopped fighting it."

He pulled her over so she leaned against him. "You've got some kind of weird wisdom inside you. You seem to be able to read me, help me smooth out when the going gets bumpy." He slid his hand up and down her arm. "You're good for me."

Alex's heart bumped crazily. Did she dare tell him he felt like home to her? She thought about it too long, and the moment got away while silence stretched between them.

Ryder's laughter bounced down the hall and made Alex smile. "He's going to be okay, isn't he?"

"Yeah. Gonna have some hard days, really hard days, along the way, but he'll be okay once he has his mom and dad to lean on."

"You lost your parents around the same age he did."

"And went to live with my granny—a tough old boot."

"You love Consuelo."

"What's not to love? She runs a tight ship, and no one slips through the cracks. Ever."

Had Broughton slipped through cracks? Is that what contributed to him being so guarded?

"You lost your mom too," he said.

"A few years ago. It was long and slow, and I was glad for her when it was over. She used to kid with me and say how we'd never make the cat suffer what she was going through, but people didn't get an easy out. She was so ready when she finally got to go."

"What about you? Were you ready?"

She shook her head, unable to speak for a minute. "I didn't want her to be in pain anymore, but the world was too bright when she was gone. Like I'd taken off my sunglasses and there was no place to find shade. There was openness, emptiness, and I suddenly had nothing to do. They came and picked up the hospital bed we'd rented, and her room was empty." She shook her head at the flood of memories.

"I nursed her to the very end. She had four PICC lines where I put her meds, and there were tubes, bags, stacks of sheets and pressure pillows. And all of it was gone."

She wanted to stop, but the words kept coming. "I came home from work one day and found the cat playing with something. When I picked it up, I fell in a heap, weeping over the tiny silver thing you pull off a bottle of injectable meds so you can stick a needle through the rubber top. It wasn't any different from the ones I pulled off bottles all day long at my job, but it was different because it was hers… It was the first time I cried."

Broughton wrapped his arms around her and held on while she soaked in his warmth. It was nice to have someone to talk to this way, not that she'd probably rehash the loss of her mother with him ever again, but it felt right tonight. Unplanned, unexpected. And real.

He rested his chin on the top of her head like he'd done all those months ago when he held her in the night because she was scared. Terrified she'd never be able to move again. She remembered how she'd longed to tip her head back and kiss that chin. So she did.

And he twisted to meet her mouth with his own in a kiss filled with everything she longed for from him. Her heart swelled and their tongues dueled for supremacy, and she slid her hands under his shirt, discovering hard muscles and smooth skin…exploring, and holding on.

He eased back. "Kid in the house."

Oh, hell. "Damn."

His chuckle warmed her even more. "I'll second that, and I won't even ask for an invite to your room, because I know what the answer will be."

"I should turn in before this gets worse."

"Or better, depending on your perspective," he

wiggled his eyebrows, and she laughed, pushed herself up to her feet.

"See you in the morning."

He didn't respond. Just gazed at her until she turned and headed down the hall, even though her heart was screaming at her to drag him to her bed. They were on a job. And besides, she was holding out for more…wasn't she?

With her hand on the doorknob she was suddenly grabbed and spun around. His mouth landed on hers, and he plundered, taking, taking, giving, and taking some more. Then she was just as suddenly standing alone, wondering what the hell just happened.

#

Morning brought clarity. This was the day.

He could feel in his bones that this would be a special day.

Once they had Ryder back in the hands of his parents, Broughton was going to ask Trent to drop them at his favorite hideaway in the Kootneys, and he was going to take her up his mountain. Show her the view.

But first they had to get the kid handled.

"You wanna hike it or use the ATVs?" Broughton asked.

"The four-wheelers will be fun." That the kid was thinking about fun was a good thing, a positive on his road to recovery.

It took less than an hour to reach the cabin high on the mountain, and they let themselves in to wait for Murray and the others Ryder didn't know about.

It wasn't long before they heard the sound of

machines approaching.

This was it. Ryder had been quiet since they arrived, and now he'd even paled.

"What's the matter?"

He shrugged. "Scared all of a sudden. Like when there were voices in the hall where they kept me and Del, and I was scared they'd take him and leave me alone."

"We're not going anywhere, bro. We're here for you."

"There's more than one ATV, or bike. I can't tell which, but there's more. Like three, maybe." Panic flitted across his face.

"I guess Dusty and Chase came after all," said Alex. "I know they really wanted to see you, welcome you back to Sunrise if you want to stay."

He nodded, and his shoulders lowered a bit until the machines shut off, and then he tightened up again. Alex touched the back of his clenched fist. "You're going to be okay, Ryder. We're here for you, and Meyers is your home team. You're safe with us."

He sucked in a hard breath, the door swung inward, and there stood a woman who looked just like her son.

Ryder's mouth moved, silently repeating one word, Mom, Mom, Mom. Then he walked straight into her arms, and Dayson came through the doorway to wrap his arms around both of them for a minute before stepping back.

"I knew it," said Ryder. "I knew you weren't dead. Why didn't you tell me you weren't dead? Take me with you?"

"The story is long and convoluted, and we did what we thought was best for you. We were wrong."

"You can come with us now," said Mae.

"But we have to go right away." Strain marred Dayson's face. "Coming to get you was worth the risk, but we have to go right now."

"Then let's go," said Ryder, and he headed straight for the machines. Stopped and swung around to Broughton and Alex, who had followed them out. "I need to take the four-wheeler. Is that okay?"

"I guess this means you're sure."

"Yep. Thanks, eh, for everything."

"Have a great life, kid."

With a roar, they started up and headed out. To where? Who knew? Didn't matter. He turned to Alex, and was just about to say something when he heard a footstep behind him and wheeled, dropping to one knee and reaching for his weapon.

"I guess I asked for that." The voice was low, and familiar. One Broughton hadn't heard in years. He blinked at the man who stepped out from behind a tree. He didn't look like the person who belonged to the voice.

Broughton took a step toward the stranger. Searched the face of a man about his own height and build.

Skin the color of copper, hair black and silver, and eyes he would never forget.

"Sorry about the surprise. How are you, son?"

"What the fuck?"

His dad laughed. "You've still got a mouth on

you."

Broughton took a step forward, another, and then more until he was in his father's arms, holding on like he'd never let go. "You were dead. I buried you beside mom."

"You buried Murray Swansen and he was a good man. Deserved a decent resting place, and your mother wouldn't mind since he saved my life. Died in my place. Let's sit, and I'll tell you the story."

Broughton turned and saw Alex, with tears dripping off her chin. "This is Alex. She usually doesn't leak like this," he said, using his sleeve to mop her face.

She sniffed and dug out a tissue. "He's right. Leaking isn't my thing. It's really nice to meet you."

"Likewise. Kind of surreal to meet my grown son and his lady."

She shot a glance at Broughton, and he winked at her.

When they were all seated, his dad explained how his life on the streets ended when someone was murdered while wearing a coat he'd traded away only the day before. Not taking any chances he switched ID with the dead man, and took off.

"I headed out of the city, looking for work, and encountered Chase. He hired me on as a handyman, and I never looked back."

"You stopped drinking." Broughton had to say it.

"I never drank. I was just a hell of an actor."

"You let me...no made me believe you were a

drunken street bum."

"Got ya to give up on me and go away, didn't I? If the Minnows had got wind of you, they'd have grabbed you and used you to draw me out. I had to make you give up and go away. You had—have—a good life."

"How do you know?"

"I still have a couple of contacts. Met James Meyers some years back, when he was going through a hard time. We got to shootin' the shit one night, and he said a name, made me sit up and forget I was supposed to be falling-down drunk. Not many men I know named Broughton.

"James knew. All this time he knew?"

"He did. Helluva man, your friend is. Backed me into a corner not long ago and said it was time. The Minnows were out of commission, so there was no danger to you and me getting to know each another again. Today seemed like good timing all round."

"You knew how to find Ryder's parents."

"I know a lot about a lot of things, people. Comes from being an observer for a very long time. We've got a network, some off the grid, some not. Some hiding, being hidden, and others looking. An interesting underworld."

"Freaking amazing how many of those there are."

"Too true." He turned his wrist to look at his watch, a move so familiar it put a lump in Broughton's throat. "I need to get back, to keep the cover clean. The loop up and back rarely takes more than an hour. But I want to spend some real time with you, away from here."

"Come to Texas, to Meyers. Or wherever. Just say when and where, and I'll meet you."

"Texas would be good in a couple of weeks." He handed Broughton a card. "Those are my numbers."

"Do you have a contact number for James?" His dad nodded. "Good, you can reach me any time through him. I don't have a regular cell."

"I do," said Alex, and she pulled a pen and card from her pocket. She put a line across the front and turned it over, wrote a number and passed it to him.

Then he was heading for the door.

"Dad."

He turned, and Broughton hugged him one more time. "I'm really glad you're not dead."

He laughed. "Me too."

#

Watching the reunion, and then the departure, wreaked havoc with Alex's insides. And now she was at a loss for what to say to the man standing in front of her, looking slightly shell-shocked.

She went to him.

"You okay?"

He pulled her in and hung on to her. Buried his face in her hair. "I am. I really am." And rocking her slightly from side to side, he said, "What an amazing day." He kissed her hard and let her go.

"My dad is alive and well and living in Canada." He half laughed. "And not because he's a draft dodger." He shook his head. "The last time we came to the mountain house, I was only a few miles away from him and didn't even know it."

"I wonder if that was the weird feeling you were getting on that trip."

"Entirely possible." He smiled at her. "You ever been to the Kootneys?"

"What's a Kootney?"

"A mountain. A bunch of them just before you get to the Rockies."

"Never been."

"I've got a cabin there. My favorite place on the planet. If I can convince Trent to drop us off, would you come? See my mountain? Hike with me? Maybe marry me someday?"

She blinked and shook her head as though to clear cobwebs.

"What did you say?"

"I'm done running. I know I want you to be a part of my life. I want to hold onto you when times are fucked up, and laugh with you, and walk in the mountains with you."

"You left the 'marry' word out that time, but all the other words made up for it. Just one more and you've got a grand slam happening."

Broughton felt the smile as it came unbidden. Something inside him was suddenly lighter, brighter.

"I love you Alex, and want you beside me forever."

"About freaking time," she said and threw herself into his arms, laughing, and he spun her around, not stopping when his mouth found hers, and then he was lost.

Found.

Home.

EPILOGUE

High in the mountains of British Columbia

Broughton held out a hand to help Alex over the final edge and into his arms. “You did it.”

“Of course I did, but for the record? Holy cow, that last bit was harder than I expected.” It wasn’t straight up, because, hey, she wasn’t that stupid, but the slope had seemed more gradual on paper.

“You want your prize now?”

She leaned back and studied his face. “Is this something like the mile-high club?”

He laughed. “No, actually, it’s something else. Close your eyes, and don’t open them until I tell you.” With his hands on her hips, he turned her until her back was against his front. He wrapped his arms tight around her, and whispered in her ear. “Open.”

She did, and had to blink. The world in all its glory was spread out before her in a sea of mountaintops. She could see forever, and suddenly felt as tiny and insignificant as dust.

She wanted to speak, but her voice was lodged in her throat. Instead, she wrapped her arms around his and simply savored perfection. Her life could get no better than this.

"What are you thinking?"

A half laugh escaped while joy seeped inside her. One of the promises they had made to each other was to never assume they knew what was going on in each other's heads.

"I'm thinking how freaking lucky we are to have this kind of freedom, and a love so down-to-earth, so real, nothing can ever make it darken, even at the edges.

"Perfection?"

"Nope, far from it, and a whole lot better." She tipped her head back to kiss him.

"I think you might like your other present now." His mouth burned a path down the side of her neck, his hands slid inside the waistband of her cargos, and her body began to hum.

NEW RELEASES

September 2018
Intrepid Women series, book #9

DIAMONDS TO DIE FOR
When a kickass racehorse trainer's life and livelihood are threatened she does what she has to do, and her choices don't make her ex—or any number of other people in her life—very happy. Jason made a career out of keeping people safe, and he doesn't believe anything is impossible, but Kate's choices leave him firmly wedged between a rock and a hard place.

October 2018
COPPER MILLS Shared World novellas:
Doing a favor for her sister, Calista suddenly finds herself in Arizona learning far more about chickens and goats than she ever thought possible.

November 2018
CATS: A Collection of Heartwarming Furry Tales Volume #5
Six more short stories with tear-worthy happy endings will be available before Christmas 2018.

ABOUT THE AUTHOR

Award winning author Kathryn Jane lives on the west coast of Canada with her very own prince, a sweet dog, and an obnoxious cat. Among her favorite things are the smell of the ocean, crisp sunny days, cats with a sense of humor, faithful mutts, the warm breath of a horse, music, sunflowers, orange gerbera daisies, beach glass, rocks, and kind people.

A perfect day begins with a walk alongside the Pacific Ocean with her sisters.

For more information about Kathryn and her other books, check out her website and sign up for the newsletter.

kathrynjane (dot) com

OTHER BOOKS BY KATHRYN JANE

INTREPID WOMEN SERIES

Book 1 – Do Not Tell Me No
Book 2 – Touch Me
Book 3 – Daring To Love
Book 4 – Voices
Book 5 – Lies
Book 6 – All She Wanted
Book 7 – Dance With Me
Book 8 – Missing
Book 9 – Diamonds To Die For (September, 2018)

INTO THE SUNRISE – Women's Fiction

CATS, A Collection of Heartwarming Furry-Tales

Volume #1 –2017
Volume #2 –2017
Volume #3 –2017
Volume #4 –2017
Volume #5 – (November 2018)
Volume #6 – (December 2018)

ACKNOWLEDGEMENTS

As always, I need to thank my wonderful team, because I couldn't publish these books without their help. Whether catching typos, spending weeks on full blown edits, or taking me out to lunch when I need to get away from my characters for an hour or two, each and every one of my "people" play an important role in my life. (Yes, the four-legged ones too because who doesn't need a cat walking on the keyboard now and then, or a dog passing gas for comic relief.)

Many thanks to: Demon For Details for your fantastic editing; author L. j. Charles for your wonderful critiquing skills, positive energy, and invaluable advice; Judicious Revisions LLC, and Barb for the sharp-eyed proof-reading; The Killion Group Inc. for another fabulous cover; Brenè Brown for Daring Greatly—an inspiration; Sandy James for encouraging me to rock the words; Nora Costigan and Anne Bailey, you are the eternally-brilliant smiles in the back of my mind—I'll never forget you; Al, my own charming prince, for baking me bread and keeping me warm at night; Barb and Judy—how do I put it into words? You are the constants in my journey. You've egged me on and believed in me always. I love you all.

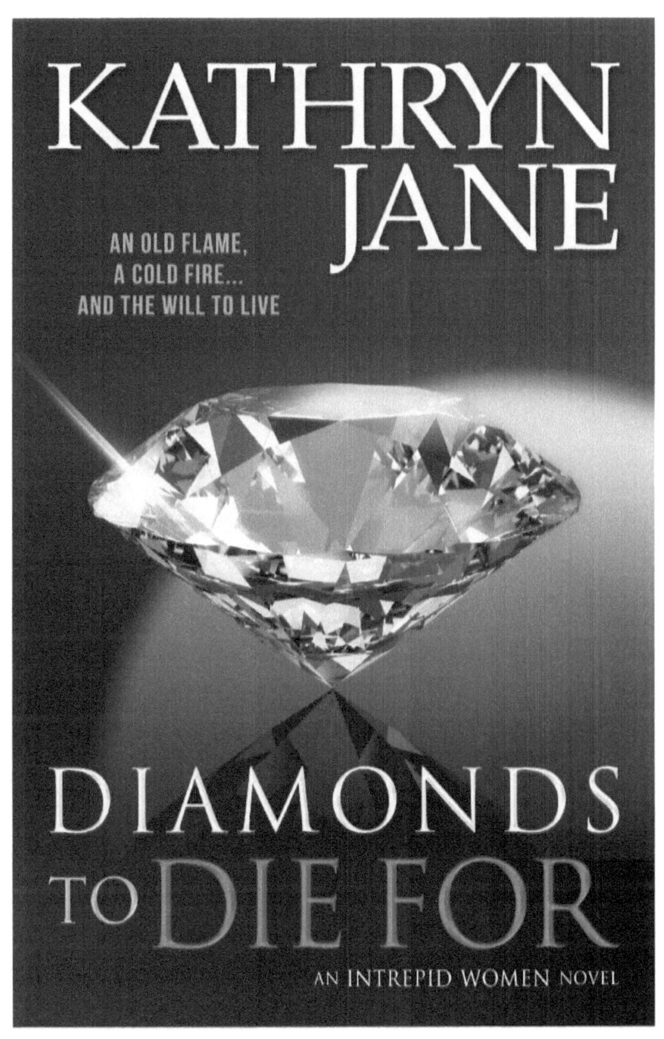
KATHRYN
JANE
AN OLD FLAME,
A COLD FIRE...
AND THE WILL TO LIVE
DIAMONDS
TO DIE FOR
AN INTREPID WOMEN NOVEL

www.ingramcontent.com/pod-product-compliance
Lightning Source LLC
Chambersburg PA
CBHW030552180626
46816CB00005B/1515

* 9 7 8 1 9 8 8 7 9 0 0 9 1 *